THE
CARBON
PAR◭DOX

A CLIMATE ACTION DRAMA

RENAT HEUBERGER
STEVE ZWICK   MARCO HIRSBRUNNER

What Readers Are Saying

The Carbon Paradox is a genre-bending triumph—blending fiction and deep expertise to illuminate the messy realities of climate finance... A vital, timely guide for navigating complexity with courage and hope.

Prof. Dr. Fabrizio Ferraro, Professor of Strategic Management, IESE Business School, Spain

It's so tempting to spend the rest of the night finishing it—just like Ella, the protagonist... My first thought was: 'I want to translate this into Vietnamese and publish it, because as many people as possible should read it.'

Dang Hanh, Co-founder and Managing Director, VNEEC, Vietnam

I would never have imagined that a story about young environmental activists navigating carbon markets—in all their technical, political and philosophical complexity—could be so gripping, informative, and hopeful. The small victories and repeated setbacks ring true, as I know from my own experience of trying to make markets and business work for people and planet.

Joshua Bishop, University of Sydney, former chief economist, IUCN, Australia

Our greatest challenge is that farmers don't speak finance; finance doesn't speak farmer; and neither speaks high-level COP jargon. Through the power of storytelling, this book bridges worlds — smallholder farmers and financiers, the Global North and the Global South, policy and practice — in a way we urgently need.

Chiyedza Heri, Founder & CEO, Ubuntu Alliance, Zimbabwe

Yin and Yang. The world works entirely based on paradoxes... Being written as a fiction is a fresh approach. A must-read!

Agus Sari, CEO, Landscape Group, Indonesia

If you think it is hard to make the world of carbon markets interesting and engaging, think again: Zwick, Heuberger and Hirsbrunner have done it in style... Part fable, part hero's journey, part documentary and part thriller. Honestly, I don't know how they came up with this chimera, but it works.

Ricardo Bayon, Partner and Co-founder, Encourage Capital and Adjunct Professor, Brown University, USA

The Carbon Paradox is not only highly readable and gripping—it is truly innovative. By weaving real-world paradoxes into a compelling story, it reshapes how we think about the challenges of CO_2 emissions.

Prof. Gregor Dorfleitner, Professor of Finance, University of Regensburg, Germany

The book perfectly captures the dreams, the intentions, the tension, the hope, the conflicts, the will for action in the face of imperfection... To date, I have not seen anything better.

Giulia Gervasoni, Executive Director, Sustainability & Climate Risk, UBS, Switzerland

Renat, Steve, Marco: your Five Elements gives us the map. I'd add one more: the Rivers, the liquidity that carries Climate Units from source to sink, so the water can circulate through the whole system. When that river flows, the price of polluting is crystal clear, and the value of reducing, avoiding, and removing it is just as tangible.

Juan Carlos Gonzalez Aybar, CEO, Fronterra, Peru

The Carbon Paradox is a fresh, refreshing, and surprisingly fun take on how to move us to action through a wild ride, semi-autobiographical allegorical MUST READ TODAY adventure!

Lisa Neuberger Fernandez, Co-Founder, SharpBrains Advisors and Professor of Strategy, IE Business School, USA

Contents

Part One

The Dream

The Clip

The little girl's head bobbed above the murky floodwaters, her arms flailing like those of a beetle on its back, her face an indecipherable mask of terror.

The image glitched—sharp one second, blurry the next.

Bits of wreckage floated past. A tire. A tree limb. The twisted skeleton of a bridge. There! Her head appeared again. Her face was down now.

She grabbed at something—a log, perhaps—before vanishing behind a rock, leaving only the empty echo of her last plea.

Robin stared at his phone and read the caption: "Tragic moment when a seven-year-old girl is dragged away in a flash flood after a powerful storm hits Demba."

A chill crept down his spine. *Not Limata*, he thought. *Please, God, don't let this be Limata.*

He turned his eyes from the grim spectacle on his phone to the creative mess of his bedroom. Hundreds of books lined the walls, and the chessboard sat mid-battle—white king in check. The old clock ticked with smug precision.

Bing.

Another message from Andy Lelong lit up his phone. Another link.

He clicked it.

> LIMATA, Demba—Dozens of people are missing after torrential rains triggered flash floods in the tropical village of Limata, where waters overwhelmed homes, swept away livestock, and collapsed a central bridge. The disaster struck after record-breaking rainfall in the region, raising questions about the interplay between climate change, deforestation, and economic pressures in this small nation.
>
> "This is a tragedy beyond words," said Wanga Namira, Executive Director of the Matipa Coalition, a local NGO. "We're doing everything we can, but many families are still searching for their loved ones."
>
> Scientists say the rains are likely linked to climate change, as warmer temperatures increase the atmosphere's capacity to hold moisture, resulting in heavier downpours, although specific attribution is difficult.
>
> Namira said there's no doubt that deforestation exacerbated the tragedy.
>
> "Forests act as natural sponges," she said.
>
> "During the rainy season, forests absorb water, slowing its flow into rivers, but in the dry season, they release that water, sustaining local ecosystems," she added. "When forests are cleared, there's nothing to hold the water back."

Robin stared at the text.

Wanga Namira? Andy's auntie?

The phone slipped from his hand and landed face down on the wine-red carpet. His gaze followed.

Did that little girl's mother find her like that, face down in the red mud?

His mind skipped to the same village one year earlier, and to the squealing children who tugged at his sleeves, tousled his hair, and practiced their English on him.

"Hello, Sir!" one would say.

"Hello!" he'd answer.

"How are you, my friend?"

"I'm good. How are you?"

"I'm fine!" followed by cascades of laughter until another child stepped forward to recite the same magical incantation they'd learned in English class.

Each round elicited the same response followed by the same peals of shy, joyous laughter—and, for Robin, a peculiar blend of warmth and alienation.

He picked up the phone and clicked on Andy's name.

"Did you watch the clip?" he heard Andy ask.

"I did. It's crazy." Robin paused. "Your family? Are they..."

"They're fine. But, Robin, this is Limata. We stood on that bridge last year."

Robin swallowed hard. "That little girl... perhaps we talked to her..." His voice faltered.

"It's a complete disaster," Andy said. "And it's killing Matipa."

"Matipa?"

"My auntie's organization. Remember, Wanga Namira? They're supposed to be building dikes, not fishing people out of the river. She just texted my mom."

Robin recalled the mottled forests between Duiba and Limata.

"If they don't finish the dikes, the next floods will be worse," Andy said, "but they've got no money left."

Robin paused. "Is your auntie still coming to the Canland Climate Summit?" he asked.

"Yeah, but now it's all about fundraising. A whole different dynamic."

"It's crazy, Andy. We have to do something. Maybe we can use our cinema to help. Maybe we can raise money?" He paused, then: "Look, Ella just wrapped up her library shift. I'm supposed to meet her at Brigitte's. Let me come to your place instead."

"No. I've been here all day and need to get out. I'll meet you both there."

Robin forwarded the video to Ella with a text:

> This is Limata, where Andy and I backpacked last year. He's joining us at the Bungalow.

He pedaled towards the Old Town, past the bridge over the old harbor, the day's heat broiling up from the streets as the sun gave way to night.

Then he crossed the park behind Niburg Central Station, and the temperature dropped like a stone.

Thank you, trees, he thought to himself. *Still working the alchemy of photosynthesis, despite the drought.*

Beyond the trees lay the University of Niburg, which sprawled along Science Square. Further down towards the harbor front, tucked away in a crooked alley that hadn't changed since the days of chivalry, was a little bar called Brigitte's Bungalow.

Everyone knew Brigitte. A flower child turned local institution, she still wore long braids from the '60s, now gray as smoke.

The Bungalow was the last surviving fragment of a textile works that her great-grandfather had founded on the waterfront, back when chimneys exhaled ambition, not planetary destruction.

At its height, the factory had employed hundreds. An old photograph, still hanging on the Bungalow wall, showed a steamer laden with raw cotton docking at the alley's end. The Bungalow, then serving as a customs office, stood watch beside a narrow yard.

The factory closed when production moved to Demba, and Brigitte's relatives all cashed in. Its shell became swanky harbor-view apartments.

Brigitte, however, cherished—and inherited—what most saw as the least valuable plot of them all: the crumbling old customs house. But instead of selling, she transformed it into the beating heart of student life: a magnet for misfits, dreamers, and rebels with half-read philosophy books in their backpacks.

A metal plaque above the bar bore the words: "All genders, races, and ages welcome—no discrimination tolerated." It sat proudly beside a faded Jimi Hendrix poster, the edges curled.

To the dismay of the neighboring tenants, Brigitte had secured permission to place a few open-air tables between the street and the entrance to her bar. The back of the bar—once a storage site for confiscated contraband—had long since been downgraded into a dumping ground for empty beer crates.

"Hey, Brigitte," Andy said one day, eyeing the space, "I think we could do something good with this."

And just like that, the Earth Cinema was born: a scrappy open-air theater showing small films with big ideas—climate change, biodiversity loss, social justice, and the messy beauty of human resilience.

It became the boys' first real social venture, and it barely broke even.

"It's a paradox," Robin said one night as they swept popcorn off the cracked concrete. "If it's fun and for a good cause, you're guaranteed to lose money."

Andy tapped his broom against the floor like a knight raising a sword.

"To paradox!" he said.

Robin had been hooked on paradox since the day his philosophy teacher scrawled on the chalkboard: "This statement is false."

"It's the liar's paradox," the teacher said.

If the statement is true, then it must be false, Robin thought. *But if it's false, then it must be true.*

The paradox initially tickled Robin the way it does all teenage brains: like the fizz of cheap champagne—a delightful riddle, nothing more. But then came others.

The sorites paradox, where a heap of sand lost one grain at a time until no one could agree when it stopped being a heap. Schrödinger's cat, sulking in its box, alive and dead at once.

To most students, these puzzles merely proved that philosophy was good at tying itself in knots, and not much else. To Robin, they exposed something more troubling and more interesting: a widening gap between the tidy systems people used to explain the world and the world's persistent refusal to cooperate.

That unease drew him into quantum physics, where paradox wasn't a distraction but a recurring feature. There, he found a dog-eared biography of Niels Bohr and the line that burned itself into his brain:

How wonderful that we have met with a paradox. Now we have some hope of making progress.

Bohr had nailed it. Paradoxes weren't roadblocks. They were invitations.

As Robin neared the park's edge, the shade peeled away like a parting curtain, spilling him back onto the heat-drenched cobblestones of

Niburg's Old Town. He zipped across Science Square, flanked by the ivy-clad facades of the old university buildings. Then he saw her.

Ella was sitting outside Brigitte's Bungalow at one of the shaded tables between the doorway and the street. She spotted him and raised a hand. Beside her, a man was gesturing sharply as he spoke.

By the time Robin dismounted and locked his bike, the man was gone.

The Bungalow

"Did you see the clip?" Robin asked, dropping into the chair beside Ella.

"There are more of them," she replied quietly, handing him her phone.

The screen lit up with fresh horrors—more footage from Demba, more chaos, more faces contorted in disbelief. Robin scrolled in silence, then slipped an arm around her shoulder. He lingered there a moment too long, not sure if he was offering comfort or asking for it.

He paused, then nodded toward the street. "And... who was that guy just now?"

"My brother," she said, her voice suddenly flat.

"Simon?" asked Robin, oddly relieved.

"Yeah. He's still furious that I moved out last year. Thinks I'm off living my best life while he's stuck with Dad."

Robin studied her face—clear gray-green eyes that missed nothing, even now. A faint spray of freckles dusted her skin, and her chestnut hair kept slipping loose from the bun she'd twisted up half an hour earlier. She wore her usual: a sunflower-yellow dress and scuffed white sneakers that somehow managed to look deliberate, like everything she did.

"I just... I don't have the bandwidth for his guilt trips right now," she muttered, shifting the conversation back to her phone.

"You know what really gets to me about these floods? It's my reaction. I saw the headlines this morning, read them all day at work—they were on every news service the library subscribes to—but until you sent this, it was just background noise. Another flood. Another tragedy. Another child who didn't make it. They all blur."

Robin barely heard her. "I think I know her."

Ella's head snapped toward him. "What?" He pulled his arm back.

"I mean... met her. The little girl in the first video. In the village. I think."

"Oh, my God."

He swallowed. "But why should it matter? Why should it change anything just because I *might* have seen her once?" His voice cracked. "I keep hoping she's not one of them. That she's some other little girl I never met, who never met me, who has—or had—no memory of me in her brain. But why does that make a difference?"

Ella rested a hand on his arm.

Just like high school, Robin thought.

"It's natural," she said. "We learned about it in econ: it's called the 'circle of moral concern'... tied to evolutionary stuff—tribalism, kinship, familiarity. We care more about what's close. What we've touched. Seen. Held."

She hesitated. "Look, I did the same. Scrolled past the headlines all day. But when I saw your clip..."

She shook her head.

"I felt it. Really felt it. And now I can't unfeel it."

Robin studied her. She had that thing people were always talking about now. *Self-awareness.* But this wasn't some social media trend. She'd always had it.

You don't lose your mom that young, get hauled off to a dead-end flat while your dad drowns in vodka, and come out untouched.

She shifted in her seat. "Are you going to help with a fundraiser? I want to do something. We can't just sit here in shock."

Over Ella's shoulder, Robin spotted Andy coming out of the bar, three beers balanced in his hands. His sharp, dark features and gray-black shirt gave him an air of sophistication that belied his 22 years.

The boys were an odd pair: best friends since kindergarten but polar opposites, like protons and electrons. Robin was all nerves and angles, his blonde hair a windswept mess. Andy radiated quiet intensity, his dark hair neatly trimmed. Robin loved the rigid patterns of chess; Andy thrived on the bluff and chaos of poker.

"Yes, we need to do something," Robin said as Andy approached. "Maybe we could promote a fundraiser for Limata during movie nights?"

Andy set the beers down harder than he needed to.

"Yes, do something," he said flatly. "Raise a few bucks, buy some shelters and water purifiers. Boom—problem solved."

Ella didn't hear the edge in Andy's voice. Robin did.

"Hey," Robin said gently, "we're just trying to help."

Andy leaned in and gave them each a quick, familiar hug, then dropped into the third chair and drained half a beer in a single pull.

"I'm not mad at you," he said finally. "I'm mad at all of it. Every time there's a disaster, people throw a few crowns at it and move on. Meanwhile, they're eating steak from the tropics, buying wood from Demba... My aunt's coming in for Niburg Climate Week. She and my mom have spent months on this, getting corporate donors lined up for sustainable investments."

His fingers curled around the beer glass. "And now? Now, it's all about plugging another hole in a sinking ship."

He paused again, then summarized:

"It's easy to raise money to address a catastrophe but almost impossible to raise money to prevent one, even though prevention is much more effective."

Robin nodded slowly. "It's a paradox," he said, almost to himself. "The worse the crisis gets, the harder it is to convince people to focus on prevention. Donors want to see action. Dikes, shelters, tents. But maybe..." His eyes brightened. "Maybe that's exactly what we should do! Launch a fundraiser for *prevention* instead of relief. Raise money for projects in Demba that tackle the root cause."

Andy bit his tongue. "Guys, did you hear what I just said? Wanga's been trying to do that for years, and it's impossible—if for no other reason than time. Charity comes for a few months, and development aid comes for a few years, while half of it gets diverted back to the donor countries, and more ends up in the pockets of local officials. Real, lasting change requires long-term, strategic investment."

He'd lifted that right from one of Wanga's speeches.

"She's always talking about the need for transitional finance that will jump-start a new economy," he said. "That won't come from passing a hat. The problem is our economic system. It's the fact that forests are worth more dead than alive."

Ella perked up. "Ah!" she said. "You're talking about externalities—Arthur Pigou!"

"Pig-who?"

"Pigou!" she said. "He was an economist who said that polluters aren't just dumping their garbage on us, they're dumping their costs on us. He said we should put the cost of cleanup into the cost of production. And he said that a hundred years ago!"

"Well, if they did that, no one could afford hamburgers, that's for sure," said Andy.

"My econ professor, Dieter Turman, talked about something else, too—payments for ecosystem services," she said. "You pay somebody to protect nature based on the services nature provides. Did you know that a lot of cities pay farmers to protect the watershed because they get clean water? And then there are carbon credits, where polluters pay for reducing greenhouse gas emissions elsewhere or even sucking greenhouse gases out of the air. If a farmer in Demba plants trees, for example, they could earn money from companies that pollute here in Canland because the trees absorb carbon."

"Wanga mentioned that," said Andy. "She said they can become providers of an ecosystem service and not just charity cases."

Before anyone could respond, a bottle of tequila plopped on the table. The hand delivering it—wrapped in fingerless leather gloves—belonged to a cowgirl with shot glasses in her bandoliers and whisky in her holsters.

The cowgirl's name was Remy Selnass.

By day, she was an ambitious economics student—one of Turman's brightest and two years ahead of Ella. Remy was obsessed with a single question: what system could come after capitalism, one that might finally deliver prosperity for all?

By night, Remy transformed into a performance artist. One evening, she'd look like she'd just ousted half a corporate board; the next, like she was about to shake you down for lunch money. Now and then, she'd add leather and a riding crop—just to keep things unpredictable.

She was also Brigitte's bona fide fixer of red tape and marketer *par excellence*. She managed the bar when Brigitte was off, sorted the cinema license with the city and the film distributors, and—most importantly—promoted the cinema while spinning records at the Laguna Club. But lately, her banter had lost some of its playfulness, edged now with urgency—as if the questions she used to perform for fun were becoming matters of necessity.

"I thought you worked at Laguna on Fridays," said Andy.

"Laguna's half empty in this heat. I don't start till late. Shots?"

Before he could answer, a crack of lightning split the sky, and a gust of cool wind swept through the alley.

Brigitte swirled out of the bar, holding up her phone.

"Holy Jesus, kiddos!" she said, "Check out this weather map."

A seething blob of red and orange storms was rolling in from the west, and the motion lines showed the whole thing barreling straight toward them. Fifteen minutes, maybe less.

She turned to the guests and held the phone up like tablets proffered by a prophet. "Okay, people, party's over. We've got a wall of weather coming in like the wrath of Gaia, and she is *pissed*. Grab your beers and get your butts inside."

Then to Remy: "You wanna cash out, Sweetie? Luke just sent a text. They'll need you early at Laguna."

Remy followed Brigitte into the bar as the others tossed their crowns on the table and sprinted for their bikes.

The Laguna Club was another local institution, and like Remy, it changed with the rotation of the planet: harbor front café by day and the closest thing in Niburg to an underground scene by night. That's when the back wall slid open to a repurposed stable, the old hayloft now a DJ booth.

The torrential rain sent the young crowd streaming into the Laguna in droves. Ella, Robin, and Andy were already standing in line when Remy appeared on the harbor promenade, soaking wet. She waved to them and slipped them past the bouncers with her staff badge.

Ella dropped off her backpack—with her laptop inside—at the cloakroom and immediately disappeared onto the dance floor. Remy's boyfriend Luke was behind the bar, mixing cocktails with impressive flair. He nodded to the guys and waved at Remy, who was now climbing up into the DJ booth.

Ella, meanwhile, had fallen into a rapture of her own near the edge of the dance floor, her head nodding softly to the beat, though her eyes were unfocused, distant. She moved as if underwater—present, but elsewhere.

"Do you know about this carbon stuff Ella was talking about?" Andy shouted at Robin. "Polluters are gonna pay Demban farmers for saving trees and stopping floods? Sounds kinda dreamy. Too good to be real, no?"

Robin shrugged, shouting back. "Maybe. We'll find out."

Robin nodded toward the dance floor. "Let's meet at my place tomorrow, ten sharp. But first—let's get Ella before she floats off completely."

"You guys launching a fundraiser for Demba?" came a voice just behind Andy.

Light and curious, the voice cut through the music like a hand on the collar, stopping them mid-step.

Andy turned, startled, and found himself staring into a pair of sharp blue eyes—playful, unblinking. Her golden hair shimmered beneath the club lights, catching every pulse of color like it knew it was being watched.

How long had she been there, watching them?

"Beatrix!" he shouted over the bass. "How do you even know about that?"

"I overheard you at Brigitte's," she said.

Beatrix Lemore had attended the parallel class at the grammar school and managed the remarkable feat of turning the rather staid school newspaper into a city-famous magazine for nightlife tips. She had a habit of showing up when least expected—and of knowing exactly how to throw Andy off balance. She was often the only girl left at the poker table, and more than once she'd lured him into going all-in when he should've folded.

"Your home country, Andy, right?" she continued. "That flood was brutal. It's awesome you're doing something about it. When you get things rolling, let me know—I landed an internship at the Niburg Daily Tribune. Maybe I could get you a little press."

Andy grinned, kissed her cheek, and drifted toward the bar, where Luke was a blur of motion—cocktails flying, spirits flowing.

After four hours, the rain eased up. Robin found Andy on a barstool, lost in thought. "Come on, let's get out of here. Where's Ella?" They scanned the dance floor and realized:

She was gone.

The Ethics Paradox

Robin pedaled along the medieval quay. The rain had stopped, the stars were out, but water still gushed from alleys and stairwells as the hills continued emptying themselves into the river.

The ancient quay had held the river back for over a thousand years. Wooden vessels had docked at its wharf. Lovers had pledged their hearts along its boardwalk. Countless times, Robin himself had run or ridden along its edge.

He froze.

The first houses began to sway. Roof tiles slipped into the flood.

Then he heard it—a dull cry from the water.

A girl's head surfaced, dark curls plastered to her face. She fought the current, clinging to a broken beam. The river tore it from her hands.

Robin's breath caught.

"Ella!" he croaked, unable to scream. His legs wouldn't move. His hands felt bound. He could only watch as she looked at him and silently mouthed his name.

"Robin."

A bell began to toll—distant at first, then sharper, more insistent.

Not a church bell.

A doorbell.

Robin jolted upright, tangled in his sheets as if still caught in the current.

The bell rang again.

He blinked at the ceiling.

10:01 a.m.

He groaned.

Seriously? Andy—on time? That never would've happened in high school.

———

Robin padded down the stairs, his feet bare, his brain foggy.

He passed his parents' "home office," formerly their dining table: a mountain of legal documents formed into peaks, promontories, and landslides, giving way on either side to a defense of territory where the couple's measured hands had made a semblance of control.

As he neared the front door, he saw Andy squinting in through the glass. Then Ella popped up beside him, in the same summer dress as the night before, her face bright despite the faint shadows under her eyes. In one hand, she held up a paper bag from Lilla Bread—the cult bakery across from Science Square.

Robin opened the door.

"Lilla Bread?" he said, looking at Ella. "Don't tell me you partied till sunrise. We lost track of you after a while."

"Not exactly," Ella smiled. "I spent the night with my laptop, my new lover. I wasn't feeling Laguna. Went out to get my bike, saw Lilla was still open... and got sucked into a black hole of carbon credit articles. Next thing I know, it's 6 a.m., and they're handing me fresh croissants. I brought them home, crashed, and just woke up."

"Well done, Ella!" Andy laughed and grabbed one from her bag. "And what did you find out? Can we fund Demban projects with these carbon credits? Or should we stick with a fundraiser?"

She drifted toward the cluttered table, searching for a flat surface amidst the outcroppings, but Robin steered them to more navigable terrain, back in their overgrown garden, an ancient wrought-iron bench under an old walnut tree, at a table whose paint had long since peeled away.

The rusty bench was clearly on the verge of collapse, but it was a keepsake from Robin's grandmother, and no one had the heart to dispose of it. Sunlight filtered through the sparse leaves, yellowed by the drought, and the air smelled of wet grass, coffee, and croissants.

"I now think," Ella began, opening her laptop, "that carbon credits could indeed help Demba. But I'm just getting my head around it myself, and it's complicated."

She launched into her explanation as if unveiling the secrets of the universe.

"So here is how I think it works. A carbon credit is basically a payment you earn for helping the planet—either by reducing green-house-gas emissions or pulling carbon out of the air," she explained.

"You can think of it like a kind of money or a voucher. The basic idea is simple: the more carbon you remove from the atmosphere or prevent from getting there in the first place, the more credits you get. For example, planting trees or switching to clean energy can earn you credits. Or replacing diesel trucks with electric ones."

"Ah!" said Andy. "So, I can get carbon credits for riding my bike?"

"No, because you're already doing that. The payments are for changing from bad to good, not for already being good."

"That's not fair!" Andy insisted. "It penalizes people who have been doing the right—"

"I know," she said, holding up her hand. "It's called 'additionality,' and I went around in circles on that all night, so I'm not going there now. The critical thing for Demba is that you can generate these credits by restoring a forest, which absorbs carbon dioxide. You can also use them to save endangered forests, which, it turns out, has an even bigger impact. Another option is transitioning to clean cooking technologies, so people rely less on firewood or charcoal. Or installing solar panels to replace diesel generators. In short, there are many different categories of carbon credit projects. The largest, by far, are nature-based solutions. These include restoring degraded forests, protecting healthy ones, and helping farmers plant trees among their crops—a practice known as *agroforestry*.

"Some of these efforts eventually pay for themselves, but not until after a long time, and most don't. That's where carbon credits come in. They provide financial incentives based on the measurable climate impact of the project—essentially turning positive environmental action into a viable revenue stream."

"How about cows?" said Andy. "Everyone talks about carbon dioxide, but methane traps something like 80 times as much heat as carbon dioxide does, and cows are burping it like mad."

"Methane, yes..." Ella continued, slightly bewildered by Andy's constant interjections. "I think you can get carbon credits also for reducing methane. If I understand correctly, there's stuff you can feed the cows so they burp less, and you can use carbon credits to pay for it."

"Could you also capture the burps and use them as fuel, and then sell cow burp credits?" laughed Robin.

"Actually," said Ella, "I think you can—"

Andy grunted. "That sounds like a distraction," he said. "We could also just stop eating meat."

"Of course—but that's exactly what makes this so complicated," said Ella. "We should fly less, fry less, and buy less. No argument there. But how do you actually get millions of people to change? It's not happening overnight. Let's be honest—most consumers respond to one thing: money. That's why carbon credits could work. At least there, you can direct money to the people actually reducing emissions."

She leaned in, energized now.

"And that's why they could be a game-changer for Demba. We could use them to fund projects that both cut emissions and make villages more resilient. The more emissions they reduce, the more funding they get. Simple, right? Cool, no?"

Robin raised an eyebrow. "And who's footing the bill for all that?"

Ella smiled. "That's the best part. The polluters pay. That's the whole idea. Companies measure their emissions—and for every ton they pump into the atmosphere, they're required to buy a carbon credit. That's where the money comes from."

Robin hesitated, then said, "I must say this is kind of paradoxical. If I get the logic right, the more we pollute in Canland, the more we need to pay, and the more money we can raise."

Ella nodded.

"From that perspective, the more we pollute, the more money we have to help Demba. That's bizarre!"

It may seem bizarre at first glance, but I think it's the other way around," Ella answered. "The fact is, pollution exists, and as long as that's the case, it is better to pay for it than not. Because if you pay for your pollution, you have an incentive to reduce it."

Andy and Robin nodded, lost in thought.

After a long silence, Andy drew in a deep breath.

"Let me come at this from another angle," he said slowly. "You're saying carbon credits put a kind of price tag on a tree, right? You get paid to plant one. You get paid to save one. It's... pricing nature."

"Yes," Ella replied cautiously, unsure where he was heading. "That's the idea."

Andy leaned forward, his voice tightening. "So—what should that price be? Is a tall, old tree worth more than a sapling just because it holds more carbon? Is a tree with a bird nest more valuable than one sheltering a butterfly colony? What if one forest purifies drinking water for a village, and another protects endangered animals? Which one deserves more money?"

He paused. "Can we really put a price on life? On nature? And if we can—what's the value of a human life? That girl in Limata in the video. Is a year of her life worth the same as mine? More? Less? You see where I'm going?"

The room had fallen still.

"Can we really boil down nature into numbers on a spreadsheet?" he asked quietly.

Ella exhaled. "I hear you. I do. Ecosystem services, human life—these things are impossible to quantify. But here's the real dilemma: if we don't put a price on nature, then the default price is zero. That's even worse. Zero means worthless. Zero means destruction."

Andy threw up his hands. "That's the madness of it! This is exactly what capitalism does—it turns everything into a transaction, and that's why we've got all the drilling, all the mining, all the injustice. Now we want to use the same system to save the forest? Does that even make sense?"

Ella leaned back, letting his words hang. "I don't disagree. But it's also the only system we have. I'm not defending it—I'm saying we're out of time. We can't wait for a perfect system to emerge."

"Governments should act," Andy said firmly. "They should ban deforestation. That's how you solve this. Just make it illegal. We know why the flood in Limata happened. The trees were gone. The land could no longer hold back the water when the rains came in."

Ella nodded. "Yes, government regulation could help. But do you honestly think Demba can afford to fix all this on its own? Their economy depends on raw material exports. It would be like asking them to cut off their own lifeline. That's not fair unless we share the burden. Help them transform. That's what I think carbon finance is supposed to do."

There was another long pause. Andy softened. "True that. Why should Demba pay for a crisis they didn't cause? But here's what keeps bothering me. In Canland, we built our wealth by burning fossil fuels. Now we offer to pay countries like Demba to absorb our emissions, while we continue to pollute. Shouldn't we be cleaning up our own mess first? Shouldn't we invest in climate solutions here at home before outsourcing the fix?"

Ella hesitated, fingertips brushing the edge of her sleeping laptop. "You're right—countries like Canland caused most of the damage. But places like Demba are suffering the most, paying the highest price! So tell me, isn't it only fair that we start by investing in Demba first? We import massive amounts of stuff from Demba, but the act of extracting that stuff generates greenhouse gas emissions there. So why exactly should we not source the emission reductions from Demba as well?"

Robin, who'd been quiet all this time, finally spoke. "There's another layer here. From a scientific perspective, carbon dioxide doesn't care about borders. Whether you cut it in Demba or Canland, the climate benefit is the same. So it makes sense to reduce emissions where it's cheapest. If a dollar cuts two tons in Demba but only half a ton in Canland... Well, the math speaks for itself."

"That's what Professor Turman said in Econ," Ella murmured.

Andy looked over. "Any chance Turman is still on campus? Or is he gone for the summer?

"He's around," Ella said. "I think he still comes in on Mondays."

"When's your next shift at the library?"

"Monday afternoon."

"Could you catch him before that? I mean, he must have thought about all these dilemmas, right?"

"I could try," she said, her smile returning faintly. "He handed out flyers for that Climate Leadership series on campus. The big summit's coming to Niburg in four weeks, and guess who's supposed to speak? Demba's Environment Minister. He said she's kind of a force."

"Amina Keita is her name," Andy said. "My mom mentioned her, but I heard she might not make it after the floods."

Robin stood and stretched. "Let's take a walk."

———

Robin shook his head as they wandered through the patch of forest behind his parents' house.

What a paradox, he thought. *Actually, three of them, all tangled up in one: the Ethics Paradox.*

First, there's the price tag. It feels wrong to put a monetary value on nature. But leave it valueless, and it gets treated like it's worthless—cut down, dug up, wiped out.

Then there's capitalism. Using the system that helped cause the crisis to solve it? That sounds backwards. But isn't it just as wrong to ignore the only engine powerful enough to drive real change—especially when time's running out?

And fairness. Poorer countries are getting paid to clean up a mess they didn't make. That stings. But if all the climate money stays in Canland, is that really any fairer? Countries like Demba are hit hardest and can often cut emissions faster and cheaper than we can here.

The Activists

Turman's office didn't reopen on Monday—or the next week, or the month after that. It was a quiet casualty of the deepening drought.

With most buildings lacking air conditioning, siestas became the norm. Doors stayed shut. Even the Laguna Club—a place built for night owls—closed after two near-fatal heatstrokes. The city gave an ultimatum: install cooling systems or shut down. The club shut down.

Niburg's few pebble beaches were twenty kilometers out and a furnace of a bus ride away. The city's pools either dried up or over-flowed, offering no comfort, only noise and heat in a different form.

Their conversation had continued into the evening, then into the days that followed—through text chains, late-night calls, and sudden silences. Could climate projects in Demba ever be ethical? Was it right to put a price on a tree, a forest, a life? Were carbon credits a genuine solution—or just a way to look busy while the planet burned?

And if not carbon credits, then what?

They talked. They argued. They circled back. And eventually, they drifted into a state of apathy.

The heat drained everything. Even their outrage began to sweat.

By early afternoon each day, the sun ruled—merciless and unyielding. By night, Brigitte's Bungalow offered a steady harbor breeze that funneled fresh air through the alley.

That kept the outdoor tables and backyard Earth Cinema hopping well into the night. Robin and Andy curated a lineup of documentaries—on colonial-era resource extraction, radical blueprints for post-capitalist societies, speculative futures where AI guided climate policy. They were heavy films. Unsettling ones. The kind that lingered. The kind that asked more than they answered.

Ella's job as an assistant librarian gave them another kind of refuge. Unlike Andy and Robin, who ran the Earth Cinema more for purpose than pay, Ella had no parental safety net—she worked to pay the rent.

The university library—chilled to preserve its brittle archives—became their unofficial daytime headquarters. The boys claimed they were only keeping Ella company, but they were doing real research—first aimless, then obsessive.

They wanted to understand the history of climate action, or inaction. One article led to another. Clear answers gave way to sharper, meaner questions. Not about the science—they had that part down. The greenhouse effect? Eunice Foote demonstrated it in 1856. John Tyndall proved it in 1859. And in 1896, Svante Arrhenius published his model explaining how CO_2 influences the Earth's temperature.

No, the mystery wasn't scientific. It was political. Why had so little been done after so much had been known?

One afternoon, Andy held up a yellowing paper, squinting at the type. "Hey, check this out—from 1976."

He began to read.

"'The long-term response to climate change must be to stop burning fossil fuels... shift to solar, geothermal, nuclear... but it can't happen overnight.' And this part—'An emergency plant-growing program would hold CO_2 at bay while the transition happens.'" He looked up. "They basically mapped out everything: cut fossil fuels, restore nature to buy time for—not replace—that cut. Nearly fifty years ago."

Robin reached for a thick black volume. "You think that's wild? Try *Proceedings of the World Climate Conference: A Conference of Experts on Climate and Mankind.*"

Andy blinked. "Modest title."

Robin smirked. "Very '70s. But it was real. Geneva, 1979. The UN gathered top scientists from around the world. They all agreed—unanimously—that climate change was a serious threat. They even listed the top human causes: fossil fuels, deforestation, land use change..."

Ella rolled up behind them with her book cart, catching the tail end of their exchange.

"I found an even crazier one yesterday," she said. "It was about the ozone hole. Scientists confirmed it in 1985—and by 1987, the world had already signed the Montreal Protocol to fix it."

Andy blinked. "Wait—so we acted within two years on ozone, but we've been dragging our feet on the rest of the climate stuff since '79?"

He shook his head. "All that talk and still no action. How does that even make sense?"

Ella tried to capture all of this in a blog post she published on the Earth Cinema site—a sharp take on the promises of market-based climate solutions to break the political deadlock.

Andy forwarded the piece to his aunt, Wanga Namira, for her take ahead of the Climate Summit. He asked whether carbon credits could help fund projects in Demba—or whether organizing a fundraiser might be more useful. And if perhaps she had time to meet up. But she didn't respond.

And so the summer wore on—interesting, but without direction.

One night, a week before the climate summit, Brigitte floated up behind Andy, like a wisp of incense. She tapped him on the shoulder.

"Hey, kiddo, got a minute?"

He turned to face her.

"So, the police stopped by earlier," she said. "Apparently, the bar is bringing too much of a good thing for the fancy flats—they've been complaining. Noise. Crowds. People lingering out front."

She gave a slight shrug. "They're threatening to shut us down unless we dial things back. No more tables out front, at least not for now."

She paused. "Which... means we'll need to put the Earth Cinema on hold. I'm really sorry. I hate to do it. But I think the backyard's our only option for now."

Andy just nodded, too tired to protest and even a little relieved. The Earth Cinema had been losing its magic for both of the boys. Even the best documentaries were starting to feel like well-worn paths to nowhere, or the roads in Kafka's *Castle*.

He, Robin, and Ella were now of the belief that the real answers lay beyond the library, beyond the conversations, beyond anything yet captured in any medium. It was still out of reach, but after weeks of drifting, they could sense it getting near. The climate summit was close, and the night before, Andy's phone had finally pinged. It was Wanga.

> Hey, my son, wonderful to hear from you. I'm glad you want to do something for your home country. Hard times here. I have a few ideas. I'll be arriving in Niburg next Tuesday at 7am. See you soon. Kisses to your mom.

Two days before the summit, Robin began dismantling the Earth Cinema.

He undusted the battered projector, folded the cracked screen, and unplugged the popcorn machine that had fed so many summer nights.

Behind the bar, Remy and Luke were washing glasses.

"Where's the cover for this machine?" Robin asked.

"In the closet, at the bottom."

Robin crouched, reached in, and bumped into a giant black box.

"Hey, what's this?" he asked, struggling to pull it out. Remy stiffened as Robin pulled it into the light. He flipped open the lid.

Inside, he found tire punchers, bottles of superglue and spray paint, flashlights. A megaphone. Padlocks. Chains. And "Climate Warriors" flags.

His stomach dropped.

"This yours?" he asked quietly.

Remy didn't answer at first. She glanced at Luke, who looked away.

Then she squared her shoulders.

"Yes," she said.

Robin stared at her. "You joined the Climate Warriors?"

"We *are* the Climate Warriors," she said. "Because somebody has to be. All this talk, these films we've been showing—decarbonize, transition, pilot projects—nothing moves the needle." She tapped the box. "So we're moving it."

Robin rested the lid on the counter. "So you're... slashing tires now? Gluing yourselves to the highways? You think that's going to help the climate?"

She folded her arms, but her tone stayed measured. "Robin, you know what I'm talking about. For how long have they held climate summits? How many times have they promised reforms, and then nothing happened? We've run out of time, Robin. A project here, an innovation there, it won't save us. We need a reset. Radical change. Systems change!"

"Look, after watching the films, I'm probably even more frustrated than you," he said, trying to keep his voice steady. "But all that anger? All that destruction? That's just gonna scare people off—"

"People are sleepwalking, Robin," Remy continued, unimpressed. "We need their attention. Our message must hit the media. The climate is collapsing! Your fundraiser for Demba is good work, I respect it. But it's a Band-Aid on a bullet wound. And there's a strange smell to it. The rich and the powerful donate some leftovers to poor Dembans? The same Dembans we colonized for centuries? Stole all their wealth? Their pride?"

"It's a start," he countered.

"It's *your* start," she said gently. "*My* start looks different."

Luke finally spoke, placing a glass upside-down. "We're on the same side, Robin. Just different fronts."

Robin looked from Luke to Remy. Their conviction was unmistakable. He swallowed. "Promise me you'll stay safe."

"No promises," Remy said, but her expression softened. "Only that I'll keep fighting, for all of us." Robin closed the box and slid it back toward her. "I guess we both keep fighting, then. Different fronts."

She offered a faint, conciliatory smile. "Different fronts."

Then she pointed to a faded poster hanging just above a row of Cuban rum bottles. "*Venceremos!*" smiled Che Guevara from the print.

The Visionary

Robin caught the first tram at 6:04 a.m.—tall, rumpled, and barely awake.

Two stops later, he spotted Andy and his father, Omar, waiting on the platform, flicking away matching cigarette butts with mirrored movements—identical lean builds, same effortless swagger.

Two of the fittest guys I know, Robin thought. *And they still smoke like chimneys.*

Omar had met Andy's mother, Midela Bahari, a fellow Demban, when they were both exchange students at Niburg University. From that first semester, they'd been inseparable—sharing cramped flats, swapping notes, planning a future that carried them between Demba and Canland. Now, decades later, he was a partner at a public relations firm, while she had worked her way up to become dean of their alma mater.

At 6:34, they pulled into Niburg Central Station, where Ella stood beneath the flickering timetable. In place of her usual summer dress, she wore a muted linen blouse and loose navy trousers—the closest thing she owned to professional wear, chosen out of quiet respect for the day ahead.

"Morning," said Omar as they approached, his voice carrying the warm, clipped rhythm of Demba. "You must be the boss."

Ella grinned.

They sprinted through the chaos and scored four seats, face-to-face, on the intercity train bound for the airport.

Wanga Namira was due to land in about 20 minutes, and the three students planned to pick her brain on the ride back.

She came to the Canland Climate Summit every year—not so much for the panels or speeches (she'd heard them all, could probably recite them backwards) but for one reason: fundraising. The summit was her hunting ground, a place to shake hands with the powerful, corner donors between coffee breaks, and quietly secure the annual lifeblood of her organization, Matipa.

But in serving that agenda, she'd developed something of a cult following, known for speaking truth to power with warmth, wit, and just enough fire to leave a mark.

To Andy, she was still Auntie Wanga.

"She used to bounce me on her knee when we visited our family in Duiba," he said. "Called me her *shadow*—said I followed her like one." He paused.

"I only started reading her speeches this year," he admitted. "Now I catch myself quoting them word for word. Then I start arguing with them."

Omar chuckled. "She'll love that. I never told you this, but she was always impressed with your argumentation—even when you were dead wrong."

Robin recalled Wanga as the friendly stranger who sensed his fish-out-of-water awkwardness in Duiba when Andy took him to his hometown for the first time. She'd nudged him, he said, gently but firmly, into the current of village life.

"One time, your other aunts told me they had prayed over me," he laughed. "I was confused. Then Wanga pulled me aside and translated: she said they asked God to protect me—and give me a bountiful harvest."

Ella raised a brow. "A harvest of what?"

"Exactly," Robin said. "I didn't get it either. She grabbed my arm, looked me dead in the eye, and said, 'You're a farmer.' Then added: *We all are. Every human is cultivating something—figuratively or literally.*"

Ella nodded thoughtfully. "The closest I came to meeting her was at a university lecture a few years ago. She told all these incredible stories—funny ones, heartbreaking ones—but what stuck with me most was how she wrapped it up."

Ella instinctively mimicked Wanga's stance, her expression shifting, a mix of warmth and motherly scold.

"She stood there, looking out at the audience like she was making eye contact with every single person. Then she raised her finger at us:

"*You people of Canland, you need the people of the forests more than we need you.*'

"Some people in the audience started clapping and cheering, but she wasn't finished. She played the audience like an instrument, let the energy build, then closed with:

"*Whether in Demba, in Lomba, or any other country of the tropics, we, the forest communities of planet Earth, are your best defense against climate change. But we can't keep doing this for free, and neither can nature. You have the resources. We have the know-how. We must work together.*'"

As the train pulled into the airport, Andy, Robin, and Omar burst into spontaneous applause.

The airport had the feel of a massive community reunion. Tens of thousands of delegates from around the world were converging for the Summit. Everywhere you looked, someone was hugging someone else like they'd been through war together. These people *knew* each other—biblically, bureaucratically, occasionally suspiciously. Ministers, negotiators, royal advisors, rewilding evangelists, blockchain prophets, climate activists, methane monks—you name it. The arrivals section was starting to look like a TED Talk with luggage.

Outside the terminal building, volunteers in branded T-shirts steered dignitaries toward their designated shuttles. And then there was security—beefy, buzzcut, and omnipresent, watching the whole carnival with the stoicism of men who knew that beneath every climate accord was a potential protocol catastrophe.

Suddenly, a ripple of movement swept through the crowd as policemen hurriedly began clearing the way, motioning people to step aside. At the far end of the arrivals hall, a discreet door swung open, and a procession of stern-faced officers filed out in formation. Behind them followed a tall woman in an elegant, flowing Belé dress —its rich patterns shimmering under the airport lights.

"Wanga's coming!" Ella exclaimed, pointing. "Look over there— wow, that outfit! I remember it from her campus speech!"

Omar chuckled. "Haha, no, Ella, that's not Wanga. That's Minister Amina Keita, straight from the VIP exit. Looks like she was on the same Demban Airways flight—though I bet she flew first class."

Omar felt a tap on his shoulder.

A poised woman stepped forward, smiling gently, dressed in a soft blazer over a well-traveled blouse, comfortable trousers, and a scarf hastily knotted at the neck—practical, not performative. Her shoes were flat and sensible, her hair slightly frayed by recycled cabin air, and the dark crescents beneath her eyes spoke of long flights and tight schedules.

Her smile widened, cracking through the fatigue like sunlight after a storm, and she pulled Omar into a hug—simple, solid, and real. No words. Just the weight of shared history.

Then she turned to Andy and kissed him.

"Wanga, remember Robin?" Andy said after a moment of emotion, gesturing toward him. "And this is Ella."

"Ella!" Wanga exclaimed, her eyes lighting up. "You wrote that blog on the potential of carbon credits in Demba. Well done. And you're trying to pull these boys into the fire?!"

Before Ella could respond, Wanga reached out and clasped her forearm—firm, steady, reassuring—drawing her in with the exact presence Robin had promised.

"Do you think they're ready for that?"

The question hung in the air, but its implication was clear: *You*, Ella, *are ready.*

"Thank you, Miss Namira."

"Call me Wanga, please," she said, her tone both kind and insistent.

The train hummed, smooth and fast, carrying them back to Niburg.

Wanga turned to Robin. "This sure beats the bumpy ride to Duiba," she said, managing a tired wink.

Andy grunted. "It helps that Demba still ships raw cocoa, palm oil, and coffee beans to Canland and buys back candy bars and espresso," he muttered.

Wanga tilted her head. "And why do you think that is?"

"You know why," Andy replied. "Colonialism destroyed Demba, and capitalism is the new colonialism."

She looked at him with weary eyes. "I *know* that?" she repeated, as though inviting him to rethink his certainties.

Andy hesitated.

"Andy, what do you think we had before colonialism?" Wanga insisted.

"Well, as far as I know, before colonialism, the people in the jungles of Demba lived in peace and harmony, helping each other out."

"Listen, Andy. A lot of people in Canland love that story. The peaceful village. The noble savage. But that wasn't the whole picture."

She leaned forward now. Just a little.

"Life in Demba was hard. Brutal. People died young. There were no hospitals, no backup plans. We had wars throughout history, and while the colonists made them worse, large parts of our society welcomed them."

Andy nodded slowly. "The colonists brought guns. Germs. Steel. And lies."

"Not just lies," Wanga replied quietly. "They brought dreams too—opportunities, hope, the illusion of something better."

She turned her gaze to the window, where wind turbines spun past in a blur of motion and noise.

"Of course, those dreams were never meant for us. Not really. Colonialism hollowed us out. And post-colonialism keeps the wound from closing. Clinging to fantasies of a stolen utopia won't help us reclaim it."

Robin and Ella went quiet.

Andy pivoted. "But now you're helping, right? Schools, clinics, flood relief—Matipa is making progress."

Wanga gave a small smile. It didn't last.

"Matipa's a patch on a cracked dam," she said, her voice edged with fatigue and a trace of bitterness. "We rely on donors. Always have. Right now, everything's going to flood recovery in Limata. Our long-term projects—to empower communities, to restore the land and forests—they're all on hold."

She looked straight at Andy. "And tonight? I'll be at the Cresta Gala. Smiling. Toasting. *Begging.* That's what I'll do. You know, looks like the world doesn't want to be saved. It just wants to feel better about itself."

Andy shook his head. "This is mad. You shouldn't have to beg for money. What about carbon credits? Can they work? What if there was a price on trees?"

Wanga didn't answer right away. Her eyes stayed on the window.

"Maybe," she said finally. "Maybe. Let's talk about it tomorrow. But right now, the fastest way to help our people is to make sure rich people feel generous, and to do that, I need some beauty rest."

They all fell silent for a moment. Outside, the windmills had vanished, replaced by rows of sprawling suburban apartment blocks. The train was closing in on Niburg Central.

Suddenly, the spark in Wanga's eyes returned. "By the way, I have three extra tickets to the Gala."

She let it hang.

"You wanna come? Meet the people who make the rules? Hear what they care about? See how this world actually works? Test your idea of carbon credits?"

It wasn't an invitation.

It was a dare.

The Lecture

Omar hustled Wanga off to a taxi, leaving Ella, Andy, and Robin on the platform.

They glanced at one another, eyes wide, their expressions caught somewhere between disbelief and giddy anticipation.

Had Wanga just invited them to the Niburg Cresta Gala? This wasn't just a gala—it was *the* gala. The legendary kickoff to the Canland Climate Summit, held each year on the eve of the official opening. A glittering vortex of wealth, influence, and exquisitely tailored ego, hosted by Cresta Software under the noble banner of raising funds for "worthy causes." It had always been a coveted ticket, but this year it practically radiated heat—figuratively, of course. In reality, it offered the rarest luxury of all: flawless air conditioning.

"I don't even own a suit," Andy spluttered. "Or a tie! Or anything remotely resembling—"

Ella cut him off. "Andy, what are you babbling about? Get one from your father! You guys look like twins."

"I will look like an idiot in a suit," grumbled Robin.

"Well, you guys figure it out. This is huge!" Ella said. "Do you realize what this means? We could meet people who might buy carbon credits, and Wanga could introduce us to organizations that are doing worthy projects!"

Andy grinned. "And all this right after Minister Keita's lecture—how cool is that? Everything we've been talking about for weeks is suddenly coming together!"

Buzzing with anticipation, Ella, Robin, and Andy lingered over a long breakfast at the Laguna Café, then got lost in a stroll along the harbor front, and ended up arriving at the Auditorium Maximum late, breathless, and slightly disheveled.

A poster of Amina Keita loomed beside the entrance—her portrait poised, eyes steady, the printed text below it reading: *Join us for the Sixth Lecture in Our Climate Leadership Series: The History of International Climate Finance.*

Cold air rushed over them the moment they stepped inside. A second later, they spotted the source: temporary ducts lashed to the ceiling, blasting relief from the heatwave into the crowded lobby and the auditorium beyond.

They slipped through the auditorium doors and into a wall of murmurs and rustling programs. The place was packed, but they found three seats in the second-to-last row. Andy grinned and whispered, "Just like high school. Always late, always in the back."

Ella scanned the room in front of her. "I've been reading up on this woman. She used to be the lead climate negotiator for the group of developing countries. She even attended the negotiations of the Montreal Protocol back in the '80s as a youth representative!"

A familiar voice sliced into her history lesson.

"Ms. Andersson," it said.

Ella turned to see Professor Dieter Turman seated right behind them —his graying hair slightly tousled, a neatly pressed blazer with elbow patches lending him an air of timeless academia. A good-natured, somewhat mischievous smile played on his lips. He had watched countless enthusiastic students pass through his classroom over the years, yet the mysteries and paradoxes of economics remained, to him, as endlessly fascinating as ever.

"I'm glad to see you here," he said. "You won't regret it—I promise. Ms. Keita is one of the sharpest minds in climate finance. Appointing her was a brilliant move by the Demban president."

"I've been reading up on her—on the whole history of the negotiations," Ella said. "There's a lot more history than I realized."

"Exactly," Turman nodded. "And without the history, the present doesn't make much sense."

Ella stood and gestured toward Andy and Robin. "These are my high-school friends. Andy's mom is Midela Lelong—the flood last week hit near her village." She hesitated, then added, "Do you think carbon credits could actually help Demba? We want to support something real—something that lasts."

Turman smiled gently. "Well, pay good attention," he whispered, "and don't let the acronyms scare you."

The lights dimmed. A hush spread across the hall.

A spotlight struck the podium. Out walked Professor Midela Lelong. Dean of the University of Niburg. Andy's mother.

"It is my honor," she said, her accent clipped and formal, "to welcome you to this afternoon's lecture in our 'Climate Leadership' series.

"You are here to hear from a woman whose influence in the field of climate science cannot be overstated—a pioneer, a mentor, a friend. Long before the term 'climate science' entered our lexicon, she was laying its moral and intellectual groundwork.

"We invited her to reflect on the arc of this field—from early doubts to today's challenges. But the urgency of the present has overtaken the calm of academic retrospection. Just last month, the Republic of Demba was devastated by catastrophic floods."

She paused, biting her tongue to keep her composure. "Floods that claimed hundreds of lives and displaced thousands more. This is not abstract. We have all lost friends, colleagues, and community members. Let there be no doubt: climate change is not a theory to be tested or a future to be forestalled. It is here. It is real. And it is reshaping the world we thought we knew."

She paused again. "But now, please join me in welcoming Minister Amina Keita, of the Republic of Demba."

The applause came softly, almost tentatively.

And there she was again. The woman who just hours ago emerged from the airport now stepped forward, her gown a cascade of deep indigo and sun-warmed earth tones, wrapped with the five elements of the Belé people—the sky, the animals, the mountains, the forest, and the ocean—stitched into every fold.

Keita moved with deliberate grace, nodding once to Midela before stepping up to the podium. She looked out across the auditorium—not just at the faces, but into the mood.

"Thank you, Midela, my sister. Thank you, Dean Lelong," she said, her voice low and resonant. "And thank you all—for being here today, and for holding space in a moment that feels, at once, historic and heartbreakingly current."

She let the silence hold.

"When we planned this lecture," she continued, "I had hoped to begin with something light—maybe a story from our early days in the field. But then, the floods came. And with them, grief."

A hush swept through the room like wind through dry grass.

"I speak to you today not only as a scientist or a minister, but as a daughter of the soil. As someone whose homeland is no longer a case study but a cautionary tale."

She inhaled slowly, eyes scanning the crowd.

"But we are not here to despair. We are here to understand. To remember that science has always warned us and that action—real, coordinated, and courageous—has always been possible."

She glanced over her shoulder. Behind her, an image emerged: a jagged red line rising across a pale graph like a scar or a heartbeat.

"This is the Keeling Curve—a record of atmospheric carbon dioxide, measured over the past sixty years."

She looked up at the red zigzag. "Like many truths, it revealed itself first as a paradox."

She told the story of how Charles Keeling set up his instrument on Mauna Loa, Hawaii, in the late 1950s; how the first readings came in steady, then dropped, then climbed again; and how even Keeling suspected the machine was broken.

"But it was not the instrument," Keita said. "It was the Earth itself— breathing in carbon during the northern summer, breathing it back in winter. What looked like error was in fact the signal. That was the first paradox."

The line on the screen pulsed upward, tooth by tooth.

"And here is the second: after Keeling proved it was real, the world nearly let it vanish. Funding collapsed, mentors passed away, and agencies turned elsewhere. The clearest record of our atmosphere almost disappeared—not from doubt, but from indifference. Certainty without urgency. Clarity without action."

She paused, letting the silence settle across the hall.

"The Keeling Curve is more than a scientific record," she concluded. "It is a parable. Progress does not come from avoiding paradoxes, but from following them."

She looked up at the red zigzag. "The pattern was clear from the start: CO_2 wasn't just fluctuating—it was rising. But those zigzags? That's a signal, not noise: the breath of the planet, trees of the temperate zones, inhaling in summer, exhaling in winter."

She paused, then let her hand fall from the screen.

"But the Keeling Curve marks only the moment we started measuring—not the moment this story began."

She then led the room back further, away from modern graphs and into the deeper past—a high-energy journey through the rise of civilization and the evolution of climate science.

She moved briskly—past the industrial revolution, past the early murmurs of concern. The crowd leaned in as she stitched together obscure milestones and familiar events, weaving them into a single thread that pulled toward the present.

Then her tone shifted.

She spoke of the 1980s, when fossil fuel companies still funded climate research and bipartisan leaders spoke openly of global cooperation—before it all unraveled.

"These same energy companies quietly slipped away and changed strategy without anyone noticing," she called out to the auditorium, raising her finger. "They launched disinformation campaigns and deliberately funded university chairs that denied climate change or downplayed its looming consequences. They succeeded in portraying the statistical uncertainties of climate science as fundamental doubts about climate change itself—and thus took the wind out of the sails of climate policy. Scientific uncertainty—once a step toward truth—was twisted into an excuse for inaction."

She pivoted to the ozone crisis. "But in this case, we listened to the scientists. We acted. In 1985, the ozone hole was discovered. In 1987, the Montreal Protocol was signed. We said, 'Let's stop using chemicals that destroy the ozone layer. And let's help each other find safer alternatives.'"

She looked out over the room, her eyes steady.

"So how was that possible? How did we act—decisively, collectively, globally? And why aren't we doing the same now, in the face of climate change?"

Ella, Andy, and Robin sat forward in their chairs. That was precisely the question they had debated in the library.

"Part of the reason is simple. The ozone problem was smaller and easier to fix. It involved just a few chemicals, and the alternatives were ready. Climate change is much bigger. It's tied to everything—energy, food, transport, money. And the industries involved are more powerful."

She paused, then shifted again—this time with conviction. "But there was something else. Something more important.

"During the ozone crisis, governments, industry, and civil society worked hand in hand. Governments set the rules. Industry responded—with innovation and alternatives. And the public supported the effort—with trust, with pressure, with purpose."

She gripped the podium, briefly, grounding the weight of her words.

"To ensure fairness, industrialized countries like Canland took the lead, phasing out harmful substances more quickly. Countries like Demba were given time, support, and funding. That's what common but differentiated responsibilities means. All nations share the burden—but not equally. Not blindly. Climate justice is not about blame—it's about balance. Those who've contributed most must lead. And those most vulnerable must be empowered—not left behind."

She moved forward again, her voice now bright with momentum.

"After Montreal came something even bigger: the UN Framework Convention on Climate Change. And in 1997, the Kyoto Protocol. It was a historic achievement for two reasons. First, it made developed countries legally responsible for cutting emissions. Second, it created a way for people in different parts of the world to work together. The Clean Development Mechanism, as it was called. A farmer in Demba. A utility company in Canland. They could cooperate on solutions."

She raised a finger.

"This was the beginning of carbon credits. In Kyoto, they were called Certified Emission Reductions. The idea was bold: you don't just reduce emissions through charity—you do it through partnership.

Business and climate action could go hand in hand. Farmers in Demba weren't just victims or aid recipients—they were stewards of the land, providers of ecosystem services. "

She let that settle, then continued:

"But the Clean Development Mechanism was historic in two other important ways," Keita continued, her voice steady.

"First, the methodologies for calculating emissions reductions weren't imposed from the top down. Everything was public. Everything was transparent. Scientists, consultants, NGOs, companies—hundreds of experts—rolled up their sleeves. They proposed methodologies, monitoring systems, and verification protocols. They debated, challenged one another, tested assumptions, refined approaches. Round after round of expert review, public consultation, pushback, revision, and more review. It was an inspiring exercise in co-creation—a global community building trust through science and open process."

She paused briefly, letting that sink in.

"And second," she continued, "participation wasn't limited to governments or companies with legal obligations. The Clean Development Mechanism was open to everyone. Any company. Any individual. A voluntary carbon market emerged, small but growing. Suddenly, the dream of a global currency to fund climate action didn't feel so far-fetched—it felt within reach."

She paused again. The auditorium was silent. Hanging on her words.

"Then, just as the protocol started to gain momentum and the price for carbon credits went up, the world hit a financial crisis. Politicians were distracted, and they couldn't agree on how to extend the protocol past its first commitment period. And yes, the Clean Development Mechanism ran into some problems. As with any novel concept, some tried to cut corners, exploiting loopholes. A lot of governments pulled out. Demand for carbon credits was gone. A bunch of projects were just left hanging—no funding, no future."

She paused. "After the collapse, all that was left was the voluntary market.

"Some companies continued buying credits—not because they had to, but because they believed it was the right thing to do. But the scale never came close to what we once dreamed of, back in those early, hopeful days."

Her eyes swept the crowd and then softened.

"Today, the Paris Agreement gives us another chance. A new path forward—based on cooperation. The agreement explicitly places carbon markets under the heading of 'cooperative approaches,' recognizing that countries can work together—across borders—to meet their climate goals more efficiently. And the research is clear: when countries cooperate, when public and private sectors team up across national lines, the cost of climate solutions can be cut in half."

She let the next line land like a drumbeat.

"And cutting the cost in half doesn't just save money. It doubles the impact."

She held up two fingers.

"Twice the trees. Twice the resilience. Twice the lives changed—for the same cost."

The Gala

A few hours later, Robin was pedaling down the boulevard to the Niburg Convention Center. Colorful banners lined the street, all shouting the same message: "Cresta—Software That Works for You!"

He swung off his bike, aiming for effortless grace. Instead, a sharp rip cut through the moment—his ill-fitting black suit trousers tangled in the chain, unraveling his dignity thread by thread.

Behind him, a cruel, crystalline sound erupted, landing somewhere between mockery and melodious schadenfreude. He spun, and there stood Andy, looking like James Bond in his father's tux, while Robin felt like a magician who specialized in the art of disappointing children.

Then came Ella, sweeping into view in a green-golden evening gown that caught the light just so.

"Behave," she said, eyes flicking between them. "Wanga's right there."

They turned to see Wanga crossing the square in her traditional Demban gown.

This was the public Wanga. The one the press called "The Princess of Belé."

Andy hated that title. But seeing her like this—he felt his Demban and familial pride.

"Ah, my dear brothers and dear sister!" Wanga called. "Come over here!"

She turned gracefully to the man beside her, tall and composed, with salt-and-pepper hair brushed back from a high forehead and a navy suit that seemed tailored by algorithm.

"Doctor Cresta, please meet my friends. This is Andy, my nephew. His mom, Professor Lelong, is a fellow Belé from Demba. My sister is now Dean of the University of Niburg!"

Andy extended his hand, eyes wide, but his greeting jammed somewhere between his brain and his throat. He managed a nod and a dry "Good ev—" before falling silent.

Ella slipped into the smile that had won so many debates before they even began. "Good evening, Dr. Cresta," she said cheerfully. "It's a great pleasure to meet you. My name is Ella Andersson. We work on environmental projects aimed at reducing greenhouse gas emissions. We—"

"Wonderful," Cresta interrupted, glancing at his watch. "A very important issue indeed. Climate change is out of control, as we all know. You should talk to Matt about that." He gestured toward a deeply tanned man in his mid-thirties with a perfectly groomed mustache, standing a few meters away and—Robin immediately noticed—looking impeccable in his tuxedo and silver cufflinks. "Matt leads our company's sustainability strategy."

Matt stepped closer as Cresta was already turning to a slender man flanked by two bodyguards.

Robin narrowed his eyes. "Isn't that our environment minister?"

"Paul Becker, yes," Andy said. "And look—Minister Keita is over there too. Incredible. Does she have infinite energy reserves or something?"

Matthew Carter greeted Ella with a casual, carefully performed indifference. In reality, he had been watching the green-and-gold evening gown—and the young woman wearing it—out of the corner of his eye for quite some time.

Ella didn't let herself be distracted for a second and launched straight into her presentation: climate change, CO_2 certificates, the local population in Demba, the long-term vision. Andy and Robin stood beside her like stunned schoolboys. Had she secretly memorized Keita's speech that afternoon? Matt listened attentively, his head slightly tilted. He was visibly impressed—and no longer just by Ella's evening gown.

"Cresta has been carbon neutral for five years," he said, with restrained pride. "We buy CO_2 certificates all over the world. First tech group to take that step. Believe me, I had to fight internal resistance." He gave a brief laugh. "My goal is to support at least one project in every country where we operate. Well, that's my vision, anyway."

He leaned closer. "You should meet Ross Murphy. CEO of Rower. The oil company drilling off Demba's coast."

All three froze.

"I know what you're thinking," Matt laughed. "Oil and gas—the villains. But I'm telling you, Murphy is also a huge philanthropist!" He lowered his voice. "He has an unbelievable amount of money. He funds orphanages, hospitals, schools—everything imaginable. He's giving the keynote tonight, right after Wanga's opening remarks. If anyone is going to buy your CO_2 certificates, Murphy is your best bet!"

The security line crawled past metal detectors and armed guards. Inside, the grand hall shimmered: chandeliers blazed above polished marble, enormous photographs of smiling Demban children lined the walls. Waiters in black and white moved like insects through the crowd, balancing cocktails topped with tiny umbrellas in the colors of the Dembanian flag.

Behind the bar, they spotted a familiar face.

"Luke!"

He winked at Andy, and moments later, they were holding perfect cocktails. Ella took a sip and coughed.

"Jesus, that's strong."

Matt smiled. "That's intentional. Donations increase when the better halves feel festive."

Ella shot him a look. An usher appeared, sparing her from replying.

Table 27—near the back. Matt's seat was at table 26.

The lights in the hall were dimmed, the background music faded, and the murmur of voices gradually died down. The waitstaff lined up along the walls, beneath enormous images of smiling Dembanian children. Two magnificent candelabra on the stage flanked the lectern, which glowed in a warm, almost romantic candlelight.

Then Luke appeared again—not along the wall, but at Wanga's side, escorting her gallantly onto the stage.

Robin raised an eyebrow. "Seriously? Luke—our rebel? If the Climate Warriors knew about this!"

Wanga approached the dais with the calm confidence of someone used to commanding attention. The polished wood of the podium caught the shimmer of her gown, dazzling in the candlelight, as she turned to face the crowd.

At the podium, Wanga scanned the audience—a mosaic of ambassadors, CEOs, ministers, and dignitaries—and began.

"Minister Keita, Minister Becker, Excellencies, Ambassadors, Directors, and honored guests," she began. "It is my privilege to welcome you tonight in the name of the Belé and Nolé people. May the five elements inspire you—the sky, the animals, the mountains, the forest, and the ocean!"

Polite applause rippled through the hall, quickly overtaken by the clink of cutlery and resumed conversation. Wanga pressed on, detailing the impact of their generous donations, especially in the aftermath of the Limata floods.

Ella frowned. "No one's listening to Wanga."

"They will," Matt said. "She's laying the groundwork. Ross comes next. He'll brag about his generous donations. Then Becker. Brainy and boring. After that, Wanga will thank him for taking time out of his busy schedule to join us, and then she and Ross will sit right there."

He pointed to the two empty chairs at table one, right in front of the stage. "They'll stay through the main course, and then, before dessert, Minister Keita will give her keynote. Provided she hasn't fallen asleep by then. Thomas Cresta will follow, reintroduce Wanga, and that's when she'll lower the boom. Then come the Demban dancers and artists—they're the real heart of the evening."

He glanced at Ella, paused, then continued.

"After that, they'll auction ancient Demban jewelry, VIP safari trips, expensive paintings, private dinners with celebrities... Believe me, no successful husband leaves untouched."

A sharp "Shhh!" cut through his running commentary from the grand dames at the neighboring table.

Matt only smiled, catching the look on Ella's face.

Ella, Andy, and Robin sat uncomfortably in their chairs.

Luke helped Wanga down from the dais and took a position between her and one of the venue's uniformed private guards while she chatted with Paul Becker.

Andy glanced to the other side of the dais, where a female server took Ross Murphy's hand and began guiding him up the stairs.

"Wow, looks like they ordered the staff straight out of a fashion catalog," Robin muttered.

Andy squinted. "Holy crap, Robin—that's Remy! On the arm of the oil boss! I'm losing my shit!"

She was wearing a spectacular hairstyle and heavy makeup—but it was unmistakably Remy.

Ross Murphy took his spot at the dais as two banners unfurled dramatically on either side of him.

"Thank You Rower!" they proclaimed.

The oil boss began his speech exactly as Matt had predicted. Clinics. Trees. Orphans. Poverty. Generosity. Hope. The future. He sounded like a preacher at an evangelical service. The audience listened, hanging on his every word, breaking into spontaneous applause again and again.

Until suddenly, two more banners descended from the ceiling—also emblazoned with words in giant capital letters.

One read: CLIMATE.

The other: WARRIORS.

Remy and Luke vaulted onto the stage, fists thrust high into the air.

"What do we waaaant?" Remy screamed, her voice slicing through the stunned silence.

"Climate justice!" Luke thundered back.

"Wheeeen do we want it?"

"NOW!"

Two guards moved towards the stage but stopped. They knew the drill: wait for the protest to end, then politely escort them out the door.

But Ross Murphy flinched. His microphone slipped from his grasp, clattering to the floor and rolling toward Remy. Without missing a beat, she stomped it under her foot—calm, sharp, deliberate. Not a tantrum. A message.

Then Luke, his face tight with nerves, fumbled out his smartphone. His thumb jabbed frantically at the screen.

"What the hell!" whispered Ella. "What is he doing?"

Boom!

All the lights went out. Only the flickering flames from the massive candelabras cast an eerie glow across the stage.

Screams. Shattering glass. Panic.

Exit signs glowed red like eyes in the night. Remy's voice cut through the darkness—unnaturally loud, magnified through the hijacked sound system:

"Climate justice! Rower, stop drilling! Rower, stop killing!"

The two security guards jumped on stage.

"Rower, stop drilling! Rower, stop—" Remy's voice disappeared in a clunk. A guard had captured her arm and her microphone.

The second guard ran towards Luke. He twisted, brushing against the middle candelabra, and one of the candles tilted sideways—straight into the edge of the 'WARRIORS' banner.

The acrylic went up like a polyester piñata soaked in rocket fuel, and the ballroom bloomed with smoke. The curtain above the banner caught fire. Alarms wailed, and sprinklers burst open in synchronized panic, baptizing the chaos.

The two guards flung Remy and Luke to the ground as their colleagues flooded to drag them out.

"Evacuation! Evacuation!"

Keita and Becker's bodyguards snapped into action. So did Murphy's. Grabbing their arms. Identifying an exit. Scanning the crowd—hands near hips, ready for anything. More bodyguards jumped up to rescue their own dignitaries.

In the center of it all stood Wanga, alone. No security. No backup. Just her and the weight of everything she carried.

The Plunge

The morning sun caught the edges of the coffee table, glinted off the rim of Robin's empty tea mug, then settled on his half-eaten croissant. It illuminated ceremonial masks from Midela's hometown, bold posters from Omar's old campaigns, and a folded gala program from the night before.

"It still doesn't feel real," Andy said. "What an unbelievably bizarre scene that was. Fully air-conditioned room in the heat. Wanga begging for money. An oil company boss posturing as a noble donor. And then Remy and Luke come in and crash the party. In the end, no winners. Only losers."

Ella sat cross-legged on the floor, her laptop on the coffee table, perusing headlines from around the world. "Everyone's reporting the chaos. Arrests, protests, the auction that never happened. No one's talking about why Wanga was there in the first place."

She tapped her screen.

"Hey, listen to this!" said Ella. "Luke and Remy got arrested and ended up in Harborview Jail. The city wants to sue them and the Climate Warriors."

"I'm not sure about that," Robin mused. "Yeah, Remy and Luke acted like idiots, but Luke didn't mean to set the whole place on fire

—it was more of a dumb accident than anything else. I doubt they'll be stuck behind bars for long. Probably just a slap on the wrist and a good story to tell."

The doorbell rang, and there was Wanga—the informal Wanga, in jeans and T-shirt, a bandage peeking out from under her headscarf.

"I hope I'm not too early," she said.

A few moments later, she was on the sofa beside Robin.

"I feel sorry for the young protesters," she said, her voice soft but firm. "I feel their pain. And let's face it, they have a point. But what to do now? The fundraising gala has collapsed."

She paused, exhaling with purpose before continuing, sipping the herbal tea Andy had offered. "Listen, you asked me if I knew of any projects in Demba you could raise money for, and the answer is yes. There are many. Disaster relief. Education. Local health centers. Many things you could support."

She nodded slowly, her gaze drifting toward some distant point only she could see.

"It's just that... honestly..." she began, then trailed off.

"It's just that it doesn't move the needle," Ella finished, her voice steady.

"Exactly. It doesn't," Wanga replied. "We're stuck in a hamster wheel. A disaster strikes, donations come in. Some people get funding, others get nothing. But nothing truly changes—nothing fundamental. You all heard Minister Keita yesterday, right?"

They nodded.

"She must've talked about international climate finance. About turning climate action into a business case. About giving every farmer, every project developer, every entrepreneur in Demba a real shot—not as beneficiaries, but as partners. To get paid for reducing emissions. That's what carbon credits were supposed to do."

"*Double the impact for every crown spent. All while creating jobs, restoring dignity, and building opportunity,*" Ella whispered, almost to herself.

Wanga sighed. "Sadly, it never really took off."

Andy moved in his chair. "Look, I know I've been skeptical about carbon credits—probably the loudest in the room—but we've been wrestling with this for weeks, and after last night... I don't think there's a clean right or wrong. Not yet. So I say, we take the plunge. Give these carbon credits a shot."

Ella and Robin looked at him.

"That's my thinking, too," said Wanga.

"But where to start?" said Ella, turning to Wanga. "Do you have any ideas for projects we could fund with carbon credits?"

"That," said Wanga, "is the important question. Let me tell you what we need, and then we'll see what we can do."

They leaned forward like children at story time.

"Most people think Matipa is about building dams and helping the poor. But the real mission is both broader and more focused: it's about helping subsistence communities shift to sustainable land use. Agroforestry, rotational grazing, integrated pest management. Protecting what forests remain. Re-growing what we've lost."

She looked each of them in the eye. "But reforestation and conservation aren't just about planting trees or saving forests. Both start with people. You can't save a forest unless you change the pressures that destroy it, and you can't just plant trees for the same reason: if you don't address the root cause, they'll just chop the trees again."

She sat back.

"Here's what you need to understand about Demba. Yes, big timber and palm oil companies are driving deforestation—but so are poor farmers. People pushed into the forest out of desperation. That's why we call it a *wicked problem*. Do you know what a wicked problem is?"

"A complex challenge with no clean solution," said Ella. "Fixing one part creates problems elsewhere."

"It's also called a paradox," added Robin.

"Exactly. One major player is the company Walmera. It's a large conglomerate. They are big in palm oil, soybeans, rubber, and sugarcane. They hold palm oil and timber concessions across the country. Over the past decades, a large part of Demba's forests has been converted to agricultural land. One exception is the region Coltra East. It's a remote area. Walmera holds logging concessions there as well."

Her voice dropped. "And here, perhaps, we might have a big opportunity. Their CEO—Hubert Spencer—told me privately they might be willing to give up those concessions. But only if someone's able to cover their losses."

"I see. So the idea could be to sell carbon credits to cover these losses?" asked Ella.

"Yes. They're open to licensing part of the forest to Matipa—if we secure carbon finance. In exchange, they'd cancel development plans and help us turn it into a national park."

Andy frowned. "So we pay them *not* to destroy the forest? That's not climate finance—that's ransom."

"They should just hand back the concessions," Ella agreed. "But I suppose that's not going to happen. They paid for those concessions. Their shareholders expect something in return. And expropriations are not an option either, as they would drive the country straight into a financial crisis. No one would invest anymore."

"Correct," said Wanga. "But that's only the first part of the problem. The bigger one is that letting go of the concession isn't enough. Turning it into a national park isn't just a declaration. The government won't approve it unless we can show how it will be managed and funded for at least thirty years. That means we have to work with communities to create a long-term management plan and show we can pay for management, monitoring, fire control—that sort of thing. Without all that, it's just a 'paper park'."

She looked at Andy.

"So even if Walmera walked away tomorrow, we'd still need an endowment or some guaranteed revenue stream. Without that, the government won't sign off on national park status, and we can't get there without carbon finance."

Robin, sensing a rabbit hole, interjected. "You mentioned reforestation, too?" he said. "The horrible Limata flood happened mainly because all the trees in the surrounding hills got cut, right? How about a project to restore those trees?"

Wanga's face softened. "Yes. Indeed. That could be a second opportunity. And this one's personal."

Robin nodded. "The Lester Hills, right? Andy took me there last year."

"When I was a child, those forests were magic," Wanga said. "My uncle built us a treehouse up there. One morning, we woke to the sounds of chainsaws and bulldozers. Two months later, they were all gone."

She looked down.

"The river turned brown. The land was stripped bare. All for a development project that people thought would help. We were promised profits from export crops—sugar, tobacco, palm oil. And for a while, it worked.

"But the soil washed away. Yields dropped. People moved uphill to farm, clearing more forest, creating more runoff. Flash floods became common. The fish died. And now, we've got the Limata flood."

Robin shook his head. "Insane. Cutting the trees was supposed to make people rich. But it made them even poorer."

"Yes. And Walmera still holds the Lester Hills. The land's too depleted even for oil palm. They'd gladly sublet it—if we use it to grow the forest back."

"That would make so much sense," Andy said, increasingly enthusiastic. "Restore habitat. Store carbon."

"It won't be easy," Wanga said. "Planting trees is one thing. Helping them survive—and helping people thrive alongside them—is another."

She paused, letting that land.

"Carbon finance can make this possible. It's not a silver bullet, but it can support local leadership and restore balance—if the communities are on board."

"How do we get them on board?" asked Ella.

"By listening first. And then by offering opportunities," said Wanga.

How much do you know about Demba's history?"

"Not much, beyond what you told us on the train," Robin replied.

"Then let me expand on that, because history here isn't background —it's the terrain you're walking on."

She leaned forward.

"Demba isn't a country that was colonized; it's a country created by colonialism. The borders are arbitrary because we never used to organize ourselves by geography. We organized by tribe, and those tribes were and still are the Belé and the Nolé. Our communities stretch far into what is now the Republic of Lomba."

"Is 'tribe' the right word?" asked Robin.

"It's the word we use," she answered. "You can say peoples, nations, tribes... either way, both groups lived by a mix of slash-and-burn farming and pastoralism. You clear a patch, burn it, use the ash to grow food, then let the land heal. Meanwhile, you herd goats, cows, sheep across the grasslands. And the men hunted. My uncle Duolo used to go off with Grandpa for days. He wore his pride like a medal."

"Good old Uncle Duolo... I can imagine..." Andy said with a smile.

"Andy, you talked about *the ancient Demba*, and I hit you kind of hard because I've never seen any good come from mythologizing the past, but there's truth in what you said as well. One is this: over many centuries, the land was not owned by anybody, at least not in the sense we understand ownership today. The two peoples were subdivided into smaller tribes and clans, and the idea was that each clan occupied the land it needed to get along. When there were conflicts, the Elders' Councils met and tried to resolve the dispute. That didn't always go well, though. Belé and Nolé sadly have a very long history of brutal fighting—not unlike the tribes of Europe. There are stories of rivers running red with blood.

"And then the Canlandish colonizers arrived, some two hundred years ago, with their boots and their greed and their polished lies—not to mention their guns, germs, and steel, as you pointed out the other day. It didn't take them long to figure out the cracks between the Belé and Nolé—cracks they could pry apart for their own gain.

"They approached the Elders' Council of the Nolé with a deal—a clever deal, dressed up in promises and flattery. The colonizers would hold the official land title, but—here's the hook—they swore to establish a Nolé government, ruling not just their own lands but the Belé territories as well. The Nolé celebrated. They thought they'd finally won. So they helped the colonizers conquer the rest."

Her voice turned sharp.

"But joy built on a lie never lasts. The so-called Nolé government was a hollow thing. It collapsed within decades. And when the colonizers fled, they left chaos in their wake. Belé and Nolé governments took turns—none brought peace. Each has focused primarily on funneling government contracts to their own clan. Just look at our two highways. They run parallel through the country and aren't even properly connected to each other. One was built by Belé companies, the other by Nolé companies. It's tragic."

She took a slow sip of tea.

"So now, people don't trust promises—especially from the government. They've taken most matters into their own hands. If you want their support, you have to *show* them the benefit. Not in theory. In reality."

She sat back, then leaned in again.

"So now, this brings me back to the third idea. One big problem is the lack of power—not just political power, but electricity."

Her voice grew wistful.

"When your mom and I were kids, the village turned pitch dark right after sunset: no lights, no TVs, nothing. Before elections, government officials frequently visited the town, promising to improve electricity. Yet, nothing materialized for a long time. Eventually, a few cables were installed, but the power supply was unreliable, available for a few hours each day at best. Fed up, some of the more affluent people in the village managed to purchase their power generators, which they occasionally fire up. The noise, the smoke, and the smell of the diesel are unbearable.

"The third project option is to help villagers buy solar cells to put on their roofs. This way, we could allow them to get rid of the diesel generators, which would also reduce CO_2, correct?"

"That is correct," said Ella. "Building solar power was even the example our Economics Professor used to explain how carbon credits work. You replace dirty with clean power."

"It sounds quite good, no?" Wanga laughed. "But remember, Demba isn't Canland. It has its own rhythms—its own customs and corruptions. Dance to the wrong beat, and you may send your partner tumbling—or end up on the floor yourself.

"Our five elements didn't bring us much luck last night," She continued. "Yet, I am trying again: May our elements be with you on your journey—the sky, the animals, the mountains, the forest, and the ocean!"

Her blessing lingered in the air, weaving itself into the room's quiet, as if the elements themselves were listening.

There was no time to lose now.

Ella, Andy, and Robin agreed to meet at the Bungalow later in the afternoon to discuss the next steps.

A knot began to tighten in Ella's chest. She had mapped out her summer down to the hour, each overtime shift at the library calculated to buy her breathing room once classes resumed. Now they were about to take a plunge into the unknown. A novel concept of carbon credits. A complex country full of wicked problems.

Would that risk eventually pay off? And how about Simon? How would he take it?

Part Two

The Project

The Additionality Paradox

Professor Dieter Turman leaned back in his chair, fingers steepled, a glint of amusement in his eyes as Ella finished her short presentation. The modest office was mostly swallowed up by tall, jam-packed bookshelves that stretched nearly to the ceiling.

The one patch of clear wall featured a bright, colorful chart that looked vaguely like an old-fashioned telephone pole toppled on its side—lines branching out, angles intersecting.

A Pigouvian tax graph. It illustrated how pollution drives a wedge between private gain and social cost—and how the right kind of tax could close the gap.

It was proudly framed, like a portrait of a favorite uncle who'd done the family proud, and it doubled as a quiet reminder of Turman's creed: economics should serve the common good—and making polluters pay was just sound economics.

Over the years, countless students sat across his old wooden table—pitching term papers, theses, even doctoral proposals—nervously awaiting his verdict. But this was different. This was their second meeting, and Turman was doing his best to mask his growing excitement.

These three weren't just theorizing—they were trying to put his life's work into practice: pricing externalities in the real world.

What if it actually worked? What if they succeeded in funding real projects by putting a cost on carbon emissions? His mind raced. Payments for communities that protect forests. Incentives to conserve water. Maybe even funding for rural clinics. A system that could address not just environmental harm, but inequality itself.

After a thoughtful pause, he finally spoke.

"Putting a price on carbon—clearly, that idea left a mark on you."

He glanced at each of them, then leaned forward, his tone shifting from playful to purposeful.

"Well, I have good news. I've spoken with the Faculty of Engineering. Robin and Andy, you're officially cleared to write a joint term paper with Ella from the Faculty of Economics. And the deadline's extended until the end of the year."

He paused, letting that sink in. Then, more solemnly: "Also—I'm approving your request for a research grant. We'll cover your travel to Demba. And Ella, we'll provide a stipend to support you while you step away from your job at the library."

A smile crept back to his face.

"I wish you the very best," he said, his eyes gleaming. "The world belongs to those who dare."

And then, they were on the way.

Demba calling.

Ella snagged the window seat, arguing that the others had seen the view before, then fell asleep on the oversized pillow she'd brought.

Robin, trapped in the purgatory of the middle seat, craned over her to see the forest below. He thought of elbowing her awake, but instead contented himself with the view of her hair, which tumbled like a waterfall frozen mid-cascade, framing her face with an effortless grace as the Ethics Paradox wiggled its way back into his brain.

Let's not even talk about whether it is ethical to produce so much carbon pollution by flying to Demba—when the goal is to reduce emissions, he thought, then called the flight attendant to get a beer.

Andy sat silently in his aisle seat, staring straight ahead, feeling impossibly small.

Three little students trying to change the world with a novel instrument called carbon credits, he thought, his mind churning with doubt. *What a joke. This is never going to work.*

But they'd cashed the checks and were on the hook for results.

Ella, who had the most to lose, slept more soundly than she had in weeks. No more tossing, turning, and second-guessing.

The air on the tarmac clung to them like a damp hug, and soldiers directed them towards the concrete terminal, painted in the now-familiar symbols of Demba—sky, animals, mountains, forest, and ocean. The immigration agents greeted them with grins as wide and warm as the equatorial sun.

They dragged their luggage through customs and then, amid the swirling noise and color of Port Kewala's arrivals hall, saw Wanga waving to them.

Beside her stood a wiry young man clutching a sign that read *Matipa*, his expression a mix of nerves and determination.

"In case you hadn't recognized us," Wanga said, laughing as she pulled them into a hug.

The energy of the moment swept over them, and the weight of their doubts began to lift, just a little.

"This is Nestor," said Wanga. "Andy, Nestor is a remote cousin of yours as well! He is one of our project managers at Matipa and our driver, born in Zima, not far from Duiba village."

"My pleasure," Nestor smiled, guiding them through the maze of zigzagging luggage carriers, screaming taxi drivers, and pamphlet-waving hostel promoters.

"A luxury watch for just 20 dollars, my Lady!"

Ella spun around to face the young man, who discreetly pulled back his coat to reveal a collection of expensive-looking branded watches.

"Come on, Ella, this is all fake; let's spend our money on real stuff," Andy laughed.

"It's not that I want to do business here," Ella replied, a hint of annoyance creeping into her voice. "I'm just wondering: If this guy can sell functioning fake branded watches at 20 dollars, how big a margin must the manufacturers of the real stuff make?"

Robin, meanwhile, had his eyes on a large banner stretched across the hallway.

"What does that mean, Wanga?"

DFRRU only Exit Door 12.

"DFRRU stands for Demba Flood Rapid Response Unit," she said. "Matipa is still leading the response, so this is our dedicated gate in the terminal."

Robin's mind flipped to the girl in the river, the flickering fragment of video lodged in his memory like a shard of glass.

Outside, the night had settled in over the parking lot, throwing the massive billboard into stark relief. In bold, illuminated letters, it proclaimed: *Empower Your Home.* Below that, in smaller print: *SunScore. Premium Solar Systems.*

"Wanga, look at that ad!" Andy shouted. "Is that the group you're working with?"

With a quick wave, she signaled she couldn't hear a thing. He held onto his question until they were inside the car—now a captive of the city's eternal gridlock.

"Not yet, Andy," she answered. "SunScore schemes are great, but most villagers can't afford them. It's frustrating because if we invest in a SunScore system, it would pay for itself in about two years. Plus, the distributor said if we order ten thousand units, he can cut the price by twenty percent."

"I see..." said Ella. "But I thought you wanted to use carbon finance for that."

"Exactly," said Wanga. "With a boost from carbon credits, we could increase scale and reduce the cost of the solar panels. This could actually become a great business case for the local villages!"

"But if these SunScore schemes are a great business case," said Ella. "Why, then, would the money from carbon credits be needed? We can't create carbon credits if the project is profitable."

Wanga blinked.

"Well, the problem is that most villagers don't have the cash upfront to buy the SunScore. Most people would get one if we could subsidize the initial buying price. So it's not a business case right now. But it could become one once we get going."

"But as soon as that happens, we can't generate carbon credits," Ella countered, turning to Andy and Robin. "Additionality, again," she said, as they rolled their eyes.

She turned back to Wanga.

"'Additionality' means we have to show carbon finance made the action possible. But the more successful you are, the more questionable your additionality case becomes."

"That's weird indeed," Andy said, his eyebrows lifting. "And on the flip side, it means that the more unattractive a project is, the more likely it is to be additional."

"Which again leads to the absurd conclusion," Robin chimed in, his voice tinged with disbelief, "that a project must be economically unattractive to qualify for carbon credits." He leaned back, clinching his fist. "That goes against any logic to work with the people of Demba on finding the most interesting projects, which bring them as much benefit as possible."

"Well, it is what it is," concluded Ella. "Face it, you can only call it an additional emission reduction if the project is really in need of additional funding."

Wanga glanced around at the group, her brow furrowed, then shrugged. "Most people designing projects aren't philosophers. They just want something that works—and that gets funded."

Robin's mind swirled with the realization, his thoughts like gears grinding late into the night while they drove through the vastly extending outskirts of Port Kewala, the city gradually giving way to open countryside.

The trio arrived at the Matipa Lodge in the middle of the night, their journey a four-hour crawl from the city's humming core. The first leg had sliced through the sleepless capital, neon lights flickering against the windows like restless spirits. Then came the highway—a brief and breathless stretch—before dissolving into a maze of narrowing roads, each more battered and forsaken than the last. By the time the tires crunched onto the gravel drive, they were just a few kilometers from Duiba village, where Andy's mother had been born.

"A shame Mom's not here," Andy said, turning to Robin. "She's only been back once since you and I came, and that was for those funerals."

As they stepped out of the car, now covered in dust and dirt, they heard the agitated fluttering of a bird colony, apparently startled by the crunching of the wheels.

"This is our Endangered Songbird Breeding Program," explained Nestor. "The donor here was Rower. Mr. Murphy has a big passion for birds!"

They could make out a large, unadorned building in the dim light of a streetlamp: the original head office of the Matipa Lodge. It consisted of a simple main building that housed the administration and a large meeting room. Upstairs were a few basic bedrooms and a shared bathroom for the permanent staff.

Over time, the lodge had grown significantly, with various buildings and facilities added around a large courtyard, many featuring the nameplates of respective donors. Robin spotted a large building that appeared to be an empty warehouse.

"This was the logistical headquarters of DFRRU," said Wanga. "It's where we stockpiled the tents, mosquito nets, and water purifiers that international donors sent after the big floods two months ago."

Robin's heart began to race again, and he was relieved when Wanga changed the topic.

"You will stay in the Lester Villa just behind the head office. I hope you don't mind sharing a triple room," Wanga said apologetically. "Each bed has a mosquito net, and you can lock the door, so you'll be safe!"

That night, under his mosquito net, Robin stared at the ceiling fan turning lazily above.

He shifted, restless.

"Ella," he whispered, unsure if she was asleep. "This additionality thing is really bugging me. It's such a paradox."

"I know," she said. "A project only qualifies for carbon credits if it *needs* carbon finance to exist. And that makes sense, right? If you pay for carbon credits, you want to have an additional impact. You don't want to fund projects that run anyway."

"Totally," Robin replied. "But it still creates a fascinating paradox. The Additionality Paradox. The better the project—the more obvious its benefits, the more likely it is to succeed without help—

the less likely it is to get credits. But if it *can't* stand on its own, then sure, it's 'additional'... but maybe not worth doing."

The logic twisted itself in Robin's mind, a snake devouring its own tail.

He closed his eyes, murmuring one last thought into the dark.

"It's like... this logic rewards failure. And punishes projects that actually work."

Then: silence. Just the night, the fan, and the faint rhythm of Ella's breathing in the next bed.

The Nature Paradox

After a hot and restless night, they were awakened by the sound of car tyres scratching on the gravel, followed by loud, frantic screaming.

Outside, they saw a trail of blood leading to a fenced-in, low building slightly set back from the lodge, making it invisible at night. They heard Wanga's voice from behind.

"This is so sad," she exclaimed, still dressed in her pajamas and flip-flops. "A baby chimpanzee. I hope we can save that little boy," she said, pointing at the low building. "One of our workers found him early this morning just outside Duiba, in a jackfruit plantation. His mother was shot dead, probably just a few minutes earlier, and he, too, was badly hurt. They found him clinging to his dead mother."

"Was this the work of the logging company?" asked Andy angrily.

"Well, indirectly, yes..." replied Wanga. "There is simply less and less forest left for these chimps to wander around, so they often find their way to the villages and gardens, searching for food. Last year, a little village girl was killed by a chimp; it was horrible. They found her tiny, broken body out in the field."

"Oh, my God!" blurted Ella.

"We run this little treatment and rewilding station here, but the villagers hate it," Wanga continued. "They would prefer to eliminate the chimps, so they put up traps. Sometimes, they catch baby chimps and sell them as pets in the city."

"This is crazy," said Ella, still staring at the trail of blood. "And it'll be worse if we don't save Coltra East."

"And restore the Lester Hills," added Andy.

"Well, when do we get started?" Ella said, clenching her fist.

"That's the idea, Ella," Wanga said with a slightly pained smile. "Morgan Toje will arrive in about half an hour. He is the business director of Walmera. He will show you his calculations. And later in the week, we will visit the site!"

Morgan was an impressive personality. A towering figure with a broad build, short hunting pants, and a worn polo shirt emblazoned with the Walmera company logo. His deep brown eyes radiated a warmth that comforted them all.

Like Uncle Duolo, just bigger, Andy thought.

Wanga and Morgan joked around for a while. They knew each other from high school in the capital, and some in the village disapproved —Morgan was a Nolé, and Wanga was a Belé.

Morgan pulled out a laptop and a massive workbook filled with documents and maps.

"We have done the math," Morgan began. "Coltra East is a magnificent forest, and it is full of very valuable teak wood. Due to a new access road from the North, which the government plans to build next year, it would be an excellent area for a palm or sugarcane plantation."

Morgan paused and scratched his short beard, observing their horrified reactions.

"We need to stop that!" Andy burst out. "How much would that cost?"

Morgan smiled gently. "Well, it's tricky. Essentially, you will incur costs on four levels. First, Walmera purchased a concession from the government for 50 years. We have 46 years remaining. Therefore, Walmera would have to be compensated for not cutting down and selling the trees.

"Second, Walmera could earn significant money by renting out the farmland.

"Thirdly, you will need yearly funds to maintain and manage the forest.

"And fourthly, and perhaps most importantly," he looked at Wanga, "you will need to involve the local communities. This will not be simple, I can promise you. Many villagers work for Walmera in the forest division or on one of the commercial farms. You will have to present them with real opportunities!"

"And how about the other idea, the restoration of the Lester Hills area? Would that one be less complex?" Ella asked, with a slightly worried expression.

"Oh, the Lester restoration would likely be even more complex. In addition to all the other topics, you will have to run a proper program for forest rehabilitation. That is not going to be simple," Morgan replied.

The trio spent the better part of the afternoon hunched over Morgan's documents, a tangle of spreadsheets and topographic maps. The evening sun was already seducing the Matipa forest with hues no paintbox could capture when Morgan left.

"If I get it right," Ella concluded, looking up from her laptop, "in the case of Coltra East conservation, we would need at least 200 dollars for every hectare, every year, to run that project. And in case of the restoration of Lester Hills," she frowned, "the price would amount to at least 1200 dollars for every hectare annually, at least in the beginning, when we have to plant the trees."

"And what happens after the trees have grown back?" asked Andy.

"We would still need money every year," replied Ella. "Because if you don't continue to fund the protection of the trees, then someone will surely think about cutting them down again."

"But then we have a logical problem here," reflected Andy. "Let's say we succeed in re-growing the trees at Lester Hills. When these trees grow, they absorb carbon dioxide. For every ton they absorb, we get our carbon credits. But what happens once the trees are standing? They won't absorb any new carbon, and we won't get more credits. So there will be no more money to protect those trees!"

"You're right," Ella said thoughtfully. "And look at Coltra East. We earn certificates for preventing trees from being cut down. But it's absurd in a way, because it means we depend on Walmera always being a threat."

"I thought we were trying to turn that into a national park," said Andy.

"We are," she replied. "But it's complicated. If Coltra East is officially declared a national park, the forest can no longer be logged. It's legally safe. And if it's safe, there are no more certificates—because there's no longer anything to prevent. The project financing would come to an end."

"Safe?" said Wanga, sharply. "We dealt with this already—like a million times: Without long-term funding, there's no money to maintain the park—let alone support people in the buffer zone. The government won't even gazette the park unless we show something like an endowment. And if they did gazette it without long-term funding, it would become a paper park—which is anything but 'safe.'"

Andy frowned. "So, to qualify for carbon finance, the forest has to be threatened," he said. "But to protect it permanently, it can't be."

Ella looked at him.

"The forest has to be protected and not protected at the same time for the project to work," she said.

They stared at each other in disbelief, as if they had just glimpsed Schrödinger's cat inside its steel chamber.

———

That night, back in their mesh cocoons, Robin contemplated the day's lesson.

"It's another paradox," he said. "The Nature Paradox."

"Here we go," said Andy.

"Like, how protecting a forest only gets you money if the forest's in danger," said Robin. "But once it's safe—poof! No more funding."

Ella rolled over in her cot. "Yeah. It's like a protection racket. 'Nice forest you've got there. Be a shame if something happened to it.'"

Andy chuckled. "Exactly! You're basically forced to hope there's some guy with a chainsaw lurking in the bushes just to keep the money flowing."

Robin sat up, his silhouette flickering in the moonlight. "And it's the same with planting trees. You get carbon credits while they're growing. But once they're fully grown and just... existing, holding all that carbon? That's when the funding stops. No more credits."

"Which, paradoxically, creates a risk that the forests could be cut down all over again!" concluded Andy.

"Look at you, getting the hang of the paradoxes," Robin said with a grin.

The Control Paradox

It was nearly 10 am, and the three had slept in after a long night of debate. They had spent hours wrestling with the Nature Paradox, grappling with the frustrating truth that credits for tree-planting only rewarded removal, not storage, of CO_2.

There was no perfect solution, they had agreed, but the advantages of planting and preserving trees—for the climate, for wildlife, for the people living alongside them—were undeniable. Somehow, they had to find a way to protect Coltra East and restore the Lester Hills.

"Come, take a look!" Wanga shouted from outside the Lester Villa.

Robin opened the door, fearing another trail of blood.

"Come out and see," she said. "It's Bobby, the baby chimp. He survived! He is trying to hop around the courtyard now!"

Fully awake, they hurried outside. The blood had been scrubbed clean, and there was Bobby, wobbling on spindly legs, a thick bandage wrapped around his head and another around his left leg. A Matipa staff member—the same one who had cooked their dinner the night before—was crouched beside him, holding a tiny bottle and coaxing him to drink. *The cutest thing I've ever seen*, thought Robin.

"What's going to happen to him now?" Ella asked, her eyes fixed on the fragile creature.

Wanga sighed, her shoulders rising and falling in a weary shrug. "That's a good question. Without a family, he'll struggle to return to the forest. And we can't bring him anywhere close to the village. The communities hate chimps, particularly the males, ever since that attack on the girl last year. It will take some time to find a solution," she shrugged.

Bobby blinked up at them, his tiny fingers curling around the bottle, as if waiting for someone to decide his fate.

The faint scent of tea lingered in the air as staff cleared the breakfast table. Wanga leaned back in her chair, arms crossed, and eyed the group.

"So, because of the additionality issue, do you think we should prioritize reforestation?" Wanga said. "How quickly do you think we could get things flowing? How fast could you raise the money for the carbon credits?"

"Well, we have to get some other things sorted first," said Ella. "We haven't even touched the hardest question yet: what exactly will happen with the money?"

Andy laughed. "What money? The money we don't have? Shouldn't we try to find that first?"

Ella shook her head. "How is anyone going to give us money if we can't demonstrate exactly how our model works—where the funds will go, who they'll benefit, and the timeline for all this? The minute we get back to Niburg, we need to create a company. That's the easy part," she said, pressing forward. "The harder question is here in Demba: who exactly owns and sells the credits? How is the money handled? Our buyers will want to know all that."

Wanga frowned. "Wait, didn't we agree that Matipa would take over that part? I mean, wasn't that the whole idea in the first place?"

"Absolutely," Ella said quickly, nodding. "Matipa would coordinate all the on-the-ground work, but wouldn't it be much cleaner and more transparent if we created a separate company, or perhaps a foundation, right here in Demba to coordinate all the carbon credits we're planning? That company could maintain relations with the various community leaders. It would hold the contracts with Walmera and track the flow of money. Plus, buyers of the carbon credits could have a seat on the board to ensure they feel comfortable."

Ella faltered as she saw Wanga's expression. "That's... well, it's what I read...," she added weakly. "That's apparently how donors want things to work... I mean, some control over how the money is used, you know..."

"Yes, it is. This is the way donors want to have it," Wanga said coldly, her expression suddenly changed. "And why? Because they don't trust us!"

Robin and Ella sat open-mouthed, but Andy nodded. He remembered the day local media in Niburg questioned whether his mother, as a female Demban national, could successfully lead the research institute as its new Dean. God, she had been furious that day, too.

"You think we in Demba can't handle a complex project without squandering the money, don't you? You're acting just like every other donor who parachutes in," Wanga snapped.

"You throw some money at us, feel good about it, but never trust us to manage it properly. Year after year, my team and I waste weeks on useless evaluation forms, justifying every expense, then hosting delegation after delegation of donors who want to be shown everything. They pepper us with questions and offer advice they have no business giving—convinced they could run our programs better, when in truth, they have no clue about what's happening on the ground."

Wanga's voice echoed through the room, heavy with anger and something more—something raw and unspoken that made the air feel charged, like the second before a storm. Ella sat frozen.

"Listen, I'm not mad at you all personally, but carbon credits are supposed to be different," she continued, her voice softening but still sharp enough to cut. "The whole point is that credits are awarded to whoever delivers results, and those results are certified under international standards and not at the whim of some billionaire. Isn't the idea to empower the project developer on the ground, in this case, Matipa and the communities? Isn't this supposed to finally break from this post-colonialist idea of wealthy donors telling us 'poor Dembans' what to do and how to behave?

"Matipa has already done the hard part: we've persuaded Walmera not only to assign the Coltra East and Lester Hills concessions but also to invest in the projects, and we've also been teaching farmers around the country agroforestry for decades. A random new company won't be able to pull that off. Forget it!"

Robin and Ella looked to Andy, who stared back at them.

"Wanga's right," he said. "That's what she's been saying for years... The idea that we're helping people shift from being charity cases to providers of an ecosystem service. Then again, it's complex. Just imagine if we're lucky and the price of carbon credits skyrockets— some people here in Demba could make a lot of money. The buyers in Canland could worry that..."

"Worry that what exactly?" Wanga snapped. "Why shouldn't some people here in Demba profit from protecting and restoring forests? Why shouldn't this become a great business—one we can be proud of, one that other countries might learn from? Why should we be expected to remain poor and hungry?"

She paused to let her points settle.

"That's actually true," said Ella, as a bird screeched from the jungle— unimpressed by human theories of justice or markets. "Do you remember what you said about Earth Cinema back then, Robin? If it's for a good cause, you're guaranteed to lose money on it. I think this expectation is deeply ingrained in our society. In contrast, the idea of making money from something good is considered suspi- cious. The result: if you want to earn money and avoid stress, you'd better find another career—in an industry where it's perfectly normal to collect a fat bonus, even if you're exploiting the planet. That's crazy, isn't it?"

"I hope we'll be so successful that we'll find out whether you're right or not!" Andy laughed.

"It's yet another paradox," Robin said after a pause. "I'm pretty sure our carbon credit buyers will want to know exactly where their money's going. Otherwise, if anything gets questioned, they're easy targets. But paradoxically, if they do try to control how the funds are used, they'll get slammed for being paternalistic—acting like neocolonial overlords."

"True," Ella nodded. "Control or not, you're always at risk of being accused."

She gave a half-smile. "Guess we can call that the Control Paradox."

"Maybe we can work out a simple structure," said Robin. "Just a framework to get things started."

"That's a wise proposal," Wanga said. "Tomorrow is the big event—when we finally meet the village and the Council of Elders."

At dinner, Robin swirled the last of his rice. "Anyone here know Russell's Paradox?"

Andy raised an eyebrow. "Is that the one with the barber who only shaves men who don't shave themselves?"

"And then the question is: Does the barber shave himself? Close enough," Robin said. "But there's an even more abstract version of that paradox. It's the set of all sets that don't contain themselves. The question is: does it contain itself?"

Ella blinked. "I'm too tired for riddles."

"No, listen," he said. "If it contains itself, it breaks the rule. But if it doesn't, then by definition it qualifies to be in the set—so it must contain itself. It's a loop. Just like in the barber's case, whatever you answer, you always get it wrong."

Andy rolled his eyes. "Where are you going with this, Robin?"

He looked around the table. "Today's argument—about who should control the money from carbon credits. The Control Paradox. It works quite similarly."

The other two stared at him expectantly.

"Whatever you answer to the control question, you're always getting it wrong. You insist on controlling how the money is spent here in Demba? You are paternalistic. A neocolonialist. You trust Demban partners to take control on their own? You risk enabling dodgy dealings. Even corruption. But it gets even more entangled. You say, ok, let's find a compromise. Let Demban partners take the lead, but establish clear guardrails. So you establish criteria sets, you set up boards, ask for audits, create advisory panels—you set up more and more layers of control, just to show you're not in control," said Robin.

Andy nodded slowly. "And in doing all that, we prove we don't trust them. Which defeats the point."

Robin leaned forward. "Exactly. The more we try to remove ourselves from the center, the more we seem to reinforce our position. Like a loop we can't escape."

Andy tapped his spoon on the edge of his plate. "So what do we do? We'd need to design something that includes and builds confidence without being patronizing."

The candle guttered slightly, as if acknowledging his point.

The Communities Paradox

They awoke to the roar of rain and the sight of roads melting into rivers.

The memory of the girl in the flood shot through Robin's mind, but this storm only threatened inconvenience, not erasure. "How are we supposed to get to Duiba now?" Andy asked, peering out the window.

Nestor chuckled. "Don't worry. I'll get the Jeep." He grinned. "Poor Ross got stuck in the mud last year. Ordered the jeep a day later."

Wanga said nothing. Her thoughts were on the other roads—the ones less likely to host Jeeps. She pictured the Elders from the Lester Hills, already on the move: packed into sputtering pickups, straddling rusted motorcycles, or walking, bare feet pressing into the soaked clay.

Today was the meeting of the Council of Elders, and all the communities of Lester Hills were sending delegates, while the Nolé communities of Coltra East were slated for later in the week.

The rain could wash away months of planning and preparation.

Andy stared ahead, jaw tight, as the Jeep growled forward, tires sinking, spinning, catching again. Mud flew in clots and ribbons. The forest pressed close—slick leaves slapping the windshield like wet towels. Wanga leaned forward, scanning each bend. And then—like breath after long effort—they crested a hill. Duiba opened below them, rain-slick and glinting as the clouds broke.

Their Jeep, caked in red-brown mud, wheezed into the village like an old beast at its last mile. Suddenly—children. A rushing tide of them, laughter spilling in bright waves, pure as birdsong after a storm. Bare feet slapped through puddles, launching arcs of muddy water into the air. Ignoring the rain and the mud, a few sprang onto the roof—sure-footed, fearless—perching like young gods until Wanga waved them off with a laugh. The Jeep shuddered to a stop in the village square.

Wanga was relieved to see most of the Elders already there. The team climbed out to handshakes, slow nods, and the kind of measured warmth of people accustomed to the weight of time.

Ella took it all in—the corrugated iron roof of the assembly hall, the packed earth beneath her feet, and, most of all, the Elders themselves. They sat on wooden benches, faces lined by years and seasons, eyes sharp with the quiet wisdom of those who had seen too much and endured it all.

She felt a slow heat rise in her chest, a flicker of shame, the echo of yesterday's argument with Wanga. She saw these men and women now—really saw them—and something in her shifted. How many waves of outsiders had come through here? Colonizers, bureaucrats, developers—each one certain they knew best, each one offering instructions on how to live, how to farm, how to grow. And yet here they sat, unbending, unmoved, with a dignity that needed no validation.

And suddenly, Ella understood. She understood why Wanga bristled at the idea of yet another foreign company arriving with solutions wrapped in fine words. These people didn't need instruction; they had outlasted empires. The lesson wasn't theirs to learn. It was hers.

And then Andy saw him—the eyes, deep and kind, mirrors of his mother's. Uncle Duolo.

Now one of Duiba's longest-serving Elders, he moved through the crowd with purpose, tears carving paths through the rugged lines of his face. He reached Wanga first, embracing her with a fierce tenderness, then pulled Andy into a grip that felt primal. For a moment, Andy could only cling to him, the smells of sweat, smoke, and the red earth filling his senses. It felt like stepping back into a part of himself he'd nearly forgotten.

"Andy, so good to have you and your friends here with us," he said, then whispered, "How is Midela doing? We are all so proud of your mom."

He turned again to the others. "Welcome to Duiba, my dears. I hear you come with big plans to restore our land. Very good."

The rain lifted, leaving the air thick with the scent of wet earth and expectation. Sunlight spilled over the village, igniting the painted walls in a riot of color.

Around the assembly fence, children gathered in wild clusters, their hands waving, voices tumbling over each other in a joyous racket. They hopped as if the earth beneath them burned.

Even as he poured tea with practiced ease, Duolo's eyes roamed the crowd, scanning for the remaining Elders, responding to nods and signals from others who needed him. Though easing out of his council role, he's the one who signaled the meeting to begin.

Finally, he nodded to Tinlope, his successor as chief of the Duiba Elders' Council. Tinlope rose—tall, deliberate, each word slicing like a machete through undergrowth—and welcomed each council in turn: Letonga, Zima, Limata, Cimahe, and Sorang. His voice bestowed their names like blessings.

"May the sky, the animals, the mountains, the forest, and the ocean all be with us today," he finished, and for a moment, it felt like they were.

Next came Morgan, stepping onto the stage with the measured gait of a man who had practiced too much and still wasn't quite sure it would land. He spoke of Walmera's achievements—roads from

Sorang to Cimahe, a new elementary school in Zima, jackfruit and rubber plantations humming outside Duiba. His tone was polished, his delivery careful. No mention of the chimpanzee incident. No mention of the floods from just a few months back.

Robin, Ella, and Andy searched the Elders' faces, but their expressions were masks of patience honed over generations. A few shifted, their discomfort subtle, like shadows moving with the sun. Others nodded, listening with a politeness that might have been interest, or just tolerance.

Was it Walmera they distrusted—the sprawling timber and agricultural giant that loomed over the region? Or was it Morgan himself, a Nolé standing in a room of Belé people?

Then came the real business.

"Walmera has been your partner in forest management for several decades, and I've enjoyed meeting you in our contact group meetings," Morgan began. "As part of a strategy review, our Board has asked us to explore other uses for our forestry concessions. One option is to scale back forestry in Coltra East and instead expand the wildlife reserve. As for the Lester Hills,"—he cleared his throat, watching the Elders whose villages encircled the Hills—"yes, regarding our beloved Lester Hills, we are considering a restoration of the forest cover."

A murmur rippled through the crowd.

"We know this may shift the livelihoods of some of our brothers and sisters," he continued. "But new possibilities will open. To this end, we also explore the launch of a SunScore subsidy program, which we hope will soon bring solar power to our villages!"

Cautious applause followed, scattered and polite. Morgan pressed on. "To make these programs a reality, we consider partnering with Matipa and your great sister Wanga, whom you all know so well."

Wanga, seated beside him, dipped her head, a smile tugging at her lips, though Robin caught something in her eyes—hesitation?

Strange, he thought. *She'd been so confident back at the gala in Canland, a force of nature in a silk dress, charming the big shots without breaking a sweat.*

"And finally," Morgan now smiled at Robin, Ella, and Andy, signaling them to stand up, "for the funding of these programs, we plan to work with our young friends from Canland, who are helping us explore the concept of carbon credits. For every ton of CO_2 we manage to reduce, their company will pay us in cash... ehm..."

He turned his head towards them.

"What again was the name of your company?" he whispered.

"Five Elements!" Ella shouted, the words bursting from her like a spark escaping a fire.

Robin blinked. What was that? Did Ella just invent a company name out of the blue?

"Exactly, Five Elements, thank you, Ella," Morgan repeated with a smile.

Then Wanga stood. And when she spoke, everything else faded. Her voice held no hesitation now, only certainty, only purpose.

"Thank you, Morgan," Wanga began. "When I grew up here in this village, just behind the little yellow church, my uncle used to take us kids to the Lester Hills, a beautiful, impenetrable forest full of trees and animals. I remember searching for birds with my sister and joining my brother Duolo at his forest camp."

Duolo smiled at her.

"Today, it's mostly scrub. The good soil is gone, washed away. We tried to turn it into farmland, but the harvests failed. Now that the trees are gone, they no longer hold back the water. We are all aware of the horrible flood at Limata. So let us restore the Lester Hills and protect Coltra East."

Morgan looked down nervously. His boss at Walmera had instructed him to avoid the awkward Limata flood.

"But we cannot do this without you. We need your help—your ideas, your priorities. The carbon money gives us a chance to implement them, but the future is ours to shape."

That's the Wanga I know, thought Robin.

"So let the discussion begin," she concluded. "This is only the first of many gatherings. This process will take time. We need to hear from all the Elders' Councils!"

A tiny woman with curly gray hair stood up first. As she spoke, Nestor translated for Robin and Ella.

"We are thankful for your efforts, dear sister Wanga and dear friends from Canland," he said in lockstep with her words.

"In Zima, we are skeptical that growing back the forests of Lester Hills makes sense. Yes, the new farmland is disappointing. Hardly anything grows there today. Something must be done. But I don't think anybody wants the old forest back. It was full of dangerous animals, poisonous snakes, and deadly insects. I believe we should explore regenerative agriculture."

"I agree with your skepticism," said a man standing in the back of the room, dressed in a traditional robe. "And this is why I don't understand Walmera's decision to stop the work in Coltra East. In Cimahe, many of our men found jobs in the palm oil and rubber fields. They have brick houses now. Motorbikes. Dignity."

Then, cutting through the silence, a younger voice rose.

"Good for Cimahe. Good for Sorong. But how about us in Limata?"

Everyone turned.

The speaker was a young man—too young, Robin thought, for an Elders' Council. And yet his voice carried authority.

"Walmera promised us the same and gave us nothing," Nestor translated, struggling to keep up. "Why? Because we are Belé. Walmera is run by Nolé. And now they come to Coltra East to take the teak, to farm the best land, and leave the rest of us behind.

"Look at Lester Hills—only empty promises. All we get is destroyed land. And floods! Whatever their plan is now..." the young speaker turned from Morgan to Wanga and the three students, "...let's give Matipa and their Canlandish friends a chance. It can't get worse," Nestor translated.

The room cracked open—anger, frustration, accusation. Voices overlapping, fingers pointed. Tinlope slammed his stick against the bell to restore order.

Nestor threw his hands up in frustration.

"I can't keep up," he said. "But what it comes down to is everyone seems to agree that deforestation is a disaster. People don't trust Walmira... too many broken promises... That guy just talked about the flood in Limata. He said everyone knows the cause, but Walmera won't say it aloud. They trust Matipa, and they like the... how do you say it? Dams?"

"Retaining walls," said Andy. "Or levees..."

"Yes—retaining walls. Matipa is building retaining walls, but everyone knows they won't hold forever. This group wants floodplains... Those people over there live up in the hills and want terraced farming, and Wanga has been trying to get them to try regenerative agriculture. Trouble is, they don't trust that, either."

Then, a new voice—older, calmer, unmoved—sliced through the cacophony. Nestor fell back into translation.

"And what happens when the hills chase you out?" Nestor said, adding: "He's responding to someone who said the carbon project wants to throw people out of the hills... he's saying that if we keep chopping, the hills will make their own decision."

A murmur of uncertainty spread through the villagers. Some nodded, others glanced away.

Duolo stood.

"My friends," he said, raising his hands, "no one is here to chase anyone away. We are here to find solutions, together. Tell us—what do you need to stop cutting the trees?"

Murmurs rippled through the crowd again. Finally, a young man named Kito stepped forward. "You know what we need: school fees for our children, food for our families. What else is there?"

Duolo nodded. "We have ideas. Some of you are already getting moringa from our distributors, but do you know how to use it?"

"Moringa is a cover crop," Andy whispered. "Wanga told me about it. It improves corn yields, provides fodder, and attracts bees."

"How many of you have joined our beekeeping program?" Nestor said, translating Duolo's words. "You know, moringa brings bees, and bees make honey."

"Beekeeping?" said a woman in the crowd. "But we don't know how to keep bees."

"How about tree nurseries?" a woman said. "If you're going to be planting trees down the hills, you will need saplings."

"What about bursaries?" an elderly woman suddenly spoke up, her voice carrying across the square. "If our children can get scholarships, we won't have to cut trees to pay for school."

A ripple of interest passed through the farmers. The idea of bursaries struck a chord. One young mother nodded thoughtfully. "Education means a better future."

New ideas began to surface—alternative crops, water storage tanks, solar energy. As perspectives were shared, the conversation grew animated and dynamic.

When the meeting adjourned, Andy stepped outside. His shirt clung to him like wet paper, and his legs ached from sitting on the low wooden bench. But more than that, it was the weight of the conversation—circular arguments, tangled loyalties, polite jabs wrapped in riddles—that wore him down.

Chickens pecked at the wet ground near the edge of the fence, and a group of boys was playing with a tire, shouting something too fast for Andy to catch.

Uncle Duolo was leaning against a post, his back to the hall, a faraway look in his eyes. Andy walked over.

"Too much talking?" Duolo asked without looking at him.

Andy nodded. "I'm trying to follow. But it feels like everything means three different things."

Duolo let out a soft, tired laugh. "Welcome to leadership."

They stood in silence for a moment. Then Duolo turned to him, his expression shifting, sharpening. "I shouldn't say this," he began, "but sometimes I wonder if we're wasting everyone's time in there."

Andy frowned. "But you're one of the Elders, aren't you?"

Duolo nodded slowly. "I am. And that's the problem. I've seen the promises. I've heard the speeches. Every council, every initiative, every project... We talk and we talk, and at the end, nothing trickles down to the people who need it most." He pushed himself off the post. "Come. I want to show you something."

Andy hesitated for half a second, then followed. Ella and Robin joined them near the edge of the village, curiosity flickering across their faces. Duolo said nothing—just motioned for them to come along.

They walked down a narrow, rutted path that curved behind a row of huts and then dropped steeply toward the edge of the hills. The air was thick with the scent of banana leaves, damp earth, and smoke.

Duolo stopped at a weathered gate and called out. A woman emerged from a small mud-brick house, her hair wrapped in a bright yellow cloth, a baby slung over one hip. Her name was Neema, and she smiled at Duolo with affection and fatigue.

They exchanged a few quiet words in Belém. Then Duolo gestured toward the trio.

"They're here to listen," he said.

Neema's smile faded slightly. She nodded and invited them to sit on three overturned jerrycans. A chicken strutted past. Somewhere nearby, a goat bleated. Andy tried to keep his notebook discreet, but Neema waved it away.

"No need," she said with a smile, and Duolo started translating. "I will tell you what you won't hear in the hall."

She looked over her small plot, where cassava leaves drooped under the weight of recent rains. A few banana plants stood ragged and bent.

"You ask what we want, what we need. The truth is that none of it is simple."

She shifted the baby to the other hip.

"If we keep cutting trees, our soil worsens, the rains flood our homes, and the hills send water roaring down like punishment. But if we reforest, I lose this land—this thin, stubborn patch that feeds my children. You tell me to plant trees in among my crops — this agroforestry stuff—but what if that fails?"

Robin opened his mouth, but Neema raised her hand.

"And now you speak of solar subsidies. But who can afford the down payment? Not me. Not my neighbors. It will be the rich who benefit. And when they do, they buy more fuel-efficient stoves and clean energy... but that means the fuel seller comes here less often. And the price goes up for the rest of us."

Ella leaned forward, her voice low. "So when change comes, it costs you more."

Neema nodded. "Always."

"And what about seedlings?" she continued. "The new trees? They come with new fertilizer. New instructions. We must buy what they say, plant where they say. And if we don't? They say our yields will drop. So we're trapped. Either way, we rely on outsiders—on people we'll never meet, who don't know what this hill feels like underfoot after a night of rain."

Andy felt his throat tighten. He glanced at Robin, who looked shaken. Ella was staring hard at the ground.

Duolo let out a long, slow breath.

"This is why I brought you," he said.

Neema shifted the baby again, her eyes never leaving theirs.

"Let the Elders talk. Let the consultants draw up plans. But in the end, nothing will reach us unless you understand this: we do not live in a policy brief. We live here, with the dirt, with the rain, with the price of salt rising every week."

There was nothing to say. Uncle Duolo's generation hadn't managed it, nor had their parents' generation. Now it was their turn. Would their generation succeed in enabling a fairer world for this baby and all the others, a world where they could thrive without the constant worry about the next plate of rice?

The group stood, thanked her, and made their way back up the hill, the air thicker now, not with heat, but with consequence. The chatter of the assembly hall returned in waves, but it felt far away—like something from another country, another kind of world.

As they stepped back inside, Duolo's voice was low, almost to himself.

"You came here thinking the problem was trees. But the trees are just the surface. What you're really facing is the deep root of fairness—and that grows slowly, if at all."

Andy, Robin, and Ella found their seats again. They were changed—not defeated but definitely sobered.

Whatever they would propose—whatever their carbon plan might bring—it would have to pass through hands like Neema's.

And if it didn't work for her, it didn't work at all.

After the short but arduous trip back to the Matipa Lodge, Wanga pulled out Nestor's notes.

"Ultimately, all five communities present agreed to proceed with the next round of discussions on restoring the Lester Hills, which is an enormous achievement," Wanga summarized.

"Remember that many people had visited them for centuries, promising many great investments and developments. In the end, they were always left worse off. Their skepticism is entirely understandable.

"We need to first gather the full sprawl of local urgencies—the real, raw needs of the people—before imposing any grand design of conservation or restoration."

She wouldn't let the process move in reverse, wouldn't let distant formulas dictate what the land and its people required. She held her notes up to the dim light, scanning the scribbles and margin marks, her fingers smudged with the ink of urgency. Each line, each phrase was a pressure point in the uneasy balance between survival and sustainability.

"Business opportunities and jobs come first," she said. "Paved access roads are listed next. Then it's fertilizers to improve farms. Antenna for mobile coverage. Improved houses, tiled roofs. Medical clinics. Vaccination programs. Improved school buildings. Motorbikes to bring kids to school and to have easier access to farms. Then we have seedlings, beehives, agricultural equipment. Retention basins for rainwater. That's an interesting one. With climate change raging on, it's increasingly dry here, and when the rain comes, everything gets flooded. TVs, fridges, aircon, that's what people are hoping to gain from the SunScore solar power program."

Wanga frowned. "So many different views, so many different priorities. It will be a long process," she concluded. "Let's rest and prepare for the Coltra East trip tomorrow."

"I think we've hit another paradox," Robin said at dinner.

Andy groaned. "Robin, if I had a coin for every paradox you've spotted on this trip…"

Ella laughed. "Let's hear it."

Robin leaned back, arms crossed. "We always talk about community engagement like it's this unified, sacred thing—'the community says this,' 'the community wants that.' But what did we see today? Communities aren't unified. They're fragmented. They disagree. Sometimes violently. Sometimes for good reason."

"How is that a paradox?" snapped Andy. "It's the same in Canland. Remember your mom complaining about the 'True Canlanders?' You never get consensus in any community—"

"Or any family," said Ella.

"Exactly," said Robin. "That's the paradox. The Communities Paradox. We say community support is essential—which it is—but full consensus is impossible. Paradoxically, the harder you push to include every stakeholder and reach an agreement, the more tangled and unmanageable the debate becomes. In the end, you risk achieving nothing at all."

The Baseline Paradox

With a slight turn of the yoke, the pilot veered Walmera's Cessna left, and the world outside the windows began to roll.

"You can see Duiba in the back," shouted Wanga. "And down to the left—Matipa Lodge!"

Robin spotted both—and the Lester Hills beyond, like a great, slumbering beast.

The transition was stark. The patchwork quilt of smallholder rice fields, rubber trees, jackfruit gardens, and pristine forest fragments—dotted with huts and clustered villages—gave way to the barren slopes of the concession. Stripped hills rolled to the horizon, their nakedness a raw wound on the land.

Some parts still held plantations, with narrow access roads twisting like strands of a spider's web. Even from this height, the forest degradation was glaring.

"And now, down here—Limata village," Wanga shouted. "Or what's left of it. Look there, on the western bank of the Lester River! Most settlements got washed away."

Robin turned away, looking out the opposite window. He felt a strange relief as the plane banked again. Now the ground below was all oil palm—an endless grid of uniform green that devoured the horizon.

"Coltra West," said Morgan, frowning. "One of the most efficient oil palm plantations in the country. We make a lot of money with it. Just ten years ago, this was all thick forest."

Robin stared at the neat, ruthless rows, his thoughts spiraling inward.

Is it possible? Can Coltra East be spared the fate of Coltra West? Can Morgan convince his company to generate carbon credits instead of rubber and palm oil? Can Wanga and her team run such a massive program—with so many communities, so many interests? And can we find a buyer for the carbon credits to fund this audacious plan?

The questions buzzed like gnats, as persistent as the drone of the engine, as the plane banked over the majestic Demba River, its waters snaking through the forest in wild, silver curves. Wisps of cloud drifted across the view, momentarily obscuring the scene below.

When the visibility returned, it was like entering another world.

"Wow. Just wow!" Andy shouted.

Below them, the pristine jungle stretched in an endless green carpet, unbroken and alive. Mist clung to the canopy in places, lending the landscape an almost mythical quality, as if it belonged more to dreams than to maps.

"Coltra East," said Wanga, her smile as wide as the horizon. She pointed ahead. "And back there—that's the Republic of Lomba. Twice the size of Demba, but not more than a fifth of the population. A magical, mysterious country."

Her words hung in the air as the plane soared over the untouched wilderness.

The pilot's voice crackled with excitement over the radio, and soon they understood why. Out of the endless forest, the tiny airstrip of the Coltra East Wildlife Reserve appeared—a strip of green where a few cows grazed, oblivious to the approaching plane.

The Cessna circled twice, and a ranger sprinted from a small hut that served as the terminal, wielding nothing but a stick. He charged onto the runway, flailing and shooing the cows with a kind of comic determination.

The plane touched down in a series of jolts before rolling to a stop just shy of a towering Kapok tree. Everyone but the pilot climbed out, their clothes damp and clinging, the humid air pressing down like a heavy hand. The sweat on their brows owed as much to the landing as to the heat.

A young biologist with a warm smile introduced herself as Sophy. Beside her stood Tiara, her composed assistant, who motioned toward an off-road vehicle rumbling behind the tiny terminal hut. The driver, Tuk, flashed a grin as wide as the trail ahead—his good cheer rising above the sticky, humid air.

The ride to the Coltra East Wildlife Center was long and jarring, the jeep lurching through rutted tracks that clawed at the tires and tested everyone's nerves. But as the trees gave way to a small clearing, the mood shifted.

A chorus of drums erupted. Young men in bright Nolé dresses surged from the forest, feet pounding the earth in synchronized rhythm. Their garments shimmered like precious stones against the green of the jungle.

"They're doing all this dancing for us?" Robin asked, squinting.

"Yes, they welcome you to the reserve," said Morgan. "Coltra East is a luxury lodge. Tourists pay thousands to spend a night here."

Robin raised an eyebrow.

"That money helps fund conservation," Morgan added. "The rangers, the patrols, the local outreach programs—none of this would survive without the rich tourists."

Lunch was served on an expansive terrace overlooking the Demba River, its silver current gliding below the swaying canopy. The food was simple but delicious—grilled fish, ripe fruit, greens seasoned with lemon.

As they lingered over their plates, the Nolé drums sounded again. A man appeared on the terrace. Well-built, dressed in crisp travel wear, he moved with purpose but wore a flicker of unease. Sophy and Tiara flanked him like diplomats.

Robin watched his gaze scan the table, landing on Morgan.

Recognition flared.

Morgan stiffened. The change was instant: his usual grin vanished, replaced by a blend of respect and fear.

"This is Mr. Spencer," Wanga whispered to Robin. "Walmera's CEO." Then she rose from her chair and smiled. "Great to see you, Hubert. How was your trip?"

"Thanks, Wanga, all smooth. And good afternoon," he looked at the trio. . "Welcome to Coltra East. I'm Hubert Spencer."

"Here are our friends from Five Elements," Wanga explained. "Yes. Five Elements," Spencer echoed, scanning their faces. He had clearly expected someone else—older, more corporate.

Still, he recovered quickly and took the seat Ella offered.

"I understand you want to license our concessions in Lester Hills and Coltra East," he said.

Ella introduced the team, calm and composed. Spencer listened politely, but his attention drifted.

"Morgan has told you this isn't cheap or simple," Spencer continued. "But carbon credits are interesting. Walmera is committed to the environment. Net-zero emissions are our goal. If credits let us protect more of Coltra East—maybe even all of it—we're open to that."

Over the next two hours, a tentative plan emerged. Walmera would license its concessions to the Matipa Foundation. Matipa would become the initial project owner and oversee forest restoration at Lester Hills. Five Elements—Robin, Ella, and Andy's company— would develop and sell the credits. The revenue would not only compensate Walmera but also fund various projects in the surrounding villages.

Spencer signaled for drinks. Two waiters in traditional dress rolled over a bar cart, mixing cocktails with exaggerated flair. The mood lightened. Spencer laughed easily now, leaning toward Ella, clearly impressed.

Robin watched uneasily.

"If we succeed here," Spencer said, raising his glass, "why not expand to Lomba? Walmera is acquiring concessions there, too. I'm flying out tonight."

"The Republic of Lomba?" Ella said brightly. "That place we saw from the air? Yes, we must protect it!"

"That might not work," said Andy.

Silence. Spencer's smile faded.

"Why not?"

"Because there's been little to no deforestation in Lomba," Andy explained. "It's all intact forest. There's no baseline loss to stop. No additionality, no credits."

Spencer frowned. "Coltra East is intact, too. You just spent two hours telling me we could get credits for leaving it alone."

Andy shook his head. "Coltra West and Lester Hills have already been cleared. Deforestation pressure here is real. Stopping it has a measurable impact. That's the baseline. In Lomba, the forest isn't under threat."

"Not yet." Wanga leaned forward, eyes flashing.

"So we make money because we destroyed our forests," she said. "And Lomba gets nothing because they didn't?"

"It's a paradox," said Robin after a pause. "The Baseline Paradox. Paradoxically, you only qualify for carbon credits if you've already destroyed your forest—or planned to. But if you've protected your forest, there's no baseline to improve against. So you get nothing for doing the right thing."

Ella looked down. Wanga and Morgan sat stiffly in their chairs, unsure of what to say. Then Spencer stood, suddenly remembering he had to return to the airstrip. The ice cubes in his half-finished cocktail melted quietly in the evening heat.

The Science Paradox

The first light of dawn filtered through the dense canopy, and the jungle awoke with an electrifying symphony of sound that pulled Robin from his sleep. He blinked at the empty bed in his bungalow, then stepped onto the terrace. Andy was already there, hunched over his laptop, eyes fixed on the screen.

"You were a bit of a party killer last night," Robin laughed, "but I was glad Spencer took off."

"Indeed..." Andy growled without looking up from his laptop. "Otherwise, we'd have had to lock Ella in..."

"Hope we didn't kill the projects though," replied Robin. "Wanga and Morgan looked really worried. We need Spencer. We have no choice. He calls the shots. By the way, what are you working so hard on here?" Robin asked.

Now Andy looked up. "Yesterday's conversation got to me," he said. "I'm digging into the carbon credit rules for forest conservation projects. We have to follow the Green Climate Standard exactly, or we won't qualify."

"Okay. At six in the morning?" Robin asked sleepily. "Did you have a coffee at all?"

"No. Ehm, wait. Listen, we have three different project ideas, right?"

"M-hm," replied Robin. "SunScore solar, the Lester Hills reforestation, and then Coltra East forest conservation."

"Exactly. The first two are relatively simple. The solar panels replace diesel engines—easy to measure. Trees in Lester Hills absorb carbon—also straightforward. But Coltra East?" He paused. "That's different. There, we're trying to earn credits not by planting trees, but by not cutting them down—thereby *avoiding* further deforestation."

"Yes, absolutely," said Robin, still unsure where Andy was going. "And that's the most important project of all. If they cut the trees here, as they did in Coltra West, imagine all the loss of plants and animals; imagine the damage to a forest that grew over thousands of years. You could kill all that within a few years. If we can save these trees here, we will have a massive impact on the climate. "

"Totally. It's massive. I just had those figures here, wait..." Andy opened a different window on his laptop. "'One hectare of deforestation pumps 355 metric tons of carbon dioxide into the air. Reforesting the same area absorbs just 6.7 metric tons per year. In other words, it would take around 50 years for a destroyed forest to recover.'"

Andy switched back to the Green Climate Standard methodology document. "But it's also by far the most complex project of all. The main problem is this: There are two very different reasons why trees are cut. The first is planned deforestation. That's Walmera with its logging concession. The second is *unplanned* deforestation, which, in our case, is caused by subsistence farmers, who cut trees to make a living. Here in Coltra East, we have both planned and unplanned deforestation."

Robin nodded. "I get this. But does it make a difference? Cutting trees is cutting trees, no?"

Suddenly, they heard a familiar voice behind them. Wanga smiled as they turned around. How long had she been listening to their conversation?

"I see," she said and blinked her eyes. "You are about to come up with a new paradox, aren't you? Can I ask you an honest question? Have you come to muse about paradoxes, or are we here to launch projects?"

She let the smile linger for a moment—then it faded.

"I've put some thought into this myself. From a scientific perspective, you could argue there's no difference. A tree is a tree, a ton of carbon is a ton of carbon. But economically and socially, it matters a great deal."

She stepped closer, her voice calm but clear.

"On the one side, you have Walmera with their legal logging rights—planned. On the other side, you have subsistence farming—unplanned. We'll need to buy back Walmera's concession, yes. But if we ignore the local communities, the forest will still vanish. People need alternatives. And as you saw in Duiba, there's not just one community voice. It's messy. It's layered."

Andy nodded eagerly, flipping to another browser tab.

"Exactly! Check this out—this map shows the human impact across Demba. It took researchers over a decade: foresters, economists, even sociologists. They tried everything—logic-based models, pure AI prediction, hybrid systems. The result?" He grinned. "No single calculation method works everywhere. Forests are like people—each one has its own story."

Robin leaned in. "So... there's no one-size-fits-all model."

"Right. But here's the smart part," Andy said, tapping the screen. "They realized they couldn't standardize the models. So instead, they standardized the process for choosing models—based on data, context, and evolving tools."

He turned the laptop toward them, revealing a flowchart.

"Step one: map past deforestation. Step two: identify the drivers—charcoal burning, slash-and-burn farming, illegal logging. Step three: project future risks using similar contexts. Step four: design local interventions—like promoting beekeeping or regenerative grazing. Then compare the outcomes."

He closed the lid a notch and grinned.

"This is what carbon folks call a 'counterfactual'—it's a model of what would happen without the intervention. That's your 'baseline.' Then you measure the difference if something better happens."

"That's basic causal inference," said Wanga. "For impact evaluation and stuff like that."

"Exactly," said Andy. "That's where it came from: causal inference, Bayesian logic." He glanced at Robin, who was clearly confused. "You of all people should get this. Have you ever read the children's book *Momo*?"

Robin nodded, astonished. *The children's book by Michael Ende?* Before his mind's eye appeared the Men in Grey, who were cutting down trees in Demba and smoking their leaves.

"You remember that tortoise named Cassiopeia that can see half an hour into the future? She shows what will happen by lighting up words on her shell, but she only predicts what happens if nobody intervenes. It's the same thing these standards call a 'business as usual' scenario. In the book, the moment someone does something brave or full of love, the whole thing can tip another way. Our models are the same—they only predict the forest's fate if nobody lifts a finger. Once we act, the future rewrites itself."

Robin raised an eyebrow. "Sounds like either magic or structured guesswork."

"No, it's neither magic nor guesswork," Andy said. "It's modeling what would happen without your project—the counterfactual. And by definition, that kind of modeling can never be scientifically proven. You can't split the universe in two and do some A/B testing. You can only revisit it in hindsight to see if your assumptions held up. That's what makes baseline setting so complex."

Robin thought for a long time and then whistled slowly through his teeth. "So if Cassiopeia makes a prediction on her shell about the number of trees we will lose, and we therefore launch a project to protect the forest, then her original prediction will no longer be accurate..." He narrowed his eyes and thought. "In retrospect, there are two possible reasons for this. Either our project worked, or the turtle was wrong with her prediction from the start. We'll never be able to prove which is true. This smells like some pretty heated debates to me..."

Andy went on, "And even if you could build the perfect model with today's best data and tools, science doesn't stand still. A year from now, you'll have better methods, better datasets. What seems solid today might look outdated tomorrow. The key point is that each methodology goes through public consultation, technical peer review, and third-party validation. And when flaws are found—which they always are—they are revised. Again and again.

"That's why baseline setting is so complex."

Robin whistled. "No wonder it takes years to finish the process."

"But that's why it works," Andy said. "It's slow, yeah. But it's trustworthy. Transparent. Open to challenges. That's how you should get global buy-in."

He finally closed his laptop and rubbed his face. "Okay—now I need a coffee."

Then he added, more seriously: "But this is what we need to do. For Coltra East, we have to gather national-level deforestation data —ideally going back ten years. Then model risk in both Coltra East and Coltra West. That's easy for Walmera, with clear logging plans, but estimating risk from local activity is harder. More nuanced."

"And?" Robin asked.

"And," Andy continued, "we need to measure the current carbon stock in Coltra East's trees. Then compare that to what would happen if deforestation continued. The difference between those two scenarios is what gives us carbon credits—*if* we can prove the forest was saved because of our project."

"Professor Andy," Robin said, mock-formal, as the three of them headed towards the stunning breakfast room, situated on a terrace overlooking the jungle. "Sounds like a lot of work ahead of us."

Ella had gotten a bungalow to herself this time, and she appeared on the terrace with a cup of coffee in her hands. She seemed worried.

"What's up, Ella?" Robin asked. "Dreamt of Spencer?"

She gave him a contemptuous look. "Spencer... See, I had a long conversation last night with Morgan. Deep in his heart, Spencer is a good guy, at least that's what Morgan says. But he is under enormous pressure.

"It's the first time the Walmera family has hired a foreign CEO. They're a proud Nolé clan, the Walmeras. Right after Spencer started, the price of palm oil tanked. Then, one of their refineries had some kind of technical issue and shut down—something about spare parts. I admire all your paradoxes, guys, I really do. But the purpose of the meeting last night was to win Spencer's trust, his commitment. Not to lecture about baselines."

They both blushed and looked down.

"Anyway. Morgan confirmed that Spencer is keen in principle. Low palm oil prices are probably another reason why a forest conservation project could make sense to him, rather than venturing into expanding the oil fields in Coltra East... What worries me more is my brother," she abruptly changed the topic.

"Your brother? Simon? What's up with him?" asked Robin, surprised.

"This morning, he sent me a message." She pulled out her smartphone.

> Decided to quit. Sick and tired of these bastards.
> Totally unfair, blaming me all the time. Covering
> their incompetence. Love, Sim.

"Wow, sounds like he was depressed. Where did he work?" asked Robin.

"He was part of the investment team at a health tech fund. Called it his dream job when he started—what, six months ago?. And now this... Before that, when he worked for the Ministry of Environment, he lasted less than a year...

"I hate to say it, but I kinda saw this coming," she continued. "Remember that night at Brigitte's when you showed me the clip with the drowning girl? Before you got there, he told me he hated his boss—after a few weeks on the job.

"He is brilliant and experienced, even if he is only 29 years old, and he is hard-working, but somehow he has no luck with his work colleagues..."

"Bring him into our team! We need an investment manager, and he needs decent colleagues. Win-win, right?" laughed Andy.

After 45 minutes of following a dirt road towards the East, Sophy asked Tuk to stop the Land Cruiser.

"Coordinates are correct. It's right here, 50 meters to the left into the forest," she shouted from the front seat, and jumped out of the car. Tiara packed her camera, laptop, and a long, rolled-up measuring tape into her bag and followed Sophy.

The two women stood at the edge of the forest holding a tape measure and an instrument for measuring angles, called a clinometer.

"Okay, this one," said Sophy, pointing to a sturdy tree just ahead. Tiara unspooled the tape measure and wrapped it around the trunk at chest height—roughly 1.4 meters from the ground. "Diameter, 27 centimeters," she called out, and Sophy jotted it down in her laptop.

"Got it. Now for the height," said Sophy, stepping back a good distance from the tree. She raised the clinometer to her eye, tilting it until the crosshairs lined up with the very top of the tree. "Seventeen degrees," she muttered, noting the angle. Then she tilted it down to measure the base. "And two degrees at the bottom."

While Sophy typed, Robin leaned over. "What's it say?"

"Height's about 12 meters," Sophy grinned.

Tiara nodded and switched to another app. They used it to calculate allometric equations, as the women called them, turning a tree's diameter, height, and species into an estimate of its weight, its volume, and the carbon it held inside. She looked up. "This one's got an above-ground biomass of 577 kilograms."

Sophy whistled softly. "Half the dry mass of a tree is carbon, and when we burn a tree, every kilogram of carbon mixes with 2.67 kilograms of oxygen to form 3.67 kilograms of carbon dioxide. That means you end up with almost twice as much carbon dioxide as you had in the tree—so this single tree would release more than a ton of carbon dioxide. Multiply that by how many trees there are, and we're looking at a pretty decent carbon store." She grinned. "See? Told you forest inventory wasn't boring."

Tiara laughed, brushing a leaf from her hair. "Yeah, it's kind of like solving a puzzle." She turned toward the next tree.

Over the coming hours, they helped Sophy and Tiara count and measure every bush and every tree within the marked field of 80 square meters. They repeated the process at seven other locations identified by the GPS. It was one of the most tiring but fun days of their new lives as carbon project developers.

***

The sun had set, the fading light casting a soft glow over the river. With a bunch of empty Demba Lager cans in front of them, the trio reflected on the day in the jungle.

"Sophy has a great life!" Robin mused. "Cruising around the forest, measuring trees, studying the various species..."

"Well, we might soon need many more Sophies..." Andy said. "Satellite imagery isn't enough to get carbon credits for Coltra East. We'll need hundreds of sampling plots across the region."

"Do we really?" asked Robin. "This sounds so inefficient and so prone to errors to me."

"Have you heard about carbon flux towers?" he suddenly asked.

Andy and Ella looked at him in surprise. "Carbon flux-what?" Ella asked.

"It's a scientific instrument that can measure CO_2 exchange between the Earth and the atmosphere. Sophy told me about it just now on the ride back. Ecologists use it to better understand carbon flow in plants and trees. She said they have one of these outside their conservation lab, the building down there," Robin pointed over Andy's shoulder.

"And why would that be relevant for us?" asked Ella.

"Well, if we could set up several towers across Coltra East, even across Demba, we could automatically measure the flow of CO_2 in and out of the various forests. This would give us exact data on how much carbon has been stored or released. We'd have a much more precise and robust way to measure and to obtain carbon credits!"

"Interesting," replied Ella, "but are these towers widely available? And what do they cost?"

"Sophy told me they paid more than 50,000 dollars for theirs, a donation from Walmera. It includes gas analyzers, sensors, and software."

"Fifty grand?" Ella shouted. "We would need dozens of them! If not hundreds!"

"I am sure prices will come down over the coming years," replied Robin.

"And how about the methodology itself?" intervened Andy. "According to the Green Climate Standard's current methodology, you have to do the ground samples, as we did today. Otherwise, you can't get carbon credits. I haven't seen an option that would allow the use of flux towers instead."

Robin hesitated. "Well, yes, that's the problem we discussed this morning, right? At some point, we will be able to physically measure each molecule of carbon going in and out of the forest. At that moment, any previous methodology will be outdated."

"So what do you suggest—we do nothing until we've got a flawless monitoring system?" said Ella.

"No, of course not. But it's another paradox, to be honest," Robin said. "And a dangerous one. Even if we do everything by the book today, and years from now someone will say, 'Why didn't they use the updated satellite layer?' Or, 'They didn't account for X, so it doesn't count.' If you want to avoid that risk, you'll have to wait until science delivers the perfect methodology—which, paradoxically, means you'll be waiting forever."

"The Science Paradox," Ella answered with a smile. "If we keep on discovering paradoxes at this rate, we'll need a taxonomy."

The last candle went out. They lingered in the darkness, settling into a quiet solitude. With the paradox of scientific correctness jeopardizing progress still spinning in their minds, they fell silent for a moment, tuning into the living world—the deep, rhythmic croaking of frogs by the river grounding them in something real.

The Intentions Paradox

The villages of Yolo and Mutela lay four hours north of the Coltra East Wildlife Center along a road that was more ambition than infrastructure: narrow, rutted, and barely passable in places. It ran along the Yolo River, which joined the Demba not far from the lodge.

Morgan didn't say much the night before. He didn't have to. You could see it in his hands. The way he tapped the table. The way he kept checking his phone, even when the plan for the following day had been arranged weeks in advance.

He was nervous, and no wonder—Morgan was born in Yolo. A Nolé village buried deep in the jungle, far from the chaos of Port Kewala.

Like Wanga, he'd earned a scholarship to study in the city, an opportunity that had plucked him out of his familiar world and into something bigger, sharper. After finishing his degree in international business management, Morgan slipped seamlessly into the Walmera family business, as if it were the next logical step in a life that always seemed to be following a map someone else had drawn.

It was a world the people of Yolo didn't always embrace.

"The Walmera family is Nolé, too," Morgan had said. "But that doesn't mean people trust them."

He said it flatly. Like a man stating a fact he'd rather not think about.

"Some villagers have good jobs now. Plantations. Steady income. Others have lost everything—the forests, the animals, the water."

He paused, then looked straight at them.

"Let's see how they respond to Walmera's new approach—protect most of the forest and earn income through carbon credits instead of traditional agriculture with palm oil and rubber plantations."

He shrugged.

"If it works—and that's a big if—it could change everything."

Today was a test. They were meeting with Chief Emmanuel, the head of Yolo's Elders' Council. Later, their journey would take them further north, deeper into the jungle of Coltra East, to the riverside settlement of Mutela—another community nestled along the winding banks of the Yolo River.

"Tila will take us there," Morgan said. "She's my niece. Her mother's a nurse—been caring for Emmanuel for years."

Then, more quietly:

"He has diabetes, and they are unsure how to help him."

To reach Yolo and Mutela in one day, there was no way around getting up at 4 am. Robin, Ella, and Andy fell asleep again when the Land Cruiser started moving.

After about three hours of restless sleep in the rocking car, thick smoke suddenly entered through the open windows of their vehicle. Their eyes began to hurt as if a hundred needles had pricked them.

"What the hell is going on here?" Robin shouted, trying to protect his eyes with his T-shirt.

The car accelerated, and Andy wondered how Tuk could push it through the smoke, unable to see anything.

A few minutes later, the smoke disappeared, and they stopped at a cluster of huts. Ella jumped out when she saw a small stream, eager to wash her face, but Morgan quickly called her back.

"Don't touch it! Use bottled water; this stream here is unsafe! You never know what worms or other creatures might surprise you."

After the trio had recovered from the shock, Morgan explained:

"This is a small Nolé settlement. What they do here is called slash-and-burn farming. That's also the reason for the smoke."

"Yes, Wanga has told us about it. Belé and Nolé tribes have been doing that for thousands of years, right?" Ella asked.

"Exactly," Wanga came in. "This is a traditional way of life that, in principle, is very sustainable and has been practiced in the tropics around the world. The villagers plant crops like maize or bananas on the newly cleared fields. After a few years, when the fields become less productive, the villagers abandon them, and over the years, the fields grow back into dense forests. Meanwhile, the villagers identify the next plot for burning and farming. After a few decades, the villagers might return to the plots used long ago, and the process repeats.

"However," Wanga looked at Morgan, "there are increasing conflicts on land ownership. None of these villagers has any official land title. They have simply been around for centuries. And with increasing populations, this rather inefficient way of farming is gradually becoming more problematic, as the period between land use and land recovery gets ever shorter."

Two young boys now peeked out from behind a hut. Robin waved to them. They let out a short scream and ran away.

"We should have taken the other Land Cruiser, the one without the Walmera logo on it," Morgan grumbled. "I told you, many here fear Walmera.

"Come on, let's go! Tila will meet us outside Yolo."

About one hour later, a young woman appeared on the roadside, waving.

"Uncle Morgan, Uncle Morgan!" she shouted as Morgan leaned out the window.

"Tila!" Morgan exclaimed, jumping out of the car. "My goodness, the last time I saw you was at your initiation ceremony; how many years back is that?"

Morgan and the young woman continued the conversation in Nolém, and even Wanga could no longer understand them. However, Tuk's face grew increasingly worried.

"They want us to hide the car here in a bush and walk the rest," he whispered. "Some sort of protest is going on in Yolo."

Tuk stayed behind, and the others quietly followed Tila towards the sound of chanting—rhythmic, angry, a couple of dozen voices.

Then, the banners came into view. Bright colors. Slogans. Protest signs in English and Nolé.

A diesel generator rumbled behind a livestock shelter. Wires snaked across the ground, feeding microphones and cameras.

"Are they making a movie?" Robin asked.

"No," Tila said, her English sharp and fluent. "It's a manifestation— a protest."

They entered the edge of the village—wooden huts, makeshift signs, and eventually two large buildings: the St. Lawrence School and, looming even larger, the Eternal Lights Mission Church. Both stood in stark contrast to the mud and thatch around them.

Morgan felt a twinge of nostalgia: this school had educated him as a child, lifted him out of poverty. He continued to support it financially.

The youngsters looked at Tila questioningly.

"They're protesting," she explained.

"You know, our Yolo River is poisoned, our forests are gone. And some of our people—" She looked at Morgan. "—have sold us out. But not you, Uncle Morgan, right?"

"Of course not," Morgan said quickly. "That's why I brought Wanga and our friends from Canland. We have a plan—to protect Coltra East and fund it through carbon credits."

Tila raised an eyebrow. "Canlanders, huh? That's funny. So is that woman."

She pointed to a gray-blonde Canlandish woman in her fifties, wrapped in a traditional Nolé garment, standing in front of a camera, holding a sign:

Colonization through Canlandish Food Production

Next to her:

Stop Palm Oil! Stop Killing Yolo People!

Her shirt read *FHA*.

"They've been here two weeks," Tila said. "Five Canlanders... Filming. Protesting. Sometimes here in the village, sometimes across the bridge, where the palm oil fields of Coltra West start."

"What's FHA?" asked Wanga.

"Fair Hope Alliance, from Canland. They want to help the people of Yolo and Mutela. Fight for our rights."

"And what do people here think about it?"

Tila shrugged. "Mixed. Walmera gives some of us jobs. Others just see them as thieves. But this—well, it's causing tension. A lot of it."

She turned to lead them away. "Chief Emmanuel is waiting—"

A terrified shout shattered the calm of the village. A woman, balancing a water tank on her head, froze mid-step. Her face twisted in alarm as she pointed toward the edge of the forest—the very path they had just walked.

More cries followed, sharp and panicked.

They spun around.

There it was. A plume of dark, oily smoke coiled into the sky, thick and rising fast. It was coming from the direction of the car. Where they had left Tuk.

"Goddamn it!" Morgan yelled, eyes locked on the rising smoke.

"Tuk!" Wanga cried out, panic cracking her voice.

Tila turned sharply to the students, her expression grim. "They've found the car," she said, barely above a whisper.

Without another word, Morgan bolted, boots hammering against the packed dirt as he tore toward the trees. Wanga and Tila were right behind him, sprinting into the haze of fear. Halfway there, Wanga skidded to a stop and spun around. "Ella! Stay there—with the others!" she barked.

"But—"

"No!" Wanga's voice was firm, urgent. "We don't know what we're walking into. Stay put. That's an order." Then she turned and ran, vanishing into the forest.

A muffled boom erupted from the smoke.

The gas tank! Thought Robin.

Banners hit the dirt. Microphones dropped. Villagers surged forward in panic and fury. The Canlandish woman stood frozen, mouth open, her camera still rolling—but the cameraman had vanished.

Ella locked eyes with Andy. "That woman's from Canland, right? Let's ask her if she has a place to lay low."

When the Canlandish woman heard the sound of her language, she blinked in disorientation, then snapped to awareness.

"The church. Its back door is always open. Let's go!"

Once inside, they collapsed onto wooden pews. A faded painting of Joan of Arc watched them from above.

Ella was the first to find her voice again. "What the hell was that? Why did they attack Tuk—damn it?"

"They didn't," Andy whispered. "It was the car. They must have seen the Walmera logo."

The Canlander spun around. "What? You came here in a Walmera vehicle?"

Ella nodded uncertainly. "We didn't have any other choice."

The woman snorted. "Are you out of your minds? Do you have any idea what that logo means here? What it triggers? You might as well have driven in on a Canlander navy warship!"

Ella studied her carefully. This was clearly not the right moment for an argument. She introduced herself first, then asked the woman—who in turn identified herself as Rebecca Silver—what had motivated her to stage a protest action here in Yolo.

Rebecca was a co-founder of the Fair Hope Alliance.

She spoke quickly, as if the explanation had been given many times before. The Alliance, she said, was working to protect the local population from what she described as the "illegal practices of an international palm oil cartel."

Then it was Ella's turn. Rebecca listened with her arms crossed as Ella gave a brief account—still in a slightly trembling voice—of forest protection and CO_2 certificates. Finally, Rebecca shook her head.

"Walmera destroys everything," she said. "They cleared Coltra West and turned it into palm oil plantations. Now they're cutting down forests here in the east of the Yolo River as well. No one really knows how they got those concessions. Legal? Definitely not. But one thing is clear: it's all about profit. Walmera cannot be trusted. The only solution is protest and resistance."

Ella's phone vibrated with a message from Wanga.

Tuk is injured but stable.

Andy jumped to his feet. "How bad is it?"

"I don't know."

Rebecca exhaled in relief. "Thank God—so he'll probably make it. Still, the best thing would be for all of you to get out of here as quickly as possible."

Ella looked at her coolly for a moment. "Yes, hopefully he'll make it," she said, nothing more.

A moment later, Ella's phone buzzed again.

> Tuk passed out. A few youths set the car on fire.
> Probably thought it was empty. Tuk has burns.
> Tila says he'll make it. They're taking him to
> Emmanuel now.

Rebecca remained unmoved. "She really has better things to do than take care of careless drivers."

Ella had to restrain herself. "Excuse me? An innocent driver was nearly killed by village youths!"

"Well, these people are defending their village. That's their right," Rebecca shot back.

Ella's face flushed. "And how do you know so certainly that Walmera can't change? What if they stopped the clear-cutting and instead promoted reforestation and sustainable agriculture—financed through CO_2 certificates? The villages around the Lester Hills are fundamentally on board with this; we were there ourselves just a few days ago!"

Rebecca's expression darkened again.

"You have no idea what you're talking about. How naïve can you be? This crazy idea will never work. And even if it did, the people here need to take their fate back into their own hands. And that's what we at the FHA are helping them do!"

"By pouring oil on the fire? By inciting people to violent resistance?" Ella snapped.

Now Rebecca was truly furious. "What are you accusing me of? That's outrageous! I am pouring oil on the fire? I'm helping these people. You showed up in a Walmera car—you provoked them!"

So on it went, the debate among Canlanders over the fate of Demba, here in this sanctuary of the Eternal Lights Mission Church.

Andy stared out at the empty churchyard.

"You guys wait here," he said. "I'll be back."

He navigated to Chief Emmanuel's house the old-fashioned way—by asking directions–then entered the modest but neatly decorated home where Tila was tending Tuk's wounds. He winced as the cool saline hit his arm. The pain had softened into a constant, throbbing heat that pulsed under his skin. Blisters had ruptured along the forearm, revealing red, wet tissue beneath.

Tila worked quickly but gently, rinsing away bits of ash and fabric. Her small clinic bag sat open beside her on the floor, tools and gauze spread before her. The place smelled of antiseptic and singed hair.

"You're lucky," she said without looking up. "It didn't go full thickness. You'll probably keep all the nerves, maybe even most of the skin."

Tuk managed a crooked smile. "Sounds like you've done this before."

"A few times. But usually with a backup team. We urgently need a clinic here in Yolo."

She dabbed antibiotic cream—silver sulfadiazine—over the raw flesh with gloved fingers. He flinched this time. Not much, but enough.

"Pain means the nerves are still alive," she said. "Take it as a good sign."

Wanga handed her more gauze. "Should he spend the night here?" she asked.

"He needs a clinic," Tila answered. "A real one. He'll need pain relief and more antiseptics."

"The Wildlife Center is our best option. It's a three-hour drive back," said Wanga. "The Center has a neat clinic."

"For the tourists, yes," Tila added drily. She wrapped the gauze carefully, layer over layer, sealing in the ointment and sealing out the dust. "But they might make an exception for us." She laughed briefly and looked at Andy. "You entered the country on a tourist visa and Tuk is your driver, right?"

Andy stepped out on the porch, where Emmanuel and Morgan were talking.

"Your plan makes sense," Emmanuel was saying, "but do your Canlandish friends really understand how things work here? I mean, that Rebecca woman is from Canland, too, and she's really stirred things up." He paused. "We need a real perspective for Yolo. Not more foreigners with their ideas and good intentions."

Morgan saw Andy standing in the doorway.

"Andy, you heard the question. What do you think? Do your friends understand how things work here?"

Andy didn't hesitate. "No. They don't. And honestly, I'm not sure I do either."

He paused.

"We have a tool—carbon credits. It channels funding into projects that reduce emissions. But whether that makes sense here... that's not our call. It's yours. Your land. Your future."

Chief Emanuel nodded slowly, eyes half closed.

When Wanga joined them on the porch, Emmanuel cleared his throat and began to speak with a soft but clear voice.

"I am grateful for your efforts to bring benefits to the people of Yolo and Mutela. Thanks, Morgan, for explaining your ideas to me. Before proceeding any further, I would be keen to understand the position of the Elders in Mutela. Wanga and Morgan, I would like to join you on the trip to Mutela. But let's leave tomorrow morning. As for you," he looked at Andy, "Can I please ask you and your friends to bring Tuk back to the Wildlife Center? Tila would join you. You should leave as soon as possible. And we need to find you a car."

Ten minutes later, Wanga and Andy arrived at the church, where they found Ella and Rebecca, standing in cold silence.

"Tuk is doing fine, but he needs to go to the clinic at the Wildlife Center as soon as possible. And we need a jeep," Wanga said.

Rebecca didn't blink. "You can take one of ours," she said, and for the first time, a smile appeared on her face. "I'll ask a driver to get you there. But no more Walmera cars here, please."

Wanga bit her tongue; Ella rolled her eyes.

"How the hell am I supposed to explain this to Hubert?" Morgan said as he helped Tuk and Tila into the back seat. "He wants to help —really help. He sees this project as his legacy. And now we've got a torched company vehicle and a community on edge. Walmera's already under pressure. So is he. I guess we'll say it was an accident."

Rebecca's driver put the jeep in gear, Andy riding shotgun, as they rolled out of the compound, past the smoldering skeleton of the Land Cruiser. There, they saw that the company logo had melted off the tailgate—only a few letters remained.

"Wa...r."

They drove in silence until Robin spoke.

"It's another paradox," he said. "The Intentions Paradox."

Andy turned slightly. "What's that?"

"It's when everyone involved has good intentions. The villagers want a future for their kids. Rebecca wants to protect Indigenous rights. Wanga wants to bring real value to the community. Even Walmera— at least this time—wants to do something better. And we're here trying to support all that with carbon credits. But the more good intentions you throw into the mix, the more complicated it gets."

Ella looked up. "Because everyone defines 'good' differently."

"Exactly," said Robin. "Different priorities, different worldviews—"

Andy frowned. "But isn't that just your Communities Paradox again?"

Robin shook his head. "Not quite. The Communities Paradox is about when local needs collide—like when one part of a village wants jobs in the palm oil industry, while the other part prefers to continue farming. The idea that there is just one united local community is naive.

"What we saw here is a clash of good intentions. Everybody wants to do good. But, paradoxically, the result is chaos."

"This one's also bigger," Ella added quietly. "It's not just about clashing interests. It's about clashing frameworks. People parachuting in with their own compasses—each one pointing to a different version of 'what's right.'"

They fell silent again, the road stretching ahead of them through the haze.

The Leakage Paradox

Darkness slowed their journey, and the sun was long gone by the time they got back to the Wildlife Center, where they proceeded straight to the clinic that was attached to the main building. "Thank God this wasn't a heart attack," said Andy.

"We were lucky," said Tila. "But others aren't."

Even the air smells expensive, thought Tila. *I bet they filter it through silk.*

Tuk drifted off quickly after a nurse had cleaned and redressed his wounds. Tila was just about to head back to the car to sleep in the backseat when Ella whispered, "Tila, come stay in my bungalow tonight."

She followed in silence. Inside, she stood for a long moment, not sitting—just taking it in. The sink was carved from a single block of onyx. The minibar had French mineral water chilled to exactly four degrees. The shower had three settings: Rain, Cascade, and Waterfall. All named after things that would terrify a child in her village.

She thought of Chief Emmanuel's cottage—its corrugated roof, its water tank, its crumbling walls. *And he's a chief,* she thought.

By the time they woke, lunch was already laid out on the terrace. After eating, they checked in on Tuk again.

"He'll be out in two days," the doctor told Tila. "The colleagues in Yolo stitched him up well."

Tila blushed and smiled.

That afternoon, Andy taught her how to play poker. She listened politely at first, brow furrowed, eyes serious. Then she started winning. Fast. With surgical precision.

"Don't you *dare* show up in Niburg!" Andy said, shuffling the deck with theatrical horror. "You'll have me bankrupt before I can order a beer."

They were still laughing when the tires crunched over gravel outside, announcing the return of Wanga and Morgan. Dust-covered, sun-dried, and weary from their long journey back from Mutela.

"The situation in Mutela is even more complex than what you saw in Duiba," Wanga began, as they sat around an outdoor table, bottles of cold Demba Lager sweating in the heat.

"Essentially, there are three groups—and they're pulling in different directions. Mutela is known for its hundreds of riverbank fish farms along the Yolo River. The first group is the fishing families. They've seen firsthand how the plantations across the river in Coltra West have damaged the ecosystem and hurt their catch. They're fiercely supportive of our project.

"The second group is the farmers. Many of them are undecided. For them, it all comes down to what we can offer—what their future looks like if they don't sell out to logging or agribusiness.

"And then there's a third group—vocal supporters of new plantations. Their main interest is the access road being built from the North. They see it as a path to jobs, business opportunities, motorbikes, mobility. Interestingly, a lot of the younger generation are in that camp."

Then Morgan pulled out a stack of flip chart sheets, its surfaces alive with multicolored index cards pinned in rows and columns. The word "health center" or "clinic" was written on many of them. Others read: "clean water," "seed banks," "scholarships."

"I liked how the younger people stepped up today," Morgan said. "They seem to be taking ownership—and they're not naive. A lot of them genuinely see Walmera as a gateway to a modern, stable life. We've got a real journey ahead of us. But at least one thing is certain: Chief Emmanuel is on board. He believes in the vision and wants to help make it a reality."

After breakfast, the time had come to bid farewell to Tila and Tuk. They found him propped against a foam pillow, with Tila by his side and an IV in his arm. An infection still lurked beneath his skin, but Tuk tried to high-five them when they entered.

"I hear the trip to Mutela with Chief Emmanuel went well," he said. "I guess we're good to go!"

"We've still got a lot of work to do," said Ella. "And you take it easy; don't push yourself too much."

"Don't worry about that," said Tila. "I won't let him!"

"But I'll be driving the truck that brings the first load of stones for the new health clinic," said Tuk. "Don't think you can do it without me."

They laughed. The nurse adjusted the line. And they were gone. This time, the Walmera Cessna flew them directly to Port Kewala International Airport.

———

Before checking in for their flight back to Niburg, they followed Wanga out of the terminal building and into a curious little establishment nestled just beyond the airport gates: a vegan fast-food restaurant, its sign promising speed, virtue, and a daring reinterpretation of comfort.

"Total novelty here," Wanga said, grinning.

They grabbed a table near the window, and Andy poked at his tempeh burger. "This isn't going to be easy. We arrived here with three big ideas. Solar power for villages. Reforest Lester Hills. Save Coltra East. And what did we find?"

He shook his head. "Problems everywhere."

Robin swallowed and set his spoon down.

"I wouldn't call them problems," he said. "They're paradoxes."

Ella raised an eyebrow. Andy leaned in.

Robin counted on his fingers. "Day one: If our solar program gets too successful, it's no longer additional. No carbon credits. No money."

He ticked the next one. "Day two: With reforestation, you only earn credits for *adding* carbon to forests, not *keeping* it there—unless you can prove there's a constant threat."

"Which is crazy," Andy muttered.

Robin ignored him. "Day three: We argued over who should control the projects. Locals or investors? Ideally, it's the people on the ground." He nodded to Wanga. "But that means investors have to trust people they've never met. In a country they don't understand. Taking risks they are not used to."

He wasn't done. "Community meetings? The opinions are all over the place. No consensus. Just like home."

"Just like everywhere," said Ella.

"Then came Walmera," Robin continued. "When we met Mr. Spencer, we learned you only get credits by turning a *bad* situation good. So you can't do projects in good places where the forest is untouched."

"And what about the forest measurements?" Andy cut in. "We've seen how science keeps evolving—new tech, better data, constant updates. What's considered solid today might be outdated or even flawed tomorrow. This could go on for years."

"Finally, this insane trip to Yolo," Ella added. "We watched good intentions collide in Yolo. Everyone means well. And it still turned into chaos, just like the Gala."

Then Morgan spoke. "Should we give up?"

He wasn't joking. "I have no idea how to sell this to my boss. Walmera's under pressure. Shareholders are breathing down his neck. The price of palm oil is low. Walmera hardly made any profits last year. Now, we have even lost a Land Cruiser and got an injured driver."

He turned to Wanga. "Maybe you should go back to Canland. Try fundraising again."

Wanga shook her head.

"That won't work," she said. "Forest conservation at Coltra East costs $200 per hectare. Every year. That's 200,000 hectares." She looked him in the eye. "That's $40 million. Annually."

Morgan blinked.

"And Lester Hills?" she continued. "Thirty thousand hectares. $1,200 per hectare, per year. For the first five years. That's another $36 million."

Andy whistled. "Isn't there government aid for this?"

"Sure," Wanga said. "It comes in from Canland and ends up right back in Canland, but in Demban bank accounts. Trickles in. Gets siphoned out."

She leaned forward now.

"I am convinced that only an instrument like carbon credits, used at a large scale by the polluters, and funding measurable outcomes, can bring us anywhere close to that level of money."

"I agree, we need to give it a try," concluded Ella firmly.

"If you are still up for it, then we need to be clear on what happens next," said Wanga, her voice more hopeful. "On our side, we will continue the outreach. There's still a lot of misunderstanding. Perhaps we can even win Rebecca and the FHA as partners."

Andy cleaned his mouth with a napkin, then said, "Talking about the wildlife reserve, I'll contact Sophy and Tiara again. We will need their full support with the measurements and calculations to validate our projects and verify the carbon credits we create."

"And we'll do everything possible to find buyers and investors for the carbon credits once we're back in Canland," Ella added. "We'll set up the Five Elements company—and with a bit of luck, turn this vision into something real."

Robin's gaze shifted to the growing crowd gathered at the entrance of the airport terminal building.

"We'd better get going," he said. "And as for all the paradoxes, we somehow have to find a way to live with them, try to understand and explain them, and find solutions as well as possible. It's complicated, but we have no choice."

"Remember, my friends, the sky, the animals, the mountains, the forest, and the ocean—they will be with you. Always!" said Wanga. She and Morgan smiled and waved as the trio joined the crowd at the airport entrance gate.

It was close to midnight when Robin, Ella, and Andy finally sat at gate number B8, Port Kewala International Airport, waiting for Demba Airways flight 322 bound for Niburg, Canland, to start boarding.

Ella was freezing. After spending so much time in the heat, the absurdly low temperature at the airport reminded them of a Canlandish winter day. Robin slipped off his jumper and placed it gently around her. They just sat quietly, Andy browsing a local newspaper, lost in thought.

"Look at this!" Andy shouted suddenly, jolting Ella and Robin out of their thoughts. He pointed at a large photo in the newspaper.

Hubert Spencer smiled at them, flanked by three official-looking men.

A new era for the Republic of Lomba, read the headline. Beneath it:

First forest concession awarded to leading Demba-based agricultural group Walmera, bringing prosperity to the people of Lomba.

Robin leaned in, scanning the article. "After mass protests in Port Lomba over wages and living standards, the government is promising to triple agricultural exports within five years."

Below the photo, a caption read:

Dr. Ronald Nolayo, President of the Republic of Lomba, and Hubert Spencer, CEO of Walmera, signing a Memorandum of Understanding.

Robin blinked. "Are you kidding me? After meeting us at the Wildlife Reserve, he said he was flying to Lomba—remember? We even talked about expanding conservation projects across the border. And now he's signing a deal to turn even more forest into plantations?"

Ella shook her head. "The Lomba government must've looked across the border and seen all the money Demba's making from palm and rubber. They want their share of the pie."

She paused. "And honestly, who can blame them? Lomba's even poorer than Demba. No wonder people are protesting."

"Well, those protests in Lomba were most likely staged," said a voice from the seat behind them.

Ella, Andy, and Robin turned in surprise. A woman in her late thirties sat there, friendly-looking, with curly blond hair and sharp blue eyes.

"I just came back from Port Lomba," she added, as if answering a question. "This is a stopover on my way back to Niburg."

She paused, then went on.

"President Nolayo's government is hanging by a thread. The radical Belé opposition is doing everything they can to bring him down—and from what I saw, they're even paying protesters to fuel unrest. Securing support from Nolé-owned Walmera is a smart move. Strategic, even. It could buy him backing from the Demban government."

She tilted her head. "Are you guys in development aid?"

As usual, it was Ella who responded first. "Not exactly. Something adjacent, I guess. Actually... if things go well, maybe something even bigger."

That piqued the woman's interest. She leaned in as Ella gave a quick summary of their projects.

"Five Elements, you said?" the woman asked, pulling a small notebook from her bag and jotting something down. "Interesting."

Ella hesitated, then asked, "And what took you to Port Lomba, if you don't mind me asking?"

The woman smiled and handed over a business card.

"Janice Hanratty. Chief Foreign Policy Editor, The Canland Standard. Let me know how your project develops!"

It's another paradox, thought Robin, sitting uncomfortably in his middle seat again—*the Leakage Paradox.*

We stop deforestation in one place, but what good does it do if the same guy just goes down the street and chops down different trees? Paradoxically, saving the trees in one region can drive deforestation in another one.

Robin dozed off, suspended in midair—literally and in thought.

Part Three

The Money

The Polluters Paradox

The message from Wanga popped up on Ella's screen with a loud "bing," causing several angry heads to turn toward her.

> Hope you arrived safely. Great news. Ross of
> Rower wants to meet you. Get in touch with his
> assistant. Have asked for her number. Will
> text you.

"Please! Phones in airplane mode until we have landed," shouted the stewardess sitting next to the emergency door. Ella didn't notice any of that.

"Look at this!" she said. "Wanga has already informed Ross. Remember, the boss of Rower."

Robin rolled his eyes. "How could I forget him? Worst mic drop ever."

"Anyway, this could be big," she continued, undeterred. "We need to get Five Elements set up. We need to get the calculations right. And we need a great presentation. Then we..."

"Ella. Can you slow down just a bit, please?" Andy came in. "I didn't sleep a wink in this narrow seat, and Robin constantly hijacked the armrest!"

"I told you! You should have booked a window seat and brought your pillow. Your fault," she added. "Key point is that we divide the work. I propose that you take responsibility for all the technical calculations—the methodology, the data, and so on. I can take care of the commercial figures."

Her enthusiasm was cut short by a hard landing. Then came the delays: After the severe flooding, more Dembans than ever before were trying to make their way to Canland, so police checked every passenger for a valid visa before they even left the gate. It took nearly two hours until they finally squeezed into the airport train.

"We should be good on technical and commercial calculations," Ella continued much later. "What we are seriously lacking is legal knowledge and investment experience."

"I was thinking about that, too," Robin replied. "As you know, my parents are lawyers. My mom knows a lot about contracts. Perhaps she can help and bring me up to speed with the essentials."

"That would be fantastic! So, legal matters, contracts, company setup, and so on, that would be with you, Robin, at least for now."

"And as for the investment..." Andy began, "Ella, didn't you say that your brother worked for a health tech fund but just quit his job? I mean, seriously, could we ask him?"

Ella frowned. "Simon? I am not sure... He is brilliant, absolutely. He knows what he is talking about and has led several large investment deals around the world. But for some reason, he tends to fall out with anybody over anything quickly..."

"Come on. We could give it a try," said Robin.

"Ok, why not? No harm in asking him," Ella concluded.

At that moment, Ella's phone produced another "bing" with another new message from Wanga:

> Meeting with Ross confirmed. Tuesday, Sept 21, 3 pm. Meet his assistant Ms. Laurie Zach at main lobby of Rower Tower. Be prepared!

What followed were the four busiest weeks of their lives. Andy locked himself in his bedroom and dissected the calculation methodologies of the Green Climate Standard. He had to grapple with three different methodologies: one on avoided deforestation for Coltra East, one on reforestation for the Lester Hills, and, finally, one for decentralized renewable energies for the roll-out of the SunScore program. Hundreds of pages of documents piled up in front of him.

Robin spent an entire evening in the garden lounge, at the same wrought-iron table where the adventure had begun, explaining the intricacies of carbon credits to his parents. The longer he talked, the more questions they had and the more thrilled they became.

Eventually, his mother sat upright and looked him in the eye.

"Robin, I'm so proud of you," she said. "I had no idea what you three were doing down there, but you've presented a really thoughtful plan, and this is right in my wheelhouse. Selling a carbon credit from Demba to Canland follows the rules of an international sales contract. I'm doing a lot of these at the law firm. And Dad can sort out the docs you need to register the company, right, Max?"

Professor Turman smiled and nodded with quiet satisfaction as the trio finished updating him in his office at Niburg University, two weeks after their return. Rarely had any of his lessons translated so directly into real-world impact.

Two weeks later, the trio met at the notary, along with Robin's Dad, Max, who brought all the paperwork. Half an hour later, Five Elements Limited was born, with each founder holding a third of its shares.

September 21, around 2:30 pm, the Five Elements team passed the massive glass door at the main entrance of Rower Tower, the only high-rise in the city, and sank into one of the huge sofas in the sprawling lobby. Autumn rains had rolled in, and the steaming hot summer felt like a distant memory. Laurie, Ross's assistant, recognized them immediately and welcomed them with a friendly smile.

From the large boardroom on the 56th floor, adjacent to Ross' office, the views across Niburg were stunning. Ella furtively pulled her smartphone out to sneak a selfie, but Laurie quickly saw through her intention.

"Let's do that right," she laughed, asked Ella to hand her the phone, and told them to pose near the window. "Beautiful, three-two-one-Niiiiiiburg!"

They had just taken their seats at the oversized table when suddenly the connecting door opened, and there he was, Ross Murphy, the CEO of Rower, his energy immediately filling the room. He must have been in his late fifties, his silver hair thinning just a bit at the crown, neatly combed to one side. He appeared shorter than when they saw him last time on stage. Bushy eyebrows framed his small, piercing, but friendly eyes. He wore an expensive navy-blue suit that barely concealed his rounded belly. An antique golden watch on his wrist was partially obscured by a slightly too short sleeve for his stout arms. A senior manager, introduced as Cecile, sat next to Ross. She opened her laptop and started taking notes.

"Good afternoon, welcome to Rower head office; it's a pleasure to meet you all!" Ross began. "My friend Wanga has talked about you, and I heard you attended that unfortunate Niburg Cresta Gala last month. I am thrilled to hear that you are spending your time doing useful things, not just creating chaos, unlike those self-declared climate warriors. Please, what do you have on offer?"

The Five Elements team was startled by this opening statement, but as usual, Ella gathered all her courage first and began the conversation. They had done their homework. Ella briefly introduced the concept of carbon credits, which, judging from his slightly impatient facial expression, Ross understood quite well. Then she quickly pivoted to their cooperation with Matipa and the projects they had in mind.

Andy took over and outlined the amount of CO_2 that could be saved in various project scenarios, in line with the calculation methodologies of the Green Climate Standard. Robin explained the envisaged structure. For each project, once ready to go, they proposed an initial payment upfront, followed by annual payments over twenty years. In exchange, the investor would obtain all carbon credits generated by the project. Moreover, 10% of the costs would go to their company, Five Elements, to cover their work delivering the carbon credits.

After they had finished, Ross reflected briefly, shifting back in his chair. Nervousness crept back in. Did their idea sound foolish? Did he trust them?

"You know," Ross eventually began, "Rower has been engaged in Demba for over 100 years. We have seen governments come and go, but over the years, the people of Demba have been at our heart. We operate most of the gas fields in the country and have engaged in a large contract to explore oil resources off the Demban coast. Prosperity and development of the beautiful nation of Demba is our main goal."

He paused briefly, the team sitting slightly uncomfortable in the massive armchairs.

"Now, of course, it is not only the people of Demba that are precious to us. We are also deeply concerned about the environment. We know that burning natural gas causes CO_2 emissions, even if gas is one of the cleanest fuels. We've agreed to embark on a path to achieve net-zero carbon emissions. We will invest in several measures to increase energy efficiency to achieve this mission. On top of that, we will invest in projects that reduce further CO_2 emissions outside our operations. Our priority is on projects that preserve and restore our precious nature. Since we are an energy company, we are also looking for projects in the energy space. However," he made a short break to ensure the following words carried even more weight, "what matters most is the well-being of the people in the countries where we operate, including, of course, the beautiful Republic of Demba!"

"Well... ehm... I mean, so in this case, our project ideas could be quite a good fit for your strategy, Mr. Murphy?" Ella asked.

"They could indeed," nodded Ross slowly. "We are keen to work with you. Of course, we would need to join forces and set it all up properly. It will be a long path. I trust our friend Wanga has already told you that Demba is not an easy place to work. Listen," he glanced at his golden watch, "I need to rush to a conference call in two minutes. Cecile will be your contact person. It's been a great pleasure!" And he whizzed back to his office.

An hour later, they were at Brigitte's Bungalow, where rain poured down on the stacked outdoor tables.

"To Ross Murphy!" Ella toasted, raising her glass. "Unbelievable! He didn't even blink when you presented him with the figures. Fifty million dollars in total... my goodness..."

Brigitte placed a fresh pint on the counter with a thunk. "Glad to see old Ross swinging to the good side," she said. "But those are just pennies to him, sweetheart. That man's family—and that company —have twisted roots in Demba. Don't let the polished pitch fool you."

Andy, who'd been quietly nursing his drink, finally chimed in. "It's gnawing at me, too. Do you know how much profit Rower made last year? It's nearly 30 billion. These 50 million, I mean, it's a lot of money, absolutely, but Rower makes that money in profits more or less every day. For them, it's peanuts."

Ella looked at him angrily. "Come on. Peanuts or not, this is massive! With Rower, we can start the projects. We can save the forests in Coltra East. We can restore the Lester Hills. We can roll out SunScore solar power. What's the matter with you?"

"Seriously!" Andy snapped, "Look at the situation. Rower is extracting all that natural gas. Now, they have a contract to extract oil off the Demban coast. They are among the main culprits responsible for accelerating climate change. Should the same group that produces all this CO_2 buy our carbon credits, claiming to be clean and green? And meet a net-zero emissions target? That's a complete irony, don't you see this?"

"Ah?" Ella returned. "Who causes all the CO_2 emissions? It is you, Andy. And me. All of us. We all depend on their oil! Who just flew to Demba? Who took the Cessna to reach the bush? We did!"

"Ella, this is outright greenwashing!" shouted Andy. "An oil company spends a few hours' worth of profits on carbon credits to continue drilling oil with a clear conscience!"

"Guys, this is unsolvable," Robin tried to calm the situation. "I'd call this the Polluters Paradox. On one hand, the biggest polluters *should* be buying carbon credits—they have the money, and they're fueling the crisis. But on the other hand, they *shouldn't*, because then it risks becoming greenwashing."

Brigitte leaned onto the bar and smiled. She had overheard the conversation. "No. I'd say it's the Devil's Paradox. Sometimes you gotta dance with the Devil to keep the music going. But don't forget who's calling the tune."

The table went quiet.

Then Brigitte exhaled, her hand briefly clutching the back of the nearest stool.

She lowered herself onto the seat, a little slower than usual.

"I don't know how much longer I can keep up with all this, kiddos," she murmured with a wistful smile. "Any of you in the market for a slightly used bungalow?"

The Ambitions Paradox

The Ministry of Environment occupied a modern, six-story building made entirely of wood, steel, and glass. A plaque in the lobby proudly highlighted its top-tier energy efficiency certification. But something was off this cold November morning. The automated ventilation and temperature control system had clearly failed—most people kept their jackets on, giving the place the atmosphere of a train station.

Robin, Ella, and Andy had met Simon at the suburban train station near the ministry. Despite the cold weather and morning traffic, Ella's brother insisted on using his racing bike.

Simon had become a fixture in their meetings. His role was to sharpen the investment cases, working closely with Andy, who had programmed a tool to compare carbon credit production scenarios based on various input parameters. Simon's expertise in project finance had quickly elevated their discussions, and his concept of "blended finance" had given them a structure to build on.

The idea was ambitious but elegant: First, a carbon credit buyer would agree to pay for every ton of CO_2 reduced, creating a predictable income stream. With that commitment, they could craft an investable project, attracting impact-driven investors and, in turn, securing lenders to leverage the capital further. To minimize the risk,

Simon suggested involving a government agency to provide a partial default guarantee. They were impressed with the sophistication of the framework—Simon's years of experience at the ministry were evident—but one question loomed large: Who would buy the carbon credits?

They had met Cecile of Rower already twice since their unforgettable visit to Rower Tower. Cecile reiterated her company's interest in participating, yet their concerns remained. Did they really want their first buyer to be an oil and gas company actively extracting fossil fuels in Demba?

As the days passed, anxiety grew.

Then Simon offered an alternative.

"Here is an idea," he said one morning. "Selling carbon credits to companies is controversial. Why don't we talk to the government instead? Canland has ratified the Paris Agreement. They have committed to a climate target, and everybody knows it will be impossible to achieve it only with policies and measures here at home. The Paris Agreement encourages countries to cooperate. On top of that, if we can engage the government in Demba, credibility will increase, and investors in the project will be much more comfortable."

"That would solve our problem indeed," said Andy. "Why don't you reach out to your old colleagues, Simon? You worked in the ministry, right?"

Simon made a barely noticeable grimace. "I worked for the Canland International Finance Corporation. Quite frankly, most people don't know what they are talking about. But I did briefly meet Paul Becker, the Minister of Environment, at a reception. He gave me his card. A brilliant and powerful man. Let me give it a shot!"

Becker's office was as restrained as Ross Murphy's had been lavish. No taxpayer money had been spent on frills.

Andy stood at the window, looking out on a barren field that separated the building from the nearby Ministry of Transport.

I know," Becker said, reading Andy's mind. "It's not a biodiversity hotspot—yet. But that's Ministry of Transport land. We've tried everything to get them to collaborate on some sort of improvement. No luck so far."

Becker was a calm and conscientious character. A man in his mid-forties with slightly graying hair, his face was framed by a pair of large, rectangular glasses with thick black rims that sat prominently on his nose, giving him a thoughtful, even scholarly appearance. He listened attentively to the brief presentation of the projects in Demba. Judging from his facial expression, Andy's carbon credit models caught his interest.

"Watch out, he holds a doctorate in theoretical physics," Simon had warned.

Becker nodded appreciatively when they finished. "So, you want to scale these projects. Impressive models. Very sophisticated."

He paused, then continued: "You know, carbon credits have been a hot topic at every climate conference I've attended. And believe me, I've been to many. But we don't call them carbon credits any longer. Instead, we call them *Mitigation Outcomes*."

He took off his glasses and started cleaning them with his shirt, noting the puzzled expressions of the room.

Perhaps a subtle distinction, but essential," he said. "The term *carbon credit* focuses on the usage—it implies the buyer can emit in exchange. *Mitigation Outcome*, on the other hand, emphasizes the *creation*—the reduction itself, regardless of how it's used. It shifts the focus to the environmental impact, not the transaction."

"So, you mean, ehm..." began Robin carefully. "If I got you right, you suggest that we should not have our projects create carbon credits, but rather Miti... ehm..."

"Mitigation Outcomes," Ella whispered sharply, kicking him under the table. "Of course, Mitigation Outcomes. I guess that would be possible, right, Andy? And would you then be in the position to buy these? As discussed, we would ideally need a contract for ten years. Based on such a contract, we could surely find an investor..."

Becker raised a hand. "It's not that simple. As you know, nearly every country has signed the Paris Agreement—including Canland and Demba. Each has its own climate targets. Article 6 allows countries to cooperate, but it also introduces the risk of double-counting. Let me explain."

He leaned forward.

"Let's assume our government buys Mitigation Outcomes from your projects in Demba. These emissions reductions automatically count toward Demba's target. If we, in Canland, then go out and say, 'See, we have funded and enabled all these mitigation outcomes,' and claim them as part of *our* target too, we've essentially counted the same reduction twice—once for us, once for them."

He paused, and everyone sipped from their water glasses, unsure how to continue.

Again, it was Ella who tried to insist. "Excuse me, Dr. Becker, I understand the problem, but couldn't it be solved quite easily? For instance, Demba and Canland could agree to just split the credits in half. Fifty percent belongs to Demba, and fifty percent to Canland. Or else, Canland could ask Demba not to count these credits for its target as compensation for the funding from Canland?"

"Correct, this would be possible," Becker smiled contentedly, impressed by her ability to grasp it so quickly. "Your second idea even has a name. We call it 'Corresponding Adjustment.' It's like double-entry bookkeeping, and it essentially means that if Canland claims a Mitigation Outcome from Demba, then Demba has to perform a corresponding adjustment to its climate target. In other words, Demba has to increase its emissions reduction target by the same amount of CO_2 reductions."

Ella brightened. "That shouldn't be a problem! Hubert Spencer of Walmera has excellent government connections in Demba and

Lomba. Trust he will easily be able to arrange such a Corresponding Adjust..."

This time, Robin kicked Ella under the table. Sure enough, if Spencer could arrange a forest concession, he would probably be able to arrange a Corresponding Adjustment, too. But you cannot talk openly about pulling strings in front of a government minister.

Becker seemed to have caught Ella's remark, though he didn't acknowledge it outright. Instead, he continued with deliberate precision.

"Unfortunately, there is an even bigger problem," he said, his voice deliberate. "The Paris Agreement's core idea is that each country must set and meet its own targets. If Canland starts funding large-scale mitigation in Demba, we risk weakening their incentive to act. In fact, they may *lower* their targets just to attract foreign investment. The softer their targets, the more room they have to host international projects!"

Simon, who had been mostly silent since the meeting began, sat up. This was his territory.

"Dr. Becker, if I may," Simon began, his tone measured but firm. "I used to work for the Canland International Finance Corporation, funding schools, hospitals, orphanages, malaria centers, and more. You're saying that funding climate projects abroad creates a perverse incentive because it might replace the local government's need to act. By that logic, wouldn't the same be true for all international development funding? Schools and hospitals—these are basic services governments are supposed to provide. If what you say applies to climate finance, why doesn't it also apply to funding for all those other areas?"

Becker sat quietly for a moment with half-closed eyes. "In principle, it is an issue for all development finance," he said slowly, "and this is also a reason for criticism. But we've come to accept it. When we see images of children in need, we respond. We fund schools. We send aid. And what do we get? Short-term results, but little in the way of systemic progress. We kick the can down the road. Many countries became stuck in a cycle of dependency."

He placed his glasses back on his nose.

"But climate is different. The problem is too urgent. Here, all targets require verifiable results. So all interventions must be quantified and precisely measured. That's why the system may seem technocratic. But, in my strong opinion, if we seriously want to decarbonize quickly and dramatically, we need firm rules and quantified targets. And above all: Every country must meet its own targets before looking abroad."

The discussion lingered in the air as they exited the meeting and began jogging down the ministry's stairwell. On the wall, a large plaque declared, *"Reducing carbon emissions starts here. Use the stairs —avoid the elevator!"*

"I see his point," Andy admitted, his voice heavy as they descended. "But I think it's an illusion. For Canland, I get it. But I struggle to believe that in places like Demba, you will soon have a government that can fully commit to a binding climate target and embark on quantifiable and measurable policies."

"If the government is still around next year..." added Ella.

At the suburban train station, Simon unlocked his bike.

"Robin, you've been so quiet," Ella said. "Another paradox brewing?"

Robin nodded. "Yeah, and I think this might be one of the nastiest yet."

He rubbed his temple. "Okay—countries are supposed to keep raising their ambition under the Paris Agreement, right?"

"Well, yes—that's kind of the whole point," Ella replied.

"Right. But think about what that means in practice." He exhaled. "If Demba gets really serious about cutting its own emissions, it actually has fewer carbon credit projects it can run. Why? Because there's less left to 'sell.'"

Andy's brow furrowed.

"But flip it around," Robin said. "If a country drags its feet—keeps ambition low—it has more room to host these projects and cash in on international funding. So, who does the system reward?"

A pause.

"The underachievers," Ella said.

Robin nodded. "Exactly. I'd call it the Ambitions Paradox."

"But the paradox goes even further," Andy grumbled. "If all that is true, and that's why Canland doesn't want to buy credits from Demba—then the most likely outcome is that nothing happens at all. No projects. No protection."

The Crowd Paradox

Room A13 of the University of Niburg's Faculty of Economics had all the charm of a forgotten storage closet. Located in the basement, its only natural light came from a pair of grimy, tiny windows, and the room's furnishings—a few battered wooden desks, mismatched chairs, a locked cupboard with no key, and an outdated printer— seemed plucked from the faculty's discard pile. Over it all hung a faded portrait of Adam Smith, his gaze stern and unyielding, as though unimpressed with what passed for modern economics in his name.

"It's fantastic! Many thanks, Professor," Ella said with a big smile when Turman handed her the key.

"It's the only spare room I have at the moment," he answered with a hint of apology in his voice. "But you can have it for free. Keep it for as long as you need."

Two days later, he came back with a small round table and a coffee machine. "We had two of them up in the faculty kitchen, figured you might need one over the coming months..."

The room eventually became their headquarters, a slightly shabby yet oddly comforting hub of energy and collaboration.

On the morning after their meeting at the Ministry of Environment, Ella was pouring freshly ground beans into the coffee machine when Andy arrived, a box of heart-shaped chocolates tucked under his arm.

"Ella, for you," he said, blushing. "You were brilliant at Rower. And again yesterday—with the Minister of Environment, no less. I should've stopped criticizing and just acknowledged how far we've come."

Ella looked down at the floor, slightly embarrassed. "That is so kind of you, Andy. But it was your data that won them over!" She lowered her voice. "But more importantly, in spite of all this, we seem to still be at square one. We have an oil company that wants us, but we are skeptical. We have a ministry that we want, but they are skeptical."

Andy nodded, then leaned against the desk. "I was thinking about it last night. The root of the problem is that we don't all share the same understanding of what carbon credits are actually for."

At this moment, Robin appeared in the corridor, surprised. *What was that? Did Andy bring chocolate hearts for Ella? Or had Ella offered them to Andy?*

"For all of us, the purpose of carbon credits is obvious," Andy continued—to Robin's relief. *Ah. They're just talking shop.*

"Namely," said Andy, "to ensure that polluters pay the bill and to ensure that the people of Demba earn money by saving and restoring trees. But for Rower, the purpose of carbon credits is different. Of course, Ross admires Wanga; he seems to really love Demba, and he is keen to make a difference. But for his company, Rower, carbon credits are a cost-effective way to demonstrate that they, too, have achieved carbon emissions reductions."

"But is it really just about appearances?" Ella interjected. "Let's be realistic, most people who consume their products won't give a damn whether Rower is engaged for the climate or not."

"But the regulator might care at some point," argued Andy. "A government could come out and say, 'That's it, guys, your products are polluting the climate, and we need to stop that, we are now putting a huge tax on all your oil and your gas products.' At that moment, Rower could insist and say, 'No, please, look at all the carbon credits we have bought and all the emissions we reduced, no need for this tax!'"

"It is probably even more nuanced," Robin said. "It is unclear whether the scenario you just described will ever happen. But the fact that it could theoretically happen is reason enough for many to be skeptical about an oil company engaging in carbon credits."

Ella took another heart out of the box. "I don't understand that at all. From an economic point of view, it works like this: Rower is willing to buy carbon credits. Sure, carbon prices are still low today, so only the most efficient projects can be carried out. But other companies will follow suit, either voluntarily or because they're forced to do so by the government. This will increase the demand for credits, and consequently, prices will also rise. And that, in turn, will make it possible to initiate more expensive projects!"

She pointed at the worn portrait above them. "That's what this man, Adam Smith, found out, 300 years ago. It's all about supply and demand!"

Robin grabbed a chocolate heart. He caught Ella's eye across the room—just a flash—and smiled. *Some things were still simple, even if the world wasn't.*

———————

"Shit, I've gotta run," Ella snapped. "I haven't read either of your term paper files, and I promised you an outline by tomorrow."

"Yeah, I was kinda wondering," Andy said. "Mine's a mess."

"Same," Robin said. "I kept bouncing between the communities, the science, the buyers—couldn't land on one."

Ella paused. "Maybe that *is* the point. Carbon credits are kind of everything to everyone."

Rob in stopped short. "That's it!"

"What's it?" Andy asked.

"We don't pick," Robin said. "We ask. Do a survey. We want to hear from everybody who has a view.

"Crowdsource the confusion," Andy said.

"Exactly! Use the results for the paper. Two birds with one stone!"

Ella laughed. "And accidentally promote Five Elements while we're at it."

"Three birds," Andy added.

"Minimum," Ella said, grabbing her bag.

In the days that followed, the team launched an online survey designed to gather perspectives on carbon credits. The opening section offered a concise explanation of carbon credits, along with links to additional resources for those unfamiliar with the concept. After some debate, they chose to stick with the term "carbon credits," rejecting the more technical "mitigation outcome," which they agreed would confuse anyone outside the field. Next, they introduced Five Elements with cautious humility. ("Ella, we're not calling ourselves a leading developer of carbon credits," Robin had insisted. "The company's barely two months old!") Finally, they posed their core question: "Who should buy carbon credits, under what conditions, and which types of projects should be prioritized?"

They harvested their own internal debates to provide a few answering options, but they also left ample space for respondents to present their own thoughts and views. Two days later, they fired all their guns and flooded their social media channels with invitations to participate in the survey.

The response was nothing short of overwhelming. Rower and Matipa immediately reposted the message, and so did Professor Turman and Andy's mom, Professor Lelong. Even Minister Paul Becker sent an acknowledging email and promised to share the vital survey with colleagues at the ministry. But what made the post go viral was an entirely unexpected influencer.

Robin stared at his smartphone. "College friends launching a carbon credits company. Great idea, if they get that right. Let's help them! Your chance to get heard!" he read out loud. "Guys, that repost already got over a hundred thousand likes and several thousand comments!"

"What? Who posted that?" Ella asked excitedly.

"Luke! And then Remy immediately reshared it as well! While we were in Demba, their Climate Warriors thing took off."

"Well done," laughed Robin. "Two nights at the Niburg Harborview Prison turned them into martyrs for action. "Their lawyer was a genius—turned the whole trial into a circus, blamed the authorities for lousy security and shutting out the underprivileged. Ironically, their deep-pocketed parents paid for the star lawyer. But hey, who cares? As long as they're promoting our survey now!"

Over five thousand respondents eventually participated, and Turman and his colleagues from the Faculty of Engineering conferred and agreed to grant Ella, Robin, and Andy an extension until spring to complete their term papers.

The results, as they emerged after several weeks of analytics, were bewildering. About a quarter of the replies were fundamentally opposed to carbon credits. Less than half thought that carbon credits could play a significant role, on the condition that nobody could use them as an excuse to pollute even more. Some ten percent were enthusiastic about carbon credits. And the rest left all the answering options blank, instead writing statements such as "All bullshit! Climate change is a hoax!"

The open-ended comments were even more contradictory.

"Storing carbon in wood products is the only viable solution," wrote a manager of a timber construction company.

"Promote hydrogen. Stop the horrific extraction of lithium for electric vehicle batteries," added a director in the automotive industry.

"Carbon credits are pointless if we don't solve overpopulation!" commented a retired civil servant.

"Nuclear power is the only realistic option for a carbon-free power system."

"Carbon credits are great, as long as they don't support dangerous or unproven technologies like hydrogen or nuclear power."

"A quick transition to electric mobility is the biggest opportunity."

"Wind power should be massively promoted, the cleanest and most efficient technology." "Carbon credits are great, as long as the funds are strictly used for Canlandish projects only. We must clean up ourselves!"

"Great idea, but you must avoid wind power. The plants look ugly and endanger our birdlife even more."

"Carbon credits are a promising instrument to support projects in the Global South."

And a classmate of Andy and Robin, Amy Dupont, shared: "Deep Ocean Carbon Injection is the only climate solution that brings the scale we need. Planning to launch a startup, wanna join?"

It went on and on.

"Oh my god," sighed Andy. "Where should we even start? How will we ever find a consensus here?"

"The more people we ask about climate action, the more conflicting views we seem to get," added Ella.

It's another paradox, thought Robin late that night—*the Crowd Paradox.*

Usually, big groups make things more powerful. You see it in music, sports, protests, or celebrations: crowds often amplify impact. A full orchestra playing Beethoven. A sea of football fans marching to the stadium. Even a few busloads of angry farmers showing up at city hall can shift policy. Every last Friday in Niburg, there's that Critical Mass bike ride—hundreds of riders taking over the streets.

But in the climate movement? It weirdly works the other way around. Everyone agrees the crisis is urgent. But because the movement pulls in people from so many backgrounds, with so many different ideas of what should be done, the unity fractures. Instead of one loud voice demanding action, you get a bunch of smaller ones arguing about the best strategy. And that can stall momentum right when it's needed most.

The Offset Paradox

Big Plans from a Basement Office.

The *Niburg Daily Tribune* splashed the headline across the front page, alongside a photo of Ella, Robin, Andy, and Simon crammed around their tiny coffee table in the basement of the Faculty of Economics.

The story had originated with a single text from Andy, fired off the moment their survey went viral.

> Beatrix. This thing's blowing up—wanna pitch it
> to the Tribune?

She jumped at the chance. Her internship was about to end, and this was her shot to make a mark.

The article came out polished and punchy—almost heroic.

"A wounded baby chimpanzee at a lodge in Demba made us realize: We have to do something. We have to act, not just sit and debate," Andy was quoted as saying.

"With carbon credits, we believe we can change the world," Robin apparently added.

They stared at the screen.

"Did you say that?" Robin asked.

Andy shook his head. "Did you?"

Ella laughed. "Who cares? It sounds convincing, and that's the key point! Our name is on the map now, guys!"

Andy scratched his head. "Not sure about that. My father always says you should insist on the right to approve your own quotes," he said. "It's not about positive or negative. It's about accuracy. And no pressure, guys... Now the expectations of our success are sky-high!"

"They should be," Ella said firmly, "and we need to hurry up. We are past the point of no return. We need to make this happen!"

Their survey had proven to be an excellent idea to raise publicity. Several media outlets had asked for interviews, and the Canland Business Review published a lengthy interview with Professor Turman, where he compared the advantages of carbon credits over philanthropic donations from an economic perspective. He was immensely proud of Ella and her friends.

Andy's mom also got into the act. "The case of Five Elements is another example of the vibrant startup ecosystem at the University of Niburg," she said in the Niburger Morning Chronicle.

After some hesitation, Ella decided to dig out the business card Janice Hanratty had handed her—the editor from The Canland Standard they'd met in the airport lounge. As Hanratty had accurately predicted, Demba had since announced both financial and military support for President Nolayo in Lomba.

A week later, Hanratty finally replied.

> Congratulations on your launch. I'd be happy to consider a background story once your projects are more developed and we have solid, verifiable data. Please keep me in the loop.

Something far more important soon followed the media frenzy: Several companies and even private individuals contacted Five Elements. Some asked for more information, others requested a straight-out quote.

"We need 24,000 carbon credits to offset last year's emissions. Can you send us a price proposal, please?" asked a logistics company.

"I love your forest restoration project. I would like to buy carbon credits to offset all the damage I have done with my flights. How many will I need, and where can I buy them?" wrote a retired pilot.

And a ten-year-old schoolgirl sent them a postcard: "I want carbon credits for Christmas! I want to help the Chimpanzees!"

In the meantime, Room A13 was crammed with two new colleagues who'd agreed to work for free until Five Elements started generating income. Sabina, a classmate of Ella's, handled their hastily established website and their buzzing social media channels. Maurice, who'd worked at the open-air cinema with Robin and Andy, promised to take over Andy's calculation models—a necessary handover, since the team had come to a stark realization: a decision of real consequence loomed. If their projects on the ground were to advance in any meaningful way, one of them would have to move to Demba for a stretch, and soon. Andy, with his Demban roots, was the obvious choice. The question was no longer if, but when.

"All this is fantastic, all this is promising," sighed Ella one morning, "but let's face it. We still have one problem. We lack an anchor client. We need one big name, one leader, who provides us with cash to start the projects and to operate our company. We cannot bootstrap this forever with volunteers."

Robin looked up from his laptop. Now in December, hardly any natural light penetrated their small A13 office. "One thought I had lately," he pondered. "What about Cresta? Remember Matt at the Cresta Gala? He told us to get back to him once we have carbon credits for sale. Well, we don't quite have them ready, but perhaps we can convince him to work with us? I mean, Ella, perhaps you can convince him?"

"We have only one shot with Cresta," Ella nodded. "I thought about them, too, but concluded it was better to wait. But we are under pressure. Perhaps this is the moment!"

Matt's email reply arrived after only five seconds. "Thanks for contacting Matthew Carter. I am on holiday and will return to my desk on January 10. Your email will not be forwarded. Merry Christmas and Happy New Year!"

"Bastard!" shouted Ella. "The world is on fire, and he is taking three weeks off! But he gave me his business card, and I have his mobile number. I will send him a text!" she added defiantly.

This time, Matt himself answered—nearly as quickly as his out-of-office answering machine.

> Thanks, Ella. What's up? Great move with your
> startup. Impressive! Hanging out here up in
> Sova Valley. Weather is bad. No snowboarding.
> Hang loose!

Robin was stunned. "Did he say Sova Valley? That's where my parents have a ski hut! We used to spend Christmas up there. Now they are too busy with their law firms."

"That's our chance!" shouted Ella. "Is your house free after Christmas? Let's spend a few nights up there and try to meet him on the ski slopes. This could work better than another stiff meeting in an office tower!"

Andy burst out laughing when he saw Ella's reply.

> Hi Matt, what a coincidence! Will be up in Sova
> Valley, too, right after Christmas. Would be
> lovely to meet up!

"Anytime! Let me know what works," Matt replied.

December 27 was one of those days you look back on years later—with a smile that shows up before you even realize it. Snow had fallen in thick flakes all night long. But when they opened the shutters of Robin's parents' mountain house, the gentle and diffuse dawn light of a crisp winter morning engulfed them, casting a cool, silver glow that reflected off the fresh, virgin snow, making it sparkle like a blanket of tiny diamonds.

As the first hints of sunlight broke over the horizon, Ella got restless. "Guys, let's grab our gear, we can have coffee up at the ski station! Make sure your avalanche beacons are fully charged. This is going to be a magnificent day in the powder!"

Matt proved to be an excellent skier, but even more importantly, he knew the Sova ski area like the back of his hand. They shot down hidden mountain slopes, carved through untouched forests, and jumped over small cliffs; Ella on her split board, Andy and Robin on their extra-wide powder skis.

"And how are your projects coming along?" asked Matt as they flattened themselves in four deck chairs at an outdoor snow bar, Canlandish Coffees, and the afternoon sun warming up their tired limbs.

"Super promising, Matt, but it looks like we need your help here," Ella did not beat around the bush. "We got over one hundred requests for carbon credits. But what we lack is one large company that takes the lead. We need somebody to make a significant commitment to buy a large chunk of the credits, ideally over the full ten years. You told us at that infamous gala dinner back in the summer that Cresta has been carbon neutral already for five years. How about Cresta becoming the first company to invest in carbon credits from Demba?"

Matt took a sip of his drink. "We only buy credits from operating projects," he replied after a while. "But we have been supporting your partner Matipa for many years now. We would be keen to get involved. But the real problem is different."

Ella looked at him expectantly.

"To be honest," he continued, "our climate action program recently attracted quite some criticism. Did you hear about the Climate

Warriors? They're the ones who crashed the gala." He cringed. "I have to admit, I kinda liked that show. Rower really is an example of rampant greenwashing. They talk a lot about all their green projects, and at the same time, they drill for new oil off the Demban coast. The trouble is, now the Climate Warriors have targeted Cresta. They hate our Carbon Neutral certification."

He pulled out his phone, tapped the *Business Daily* app, and handed it to Ella. *Green Group Slams Carbon Neutral Claims*, read the headline. "Why that?" asked Andy. "Isn't the 'carbon-neutral' label common by now? It proves that you have a robust climate strategy in place. You counted all your emissions, you reduced as much as reasonably possible, and you compensated for the rest with carbon credits. I recently checked online. 'Carbon neutral' gets nearly 300 million hits on search engines!"

Matt scratched his head. "Well, I agree. But the Climate Warriors argue that 'carbon-neutral' blurs the lines between genuine emissions reductions at the source and paying for emissions reductions elsewhere. Reduction and offsetting, those are closely linked. Like twins. The Warriors say that we are confusing the customer. People could think that our software and our servers are emissions-free and do not harm the climate. This is misleading, they say. We still have emissions, even if we compensate for them."

Ella insisted: "But Matt, scientifically, they're simply wrong. For the climate, it doesn't matter where you emit and where you reduce CO_2. Reduction and offsetting complement each other."

"I know, but paradoxically, the label 'climate neutral' was too successful," replied Matt. "Organizations like the Climate Warriors don't like it if companies use such labels in their communication. To them, this smells like greenwashing. They hate that."

All sat for a while and gazed at the fantastic mountain panorama. The Sova glacier, high up on the other side of the valley, shone beautifully in the fading afternoon sunlight.

"How about you switch from 'carbon-neutral' to 'carbon offset'?" Ella began again. "By calling it 'offset,' you make it very clear that the emissions are not just gone; they are still happening, but balanced out. And 'offset' sounds humbler than 'carbon-neutral.'"

Andy got excited: "Yes, and 'carbon offsetting' has nearly 200 million online hits, too!"

Matt shook his head again. "We proposed that in a recent meeting with the Climate Warriors," he replied. "They don't like 'carbon offset' either. Offsetting shifts the focus away from reductions, they say. Instead of investing in reducing emissions, companies can buy their way out. Remy Selnass—she's the head of this outfit—compared offsetting to a cheating husband, who compensates for his sins by bringing flowers to his wife."

"What a heap of nonsense! Is that supposed to be funny?" Ella shouted angrily. "They seriously compare a shagging hubby with our efforts to rescue the trees of Coltra East? Have they ever been to Demba? And besides, the example just demonstrates the stupidity of the argument. A husband should always buy his wife flowers. Regardless of an affair or not."

Andy burst out laughing, then grew serious. "Frankly, I don't get it either. Cresta spends money on so many things. They sponsor the Canland Climate Summit. They fund the Cresta AI Learning Center at the university. They donate to Matipa. They are the main sponsor of the Niburg Hockey Club. The Warriors criticize none of these. But when it comes to carbon credits that fund climate projects —that's what they criticize!"

"It's a paradox," said Robin. "The Climate Warriors hate offsetting precisely *because* it ultimately serves the same goal: to act against climate change. They fear it will be used as a substitute for deep emission cuts. You find the same pattern appearing in the debate over plastic recycling—some of the most virulent critics are activists who believe recycling distracts from the more urgent goal: to get rid of plastics altogether."

"Correct!" shouted Andy. "As Niburg HC fans, who do we hate the most? It's the fans of the fucking Niburg Ice Bears!"

"And who do we skiers think are the worst people on the mountain?" asked Matt and smiled at Ella. "Not the hikers, not the paragliders. It's you snowboarders, ruining our powder!"

"So, what do we call this paradox?" asked Ella. "The Offsets Paradox?"

"Or maybe the Proximity Paradox," said Robin.

"Snow falling, beer calling!" read a large banner above the snow bar.

"Looks like we chose the wrong business," said Ella with a smile while she pointed towards the banner. "Why don't we open a brewery instead of selling carbon credits?"

"There are indeed easier ways to make money," laughed Matt. "Let's go one more round before the chairlift stops!"

The Claims Paradox

"I've told you again and again, Andy! You're overcomplicating things!"

Andy winced and pulled the phone away from his ear. Wanga was furious. He hadn't heard her like this since that day at Matipa Lodge, when Ella suggested that Canlandish buyers should directly oversee how project funds were spent in Demba. Usually measured and composed, Wanga had snapped then—and she was snapping now.

"Listen to me," she continued, her voice rising. "It's been six months since your visit to Demba. I set up a meeting with Ross Murphy. Rower is ready to fund these projects. But now Ross is calling me—angry, frustrated. He says you've already met with his assistant twice, and still there's no proposal on his desk! Meanwhile, you've talked to journalists, run surveys, spoken with the government—fine. Great. But where are the results? What are the next steps? And now you tell me you're stuck trying to figure out whether Cresta calls it 'Carbon Neutral' or 'Offset' or 'Contribution' or 'Outcome'—who cares? Who the hell cares what it's called?"

Andy tried to interject. "But Wanga—"

"No, listen! Walmera is under pressure. Morgan called me again this morning. He can't keep Spencer waiting for much longer. They've got a palm oil planting target for this year. If he wants to propose forest conservation instead, he needs approval from his investment board—and he needs it *now*. We are running out of time!"

Andy tried again, more cautiously. "We're doing what we can. The situation is complex. Carbon credits are controversial. We don't want to rush in and get slammed right away. And we haven't given up on Matt or Cresta. Matt's still interested."

Wanga's voice softened, but the urgency remained. "Andy," she said, almost gently now, "believe me. I have spent half of my life fundraising. Whatever the science and the logic behind it, the story must be simple. Otherwise, people simply won't buy it!"

———

It was a cold, gray February, and a decision was looming. Robin, Ella, and Andy had skipped most of their classes. Their professors, including Turman, had given them ample leeway to focus on Five Elements. Their term paper, due at year's end, was little more than a messy stack of research and references, with no clear beginning or conclusion.

But the next semester would be different. They'd face finals, followed by six months of hard work for their bachelor's thesis. The question was unavoidable now: should they go all-in on the company and pause their studies? Or was their dream—brimming with complexities and contradictions—just too unrealistic?

Back in the basement office, the mood was bleak.

"Complete waste of time," Simon muttered one morning. "Voluntary carbon markets don't work. Wanga was right—it's too complicated. We should go back to Paul Becker. Regulation and government action are the only serious options. Otherwise, we should just walk away."

Ella exploded. "Did you even listen to Becker? His ideas on CO_2 emission targets and corresponding adjustments? My goodness, that was the mother of all complexity! And yes, Wanga was right. We should call Ross and apologize. He has the money and is willing to fund the projects!"

Simon shook his head. "Carbon credits are a half-measure. They don't fix the root problem. The only real solution is a global carbon tax—universally applied and high enough to reflect the true social cost of carbon. Anything less is just noise."

Something flickered in Simon's eyes—tight, almost unhinged. Ella instinctively stepped back, a chill moving through her chest.

He looked down, muttering more to himself than to her. "I'm the one holding things together, taking care of Dad while you're off chasing some fantasy where companies save forests on the other side of the world."

Robin stepped in, trying to break the tension. "Guys, stop. We're getting nowhere here. Let's just take a break. Half a day. Niburg Hill —I haven't been since I was a kid, but I used to love it. My parents and I went every Sunday."

An hour later, they met at the bus station, bundled in winter clothes. By the time the bus stopped at the forest's edge, just past the city's last villas, they were the only passengers left.

Bare oaks lined the trail up Niburg Hill, quiet and monumental. *What stories would these oak trees tell us if they could?* Robin wondered.

They had, after all, observed us for centuries, witnessed all our efforts to imagine the future, to create sophisticated and complex solutions to our self-made problems—and in the end, they see us coming back time and again, looking for simplicity, for clarity, for connectivity.

Would the trees be laughing if they could? Or feel sympathy? Or perhaps even compassion?

By the time they reached the top, twilight had fallen. A broad meadow opened before them, ringed by forest. A shuttered restaurant, an empty playground, and a locked observation tower loomed in the distance. The last sun rays pierced the fog for the first time in weeks. In the distance, Rower Tower glistened majestically in the evening light, the harbor sprawling behind it.

They stepped onto the empty viewing platform and stood quietly, soaking up the last bit of light. As they overlooked the Niburg Hill forest, the city, and the ocean, they could all feel a glimmer of hope touching their souls. Suddenly, two deer shot out of the trees below and immediately disappeared into the dense woodland.

"Remember the five elements of the Belé people?" laughed Robin. "The sky, the animals, the mountains, the forest, and the ocean. All of them are here with us!"

"Yes, it's inspiring...," said Andy after a while. "The evening sun illuminating all these millions of roofs, all these millions of trees..."

"A million trees! A million roofs!" Ella shouted suddenly, wildly gesticulating.

"Ella, Ella, what's wrong?" Everyone whirled around in shock.

"That's the solution, guys!" They all just stared at her, perplexed. "What if Cresta stops claiming that they are carbon-neutral or that they offset their emissions? What if instead, they will say: We enable one million solar roofs. And we plant one million trees. We pay for our remaining emissions. We fund projects in Demba. Simple, clear, honest. How does that sound?"

Robin and Andy stared at her. A breeze lifted her curly hair.

"I think it's genius," Robin said. "That could work. Catchy. But— isn't vagueness a problem? You once said what made offsetting powerful was the ability to make a precise claim, like *carbon-neutral.*"

Ella shook her head. "Exactly. And that's what makes it a target. The vaguer the claim, the harder it is to attack. Plus, 'solar roofs' and 'trees' sound inspiring. Not bureaucratic."

"It's a simple and convincing way to frame it," Andy agreed. "But there's a trade-off. Right now, they say they offset every ton—one-to-one. With these new claims you propose now, this strict balancing out of tons would no longer exist."

"Maybe not entirely," said Ella. "Full balancing out of tons could still be a requirement or at least a goal—just not the focus. That shift reduces complexity and controversy. I'm texting Matt. Let's see what he thinks. And let's get moving—before we're trapped in the dark."

They started back down the hill, phones lighting their path around the ancient oaks.

Humans, the trees surely whispered to each other, *sometimes depressed, sometimes in good spirits, always struggling.*

Right before they reached the bus stop, Ella's phone pinged. The glow illuminated her face in the darkness.

"Matt just replied," she said, eyes wide:

> Ella, have shown this to Lara. Her marketing team had a similar idea. They are keen. Will discuss more internally tomorrow. Please come to our office at 5 pm. Bring your gang.

It was yet another paradox, Robin thought, lying awake in bed that night—*the Claims Paradox. You'd think calling something "climate neutral" would be seen as bold and responsible: measure all your emissions, reduce what you can, offset the rest. Instead, people hate it.*

Set an ambitious goal and fall short ever so slightly, and the backlash is immediate.

Paradoxically, if you want to avoid criticism, just aim lower. Make softer, vaguer claims. Say something like "we're helping plant a million trees"—it sounds inspiring, doesn't commit you to much, and no one can really hold you accountable.

The Speed Paradox

"Nope—fifteenth floor," Matt said with a grin when Ella hit the usual button.

This was their third visit since the snowboarding trip. Matt's sustainability team shared office space on the seventh floor with dozens of software developers—slightly geeky, utterly absorbed. They worked in cluttered nests with colorful keyboards, ergonomic mice, VR headsets, USB hubs, and wireless chargers, the air filled with the hum of computer fans and the soft click of keys.

These guys probably won't notice when the world is on fire, Ella thought. And when it happens, *they'll have uploaded virtual avatars of themselves on the cloud.*

But today, Matt slid a key into the panel and unlocked access to the fifteenth floor.

"Dr. Cresta wants to see us," he smiled.

Ella blinked. *Dr. Cresta himself? The founder and chief executive of Canland's largest software development company?*

Dr. Thomas Cresta's office was a statement in yet a different way than the offices of Ross Murphy and Paul Becker. Behind the elevator doors, a spacious lounge awaited them, styled like an oversized living room. The expansive room, tall bookcases on either side, and floor-to-ceiling windows in the back created an atmosphere of openness and grandeur, combined with a peculiar sense of modesty. A stunning crystal chandelier hung above, casting a warm, ambient glow throughout the space. The floors were made of polished hardwood, "one hundred percent sustainably grown teak wood," as Cresta later eagerly explained.

In the center of the room, a plush dark-red sofa and several designer armchairs were arranged around a large coffee table. Robin glanced over some of the book titles in Cresta's extensive library. He would have expected the latest management literature or groundbreaking publications on the future of artificial intelligence. Instead, *Critique of Pure Reason* by Immanuel Kant sat next to the *Complete Works of Hermann Hesse in 20 Volumes*. Daniel Kahneman's *Thinking Fast and Slow* stood out on the shelf below, which Cresta had dedicated to modern theoretical psychology.

"If you want to understand what products people crave in the future," said a voice behind them, "you must first know how they think, feel, dream, and search for meaning in life."

It was Dr. Cresta, standing in a kitchenette tucked just off the elevator. He smiled and continued, "And talking about feelings and dreams, I think you struck a chord with your idea of launching the one million solar roofs project. Our company uses huge amounts of electric power to run our server centers. The link is obvious. I also like the idea of enabling one million new trees and saving a billion ancient trees. That would be a simple and inspiring way to talk about our engagement in carbon credits."

His marketing team had done their homework. The Climate Warriors agreed that the use of carbon credits to balance emissions was acceptable as long as there was no "carbon-neutral" or "carbon offset" label attached to it. They sat on the dark red sofa for the rest of the evening, going through Ella's financial models and Andy's calculation tool.

After two hours of testing various options, Cresta put his pen down and leaned back. "Listen, I propose the following. Cresta will commit to buying fifty percent of all your carbon credits over the first ten years. For the other fifty percent, you will have to find other buyers; we don't want to be the only risk-takers. We pay half of the money in advance to fund the projects. The rest we pay once you deliver the carbon credits. Further, we would invest in Five Elements so that you can hire a sound team. And finally," he looked at Andy and smiled, "Cresta will develop proper monitoring software so you can transparently handle all the project data. And we can encourage others to follow our example! But one more thing," Cresta looked at Matt. "We are aware that speed is of the essence. We know that Matipa and Walmera need a contract as soon as possible. But I hope you understand that before making a final decision, we have to conduct due diligence on the projects and your partners. Otherwise, we run a high risk of getting attacked by critical voices straight away."

"We are ready, Dr. Cresta," Ella said. "We commit to providing all documents and data you need as fast as possible!"

Cresta vanished into his kitchenette and returned with a bottle of Château Margaux and five glasses.

"Thanks for the inspiration and the dedication. There is a long path ahead of us, but for now, let us cheer for helping to make this world a little bit better! Oh, and one last thing," Cresta lowered his voice. "Let's be very careful with communication. Carbon credits are like onions. At first glance, they seem straightforward—a dream solution. But the more you dig into the details and the more layers you peel back, the more controversies you uncover. So let's move carefully!"

The vision was inspiring, but execution would demand meticulous work—across spreadsheets, borders, and boardrooms.

In the months that followed, Cresta's warning proved prescient. The Five Elements team—along with Robin's legal-eagle mother, Deborah—shifted into execution mode.

First came structure: dozens of contracts, new funding flows, legal entities, accounts.

Then came negotiation. And with it, the real test: calculating the deal for the village communities.

Wanga's words guided them at every step: "Remember, if the villagers don't like our ideas, it will be impossible to bring them to life. We need their involvement and must offer real opportunities for participation."

She estimated the need for at least 2,000 local employees in the Lester Hills restoration area and another 500 in Coltra East. The solar roof rollout would bring clean, affordable energy to tens of thousands of people. SunScore's rates were steep, but volume discounts helped. Every 10,000 rooftops unlocked cheaper pricing.

To ensure that, Wanga proposed the creation of two local trusts: the Lester Prosperity Fund and the Coltra Prosperity Fund, each receiving 10% of the carbon credit revenue. The Elders' Councils would manage these funds directly, allowing communities to prioritize their needs.

Once the structure was in place, the real work began, starting with Cresta's due diligence: a grueling, tedious process of verifying every claim, document, and partnership before any funds could move.

Cresta lawyers asked hundreds of questions and requested a myriad of documents. After countless video calls, emails, chats, flipchart diagrams, calculation spreadsheets, and drafts of contracts—and after hours of debate, negotiation, and copious amounts of coffee—they finally reached a compromise.

As Wanga had warned, doing business in Demba was complicated. The lawyers grumbled. The team compromised. But no one walked away. The outlines of a deal were finally visible. Cresta was ready to sign. So were SunScore, Walmera, and Matipa.

Only one hurdle remained: a final presentation to Walmera's board of directors, scheduled for Thursday, May 5th. At least one Five Elements founder would have to make the case in person in Demba.

"I'm beat," said Robin. "Let's call it a night."

Exhausted, they wandered through the Old Town, past the sleeping towers of Science Square, to Brigitte's Bungalow.

The bar was half-empty, but its punk rock playlist was still very much awake, and Brigitte herself was behind the bar—her silver hair tied up, her eyes sharp with amusement.

"Well damn," she said, narrowing her eyes. "You look like you've been chewed up by bureaucracy."

She turned away, paused the punk rock playlist mid-riff, and rummaged through a drawer behind the counter.

"You don't need punk right now," she said. "You need prophecy."

With a flourish, she pulled out a scratched old CD—Tracy Chapman, *Talkin' Bout a Revolution*.

As the opening chords played, she poured the drinks and murmured, more to herself than to anyone else: "For the many, not the few."

"Man, this has been a process," sighed Ella, taking a nip from her Bison Grass Vodka Tonic. "How many rounds of questions did we get from the Cresta lawyers? Five? Seven? I stopped counting."

"That's just the beginning, Ella," replied Andy drily over the reddish glow of a Negroni Sbagliato. "That was the easy part. It will take us at least one full year to pass the validation at the Green Climate Standard. They will need each and every detail on all projects. Each figure, each data point, everything we'll need to prove and document."

Ella emptied her glass. "Once we've verified every last detail, the final tree will be gone. This glacial pace is killing the projects. And no, Robin—I don't want to hear about a paradox."

Robin grinned as he held on to his IPA. "Too late. You walked right into it. The Speed Paradox: Rush the process and risk screwing up. Move too slow, and the project dies waiting."

"Stop it!" Ella said, half laughing. Then she leaned in. "But seriously, guys, are you aware of how close we are? If Walmera signs off, we have a deal. Cresta's money flows to Matipa, and Matipa conserves

Coltra East, restores the Lester Hills. Tens of thousands of homes go solar. And if this works, others will follow."

Andy nodded slowly. "It's almost hard to believe. Remember our blowout a few months back? We nearly gave up. And now... here we are."

He paused for a moment, then continued, more deliberately. "I've thought this through. I can go to Demba and present to the Walmera board. If we get their support, I'll stay on for the next few months to lead the work on the ground."

He turned to Simon. "Would you join me? I'll need help with the investment case."

Simon finally spoke. "Sure. If we can get those bastards to stop exploiting the communities and actually give something back, I'm all in."

At that moment, Brigitte arrived with a fourth round of drinks.

The Expectations Paradox

Nestor didn't bring his "Matipa" sign this time. A tear of joy ran down his cheek as he spotted Andy, the "lost son of Demba," as he once jokingly said.

"Please meet Simon, Ella's brother," Andy said after embracing Wanga in a long, joyful hug.

Now in March, the contrast between gray, frosty Canland and colorful, steaming Demba was even sharper than it had been last summer, the sheer vibrancy of the place almost too much to take in at once.

This time, the ride from the airport was shorter—just thirty minutes along the bayside highway. Outside the window, glittering skyscrapers sparkled like glass mosaics in the afternoon sun, their sharp edges softened by the haze of humidity. Between them, the sprawl of enormous, dark slums carved jagged interruptions into the skyline, like reminders of something more profound and unresolved. Simon glanced out the window, his silence thick with the weight of observation, but Andy was already grinning, leaning forward as the car pulled up to the grand entrance of the Port Kewala Palace Hotel.

Three uniformed concierges, impeccably dressed in tailored suits and white gloves, stepped forward with warm, welcoming smiles and opened their car doors. They swiftly loaded their bags on large trolleys. The scent of fresh flowers wafted through the air, and the soft strains of piano music drifted from the lobby.

"You are with Walmera, Sirs? Welcome to the Palace Hotel. Executive suites are all paid for, minibar and breakfast included," purred a beautiful receptionist with an unmistakable Belé accent. Andy felt awkward in his surfer shirt, smelly and sweaty from the long flight. At least he carried a brand-new tailored suit in his bag. His father's tuxedo had proven to be beyond repair after the disastrous gala dinner last summer.

After checking in at the grand marble reception desk, Andy felt hungry. "How about we grab something to eat? I saw some food stalls just before we passed through the gates." A concierge intervened as they were about to step out into the dark. "Excuse me, Sir, you cannot get out now. It is too dangerous. Don't worry, we have six different restaurants here in the Palace Hotel. You can choose whatever you prefer!" Disappointed, they settled for a posh but empty place offering Demban-Asian-fusion dishes.

"Morgan's driver will collect us in front of the Palace at eight tomorrow morning," Wanga began after they finished a shared plate of mediocre and overpriced sushi. "The Walmera Board meeting will start at nine. Let's ensure we've got all key figures ready. Please remember and pronounce their names correctly. It's important in Demba. Andy, make sure you deliver your presentation without looking at the slides. The screen will be behind you. When they give you the floor, Andy..."

"I think the deal is bad!" interrupted Simon.

"Huh? What do you mean?" asked Wanga, surprised.

"Look at the price of palm oil. It's been going down for the past six months. We are solving a problem for Walmera! Instead of wasting money on new plantations, they can now reap the benefits of carbon credits. You should have pushed them harder."

"But Simon," Wanga insisted, "believe me, we have negotiated for months. Morgan was super helpful; he played a double role.

Officially, he was Walmera's lead negotiator, but he consistently shared insider information with us regarding Spencer's red lines."

"And besides, Simon," Andy said, "I challenge your hypothesis. Yes, the price of palm oil is low right now, but it fluctuates, and that doesn't reduce the pressure to cut trees and open new plantations. Quite the contrary! Walmera shareholders want to increase returns. To achieve that, Walmera needs even more plantations since each one brings a lower contribution."

"It's simply unfair!" Simon shot back angrily. "Did you see all the slums on the bayside highway? We are hanging out in this absurd luxury hotel, eating expensive Sushi, paid for by Walmera, while those people have nothing to eat. Sure, this deal helps local communities. But Walmera exploited the land and deepened the inequality. Now they're profiting even more by selling carbon credits!"

Wanga and Andy sat silently, staring at the wasabi and soy sauce remnants on their plates. After a moment of awkward silence, Wanga looked up. "I'm with you, Simon," she said slowly. "I've dedicated my life to working with local communities, and it's brutal—inequality is everywhere. I honestly believe the deal we have now is a good start. It's better than nothing. Or do you really want to stop it now?"

The next morning, Andy stood at the ironing board, his hands moving without conviction, pressing and re-pressing the same patch of fabric. The fifty-square-meter executive suite was all polished teak wood and cold, impersonal elegance, the dark ocean stretching beyond the glass like a mute witness. He would have given it up in a heartbeat for a cramped, mosquito-netted bunk at Matipa Lodge, where the air smelled of damp earth and the laughter of strangers carried through thin walls.

The Walmera Board meeting had stalled before it began. Two hours in a windowless room on the 32nd floor of Walmera Center, the kind of place that seemed designed to absorb human warmth. Andy's suit, a supposed mark of competence, had betrayed him—it was cut too tight, and as the minutes dragged on, the collar pressed against his throat like a slow, bureaucratic noose. The tie, which only Wanga had the patience to knot properly, was a coiled snake, tightening with every swallow.

Then, abruptly, movement. The door swung open, and a tall, unsmiling Walmera officer gestured them forward. They followed down a long corridor, the hush of heavy carpet swallowing their steps.

Inside, the boardroom buzzed with the idle chatter of power at ease. A long table, surrounded by twenty-five board members, their jackets draped over chair backs, their limbs stretching like house cats mid-morning. Coffee cups in hand, they were just shaking off the stiffness of a first break, the kind that comes before the real work begins.

Andy let his eyes drift past them, past the polished surfaces and crisp papers, to the windows. Beyond the glass, the Parliament building stood in solemn grandeur, the Presidential Palace just behind it, cushioned in a sprawl of manicured green. A scene of order, of control, of a world that moved according to its own unspoken rules.

"Order, please, Sirs!" a loud and low voice raised from the far left. The chairman was Dr. Mentawa, one of the wealthiest individuals in Demba and the owner of numerous businesses, as Wanga had explained over their sushi dinner.

"Sirs?" thought Andy, surveying the room. "Did this board honestly not include a single woman?"

"We have the great pleasure of welcoming two gentlemen from Canland. They are the founders and owners of Five Elements. Mr. Andreas Lelong and Mr. Simon Andersson. Also, we have our Sister Wanga Namira, who is from the beautiful community of Duiba. Please come forward! Mr. Spencer, would you kindly introduce the next agenda item?"

Simon was awkwardly standing between the large whiteboard and the projector, whose light shone directly into his eyes, blinding him and creating an odd silhouette on the board.

Spencer rose from his seat, sweeping the room with a measured glance. "Gentlemen, with your permission, the next item on the agenda is a decision on carbon credits," he began. "The management of Walmera proposes an entirely novel type of transaction, which will be first-of-its-kind in Demba and most likely in the entire world. This initiative is part of our efforts to become one of the first agricultural companies to achieve a 'net-zero emissions' label, reinforcing our commitment to sustainability and environmental responsibility! It will further set us apart from our competitors, like Kewala Palm International.

"In short, the proposal is to license some of our forestry permits to Ms. Namira's organization, Matipa, to establish one of the largest producers of carbon credits in the world. We will achieve these CO_2 emissions reductions by restoring parts of the Lester Hills, expanding the protected area of Coltra East, and working with communities to help them manage the land more efficiently.

"Carbon credits," he paused, taking in the room, the moment, the breath before the plunge, "are projected to become a multi-billion dollar market, according to predictions from renowned analytics providers. Our projections show a significantly increasing price per carbon credit"—the blue line indicating his price predictions ran straight across Simon's white shirt, the figure 2032 appeared on his chest—"and as an early mover, Walmera could benefit dramatically from this emerging market!

"And our risk?" He turned to Andy, his smile easy, assured. "Minimal. Thanks to Five Elements, a major part of our revenues is already guaranteed in hard currency. Moreover, we will start with sublicensing only a fraction of our concessions in Lester Hills and Coltra East. In case of commercial success, of which I am convinced, we would present further proposals to the Board of Directors."

Spencer presented a few more figures and then gave the floor back to Dr. Mentawa. The chairman addressed Andy: "Mr. Lelong, would you like to say a few words?" Andy's hands were trembling with nervousness. The screensaver only projected changing photographs of massive oil palm plantations and a Walmera logo across the whiteboard. The presentation that he had prepared so carefully was nowhere to be seen. *If only Ella had been here to help out.* Andy's mind went blank.

"Thank you, Wamera... thank you for your... ehm... visionary thinking. Thank you for your willingness to... ehm... help stop climate change and help the people of Lester and Coltra..." He cast a fleeting, helpless glance at Mentawa.

The chairman smiled, slow and self-satisfied, as if indulging a small child. "It is our pleasure, Mr. Lelong. Being good and responsible citizens is always at the core of our business. Now, gentlemen, any questions?"

A murmur rippled through the room, a few knowing glances exchanged, but no hands rose.

"Let's turn to vote then," the chairman continued. "Those in favor?"

Nearly all hands went up in near-perfect synchronization.

"Those against?"

Three men in the back cautiously raised their hands halfway but took them straight back when they realized they were the only ones.

"Then this is so decided. Thank you!"

A few murmurs, a shuffle of papers. But Mentawa had no patience for second thoughts.

"Gentlemen! The next item on the agenda is the status of the Lower Coltra palm oil refinery. As you know, towers three, four, and five have been offline since last July..."

Morgan gave Wanga a quick signal. "Let's go," she whispered.

Ten minutes later, they merged with the traffic jam of Port Kewala, heading back towards the Palace Hotel.

Simon was already fuming when they reached the lobby bar. "I told you!" He slammed his glass onto the marble counter, the ice rattling. "It was a no-brainer for Walmera. Otherwise, why would they finish the topic within 30 minutes? Walmera is not serious about its net-zero emissions target. It's just about the money. And you praise them for their *visionary thinking*? It's ridiculous!"

Andy's face was still pale, his fingers absently tracing the rim of his glass. He knew his performance had been lackluster, a stumble when he needed a stride. He could feel Simon's eyes drilling into him, sharp with disappointment.

"Simon, but please see it from a different perspective," Andy replied carefully. "We've just witnessed the approval of our first carbon credits deal after months of negotiations. We will put the first parts of Coltra East under protection. Matipa can start with the forest restoration program. We can also expand the meetings with farmers outside the project areas to see what they need to stop chopping the trees. Isn't this a reason for celebrating?"

Simon exhaled sharply, shaking his head. "If they were serious, they would put all of Coltra East under protection! The government of Demba should withdraw Walmera's license! And where the hell is Canland in all this? Our country should step in and fund conservation and restoration. Instead, we're watching this disgrace play out like we have no say."

Andy tried to change the topic. "But Simon, tomorrow we will meet SunScore. It is yet another deal that we can hopefully close and then, at last, move to implementation!"

Simon let out a bitter laugh. "The SunScore deal? That one is even more unfair! A large international solar power company does a big business here. They don't even produce their solar systems here in Demba, making the country even more dependent on their imported hardware."

Andy sighed. "But Simon, nobody produces solar panels in Demba."

Simon seized on that, eyes flashing. "Exactly! That's the real project we should be fighting for! Imagine launching the first Demba-based solar production facility. That would create real jobs, real skills—something that lasts."

Andy leaned in, voice steady, trying to anchor the conversation back to reality. "But Simon, we can't do everything all at once. This is one step in the right direction. We're helping to bring reliable solar power to the villages. Many households will be able to charge their phones and do business. It's catalytic. Don't you agree that this is a good cause?"

Simon's face darkened, his voice rising. "You think that's their biggest problem? Charging their phones? Malaria is raging. HIV is rampant. Child mortality is through the roof. I just pulled the latest report from the World Health Organization. The figures are alarming. What are we doing about healthcare? Nothing!"

The bar around them hummed with quiet conversations, clinking glasses, and the low murmur of a world moving forward. Andy sat back, staring at his untouched drink. The city stretched beyond the tinted windows—flickering lights, unfolding stories, and countless problems no one could fix tonight.

———

It's another paradox, thought Robin late that night, after Andy had updated him on the Walmera board meeting and the fallout with Simon—*the Expectations Paradox.*

Carbon projects are supposed to help make the world a little fairer. We can support clean energy, restore forests, and bring some balance. But weirdly, the moment we try to solve one problem, all the other issues we haven't solved come into focus.

A project might improve energy access or protect a forest—yet suddenly people are asking why it didn't also solve poverty, gender inequality, or healthcare. It's a paradox: by making progress in one area, we unintentionally shine a light on everything that's still broken. Expectations rise, and when the project doesn't fix everything, disappointment sets in.

By trying to make things better, we end up highlighting how broken everything still is.

The Avoidance Paradox

The following weeks at Matipa Lodge passed in a blur of numbers, maps, and half-functioning broadband. Andy and Simon buried themselves in carbon project documentation, sifting through satellite images, refining carbon calculations, watching videos of canopy density and soil restoration. The weak internet strained under the weight of their work, every upload dragging like a slow tide.

Andy and Simon never revisited the thorny conversation they'd had in the bar of the Port Kewala Palace Hotel. Perhaps Simon had finally come to terms with the hard truth: their projects were, at best, modest efforts to make the world a little better—never enough to solve all of Demba's deep, persistent challenges.

In any case, Simon had found solace in Bobby, the baby chimp rescued during their visit to Demba the previous year. Now a sprightly, mischievous thing, Bobby darted around his cage, eyes full of challenge, limbs full of defiance. Simon leaned against the enclosure, watching the tiny primate at play. "Let's put it this way," he laughed, shaking his head. "Our projects won't fix the broken world, but at least they'll make more space for the chimps."

He gave a quick wave from the passenger seat of Nestor's dusty Matipa truck, bags packed, airport-bound. Andy watched him disappear down the road, clinging to the hope that Simon's trust had been mended. But as Andy was about to learn the hard way, the surface had healed, but the wound hadn't closed.

By late June, Five Elements had crossed a major threshold: the contracts with Walmera and SunScore were signed, and Cresta wired the first tranche of funding to Matipa. But the money came with a catch.

"We have to cover the restoration costs in local currency," Wanga said, rubbing her temples, "but the bank gives us a horrible government exchange rate. This way, we lose about fifty percent of the funds before we even start. If only we could pay them out directly in Canland Crowns!"

Andy had decided to stay at the Matipa lodge until at least the end of the year, helping Wanga advance the projects and continuing to collect missing data for the project documentation. He insisted on planting the first new seedling at the edge of the Lester Hills himself, just a short drive from Duiba village.

Meanwhile, at the Coltra East Wildlife Reserve, Sophy moved forward with a bold plan—two large classrooms, enough to train a hundred new rangers. Their task: to guard the newly protected forests, to halt illegal deforestation, to stand between the trees and the hungry, advancing saws. From hundreds of applicants, she chose fifty men and fifty women. The conservation area now stretched from the Yolo River airstrip up to the hills, embracing Yolo village itself.

With Chief Emmanuel's blessings, Tila, Morgan's niece, proudly assumed the role of District Coordinator of the Coltra East Emissions Reduction and Forest Conservation Project. She agreed with the Elders' Councils of Yolo and Mutela that the first disbursement from the Coltra Prosperity Fund should go toward the secondary school in Yolo, then a health center at Mutela village. Construction of the new buildings began soon thereafter.

The foundation stone was laid during the Nolé ceremony—a vibrant explosion of color, music, and community pride. Tuk's wish had finally come true. He drove the first truckload of pebble stone up to

Mutela, destined for the new health center. A year after the brutal attack on his Walmera car, Tuk's infectious wound had healed, and his contagious smile had returned, lighting up his face like it once had. Wanga, standing in the throng, grinned. "In the name of the sky, the animals, the mountains, the forest, and the ocean," she laughed, translating the prayer into English. "They use that little prayer both in Belé and Nolé tradition. It is unifying our cultures, which are much more linked than people sometimes believe."

Matipa had agreed to repurpose the empty DFRRU storage room into a warehouse for SunScore's solar power equipment. "Isn't it beautiful?" smiled Andy. "The very same warehouse, where you stored the emergency equipment for the flood disaster, now becomes the home for solar panels, a solution to climate change."

SunScore shipped truckloads of panels, inverters, batteries, and cables from the harbor at Port Kewala. Almost immediately, a new question arose: who would benefit first from reliable solar power? The answer stirred unrest among the villages.

At first, only families with a proven income could join the lending scheme set up by the local branch of the Demba Agricultural Bank. Senior employees of the plantation companies fit the bill, since their loan repayments could be deducted directly from their salaries.

That reduced the bank's risk and allowed for lower interest rates, but it was a system designed for security, not fairness.

"Andy, do you know someone named Janice Hanratty?" Wanga asked one morning in July.

"Yeah, the reporter from The Canland Standard. We met her at the Port Kewala airport last year. Why?" Andy replied.

"She just called me—apparently, Ella passed her my number. She's in Port Kewala covering the elections and interviewing Minister Keita. She said she wants to learn more about our work and asked if she could join a site visit to Yolo."

Andy's face lit up. "That's fantastic. Let's make it happen. She told us last year she might do a background piece once the projects matured. It's great she's still interested."

Janice Hanratty arrived a few days later. Wanga and Andy took her to Matipa Lodge, then on to Duiba and Limata. At the Coltra East Wildlife Center, Tila met her and gave her a tour, ending at the construction site of St. Lawrence Secondary School in Yolo.

But back in Port Kewala, the political situation was deteriorating fast. After losing the election, the opposition candidate claimed the vote had been rigged. Protesters stormed the parliament building, and the city was soon engulfed in unrest.

Hanratty shifted focus. She published a long, in-depth feature on the political and ethical tensions between the Belé and the Nolé—two groups whose cultural differences were, in truth, minimal but had been amplified by colonial powers generations ago.

The background article on Matipa and Five Elements never appeared. Overshadowed by bigger and punchier headlines, it was quietly set aside.

The team settled into months of tedium and frustration. Each of their projects had to get validated with the Green Climate Standard. This process involved a thorough review by independent experts, who assessed the documents and conducted a site visit.

The validation process was anything but linear. On paper, the carbon methodology reads like a clean set of steps—one block flowing into the next. In practice, it was more like navigating a maze with a dozen dead ends, each guarded by jargon and subjectivity. Every decision looped back on another.

And all of it was submitted in sprawling documents e-mailed back and forth with auditors. Andy once joked that validating a project felt like trying to do your taxes by Morse code—while blindfolded— during an earthquake.

In December, Andy and Simon managed to submit their project documentation to the Green Climate Standard.

Surprisingly, they didn't have to wait long for a reply.

"Rejected," read the letter that arrived at the Five Elements office just before Christmas.

"Failed to prove additionality. Projects likely to proceed without carbon finance," read the auditor's damning verdict.

How on earth was that possible? After all the calculations and documentation they had provided? Andy reviewed their last submission again. Then it clicked. He picked up the phone and called Simon in Canland.

"What the hell is going on? Have you lost your mind?" he shouted into the phone. "You changed the investment case at the last minute! In your new model, Walmera gets dismantled within three years, and the Demba government subsidizes solar power? That's insane!"

"That's exactly what will have to happen!" Simon shot back. "I've gone through everything. Demba pledged a 40% emissions cut under the Paris Agreement. There's no way they can reach that without shutting down Walmera and pouring money into solar."

Andy snorted. "Oh, really? Demba is drowning in over $20 billion of debt. They barely survived mass riots two months ago. And you think they're suddenly going to fund a solar revolution? Come on, Simon—this is fantasy."

After several rounds of back-and-forth, they finally settled on a consistent, realistic investment model. Wanga had just reported a new logging concession granted to Kewala Palm, along with government approval for two additional coal plants.

Simon seemed satisfied with the final version—at least, Andy assumed he was.

They ultimately divided their efforts into three distinct projects, each addressing a different piece of the puzzle. The Coltra East Emissions Reduction and Forest Conservation Project focused on Walmera's undeveloped concession in the pristine forest, ending deforestation and engaging local communities in conservation and promoting sustainable land use along the forest's edge.

The Lester Hills Forest Restoration Project initiated a massive ecological restoration program in the degraded foothills of the Lester Hills while working with local communities in and around the project area to train them in agroforestry, beekeeping, and other sustainable land management practices designed to prevent future losses.

Finally, the Demba Community Power Project financed the distribution of off-grid solar across the communities.

Each project carried its complexities, its struggles, but together, they formed the foundation of something bigger—a vision of balance, restoration, and possibility.

Andy was bristling with pride when Dr. Cresta himself dialed into one of their team calls to congratulate them for this achievement. Meanwhile, Ella and Robin signed up twelve new clients for the carbon credits, all of them eager to follow Cresta's example.

In March, Five Elements moved into new offices in Cresta Tower, one floor below Matt's sustainability team. Professor Turman personally brought along his coffee machine as a goodbye present.

One rainy morning in April, Ella was locking her bike in the basement of Cresta Tower when an unknown number flashed on her phone.

"Good morning. Am I talking to Ella Andersson, CEO of Five Elements?" a female voice asked, slightly broken by the poor phone reception in the basement.

"Yes, Ella here, who is calling?"

"My name is Lena Goldman of Canland National Broadcasting Network. First of all, congratulations, Ms. Andersson!"

Ella was puzzled. *No way. Was that Goldman herself? The former top model and star moderator at CNBN?*

"I am the host of the CNBN Canland Awards Night," Goldman continued. "I'm pleased to inform you that our panel of international judges has nominated Dr. Cresta and you as a finalist in the 'Leaders for a Better Planet' category. Your One Million Trees Project in Demba has convinced our judges as a particularly courageous investment. The awards night will happen on August 19 and will be broadcast live out of the Niburg Convention Center. Would you be available that night, and would you honor us with your participation?"

Ella nearly dropped her phone.

"Ehm, well, I am speechless, Ms. Goldman. It is an absolute honor."

Goldman chuckled. "It is well deserved, Ms. Andersson! With your permission, a film crew will contact you shortly. We intend to shoot a five-minute clip about you and Mr. Cresta here in Niburg, and we would also like to send a team down to Demba so we can feature your project."

Ella exhaled, collecting herself. "Many thanks, Ms. Goldman. I would be delighted to work with your team! If you allow me one question, Ms. Goldman. Five Elements runs two more projects in Demba. Our biggest one is about the conservation of forests in the Coltra East region. It's our Save a Billion Trees Project. The goal is to avoid further tree-cutting and oil palm plantations, but we're also working with communities in and around all the project areas to reduce deforestation by reducing poverty. This is currently our most advanced and impactful project. The other one is the installation of solar power in the villages, our Million Solar Roofs Project. Here, we avoid dirty diesel engines. Arguably, these two projects are even more relevant since they immediately reduce CO_2 emissions and directly bring benefits to the communities, and..."

"Certainly, Ms. Andersson," Goldman interrupted. "Our judges are fully aware of your other projects. They are outstanding, too, and they make you and Dr. Cresta even stronger candidates! However, the judges concluded that the tree-planting project at Lester Hills is, how to say that, kind of more real and easier to understand for the public, you know? New trees are growing, directly sucking CO_2 out of the air. Our film crew is excited as well. They would love to accompany your team on a planting day, along with local villagers!"

"Well done, Ella!" Robin laughed as she called with the news. "We got nominated for planting trees at Lester Hills, but not for stopping deforestation at Coltra East? That's classic. Another paradox."

Ella laughed. "Don't start with your paradoxes again."

"I'm serious," Robin said. "The Avoidance Paradox: Protecting forests does way more for the climate than planting new ones, but nobody sees it. No one celebrates what didn't happen. No headlines for 'Forest Not Destroyed.' People want something they can point to —photos, seedlings, carbon being sucked out of the air."

"It's true," Ella admitted. "But hey, we got the nomination. That counts for something."

"Sure," Robin said, mock-dramatic. "Just don't expect a prize for saving a tree. Only for planting one."

The Green Climate Standard still hadn't registered their projects. Every answered question led to two more. Their documentation swelled to thousands of pages—maps, tables, formulas, graphs, appendices. Robin and Sabina managed new client requests, fed live updates from Demba, and braced Ella for media attention. Word of the nomination had leaked, and suddenly, journalists were circling.

Beatrix Lemore published a glowing interview with Ella. Riding the carbon credit hype wave had earned her a permanent editor's chair at the Niburg Daily Tribune.

Even The Canland Standard ran a short piece on Ella—though it appeared in the "Faces & Voices" section, not under Hanratty's foreign affairs desk.

The floodgates opened. Messages poured in—old classmates, professors, even Robin's childhood pediatrician. *I always knew you'd make it!*

Only one desk at the office remained conspicuously empty.

"Where is Simon? Haven't seen him for a while?" asked Robin one morning.

"He said he was working with Andy on the investment case for an expansion of the Coltra East conservation area," Ella replied, shrugging her shoulders. "He's kind of changed ever since he came back from Demba last year."

Their primary concern, however, came from elsewhere: Andy kept reporting delays with the plantations. Two months after kick-off, they had already replaced the main planting contractor because the initial pick had only a quarter of the required workforce. The second contractor showed up with sufficient staff, but instead, they experienced a shortage of seedlings. The first contractor had removed several truckloads of seedlings overnight. On top of that, a nasty dispute between Zima and Letonga villages had emerged, the latter accusing the former of having sent youngsters to steal cattle. In revenge, a horde of Letonga youths destroyed several hundred small trees that they had just planted outside Zima.

"I don't get it!" Andy cursed the day before the film team arrived. "We are making good progress in Coltra East with the conservation program. The construction of the secondary school in Yolo is complete, and we have over 100 rangers now fully ready and equipped. Our SunScore solar program is growing nicely as well. Already, 300 houses have panels and batteries. Why do they insist on filming the Lester Hill plantations instead? Lester Hills reforestation is a long-term project. It will take years before we truly see the results!"

Luckily, it turned out that the film crew was on a very tight schedule, and their car lacked a four-wheel drive, which meant that they were unable to travel past the Matipa Lodge anyway.

"Why don't you just plant a few seedlings here in the backyard of the lodge?" the film director suggested. "We will feature Andy and three staff members from the plantation company. Then, we will interview Wanga and a few of the villagers in the area. I think that will do. The message still gets across, and that is the main thing!"

Two weeks before the Canland Awards, Ella arrived at the office to find a racing bike parked at the usual spot. Her heart skipped. When she reached her desk, Simon was already there, waiting.

"We need to talk," he said quietly—but his eyes were burning.

Just then, Robin appeared from the kitchenette, balancing two cups of tea, clearly trying to soften the tension.

"I've spent the past week recalculating everything," Simon continued. "Used an open-source platform with twenty years of satellite imagery from Demba. I rebuilt the deforestation model. The results are conclusive. The Green Climate Standard's methodology is flawed. Yes, trees are being lost. But not at the rate the model claims."

He slid a printout across the desk.

"And more than that—this," he tapped the page, "proves Walmera secured their forest concessions through bribes. They're not a legitimate partner. We can't work with them."

"But Simon—" Ella began.

"We need to stop the projects. Now. Apologize to Cresta. Return the funding. And withdraw from the Canland Awards."

Robin gently set the tea on the table. "Simon, we've followed the Green Climate Standard to the letter. You were there. You've seen the files. Thousands of pages—documentation, datasets, photo evidence."

"I know that," Simon snapped. "But the methodology itself is flawed. We have to wait for a revision!"

"The Science Paradox," Robin said, steady but firm. "There will always be a better model in the works. Science evolves. But the forests at Coltra East are under threat now. This is the best tool we have. We can't wait three years for the perfect version. We move now, and will adjust the baseline over time when more precise data becomes available. And Simon, you know very well that the method has a correction mechanism. If the model does not calculate conservatively enough, the figures are automatically adjusted later."

"And about Walmera," Ella added, "even if what you're saying is true —and it might be—they own the concessions. Who else do you suggest we work with? We can't invent a new landowner."

"These projects are morally compromised!" Simon shouted. "We have to shut them down before it's too late!"

Robin took a breath, then spoke calmly. "I'm asking you again, Simon. What's your alternative? Over one thousand farmers have enrolled in the education program for agroforestry, while a hundred or so are in the rangers training. The Yolo secondary school is about to open, and the Mutela health center is under construction. Seedlings are planted on Lester Hills. SunScore is installing solar roofs across the region. Do you want to throw all that away? What about all the effort, the sweat, and the hope of these people? What do you say to all those who are looking forward to a better future? Of course, we'll adapt when the methodology evolves—but we can't freeze everything in the meantime."

Simon's eyes flashed. "I'm here to warn you—and to help you. What you do with that is your choice."

He grabbed his helmet and stormed out.

Five days before the Canland Awards, the Green Climate Standard finally confirmed registration of all three projects. Five Elements could officially generate carbon credits.

Andy arrived back from Demba just in time to watch the final cut of the CNBN feature in the studio. An apéritif was served, a pre-celebration for all the award winners. The atmosphere was exuberant.

The Five Elements team sat in the viewing room, eyes on the screen. Tears of pride. Tears of exhaustion. Tears of joy.

"I just worry about Simon," Ella confessed as they walked towards the tram stop.

"Beer at Brigitte's?" asked Andy.

"Not tonight. Let's get some sleep," replied Ella.

Part Four

The Society

The Voluntary Paradox

The lights dimmed. A spotlight swept across the stage, and a familiar voice cut through the buzz.

"Ladies and Gentlemen. We now announce the winner of our most prestigious award category—the CNBN Canland Award for 'Leaders for a Better Planet'!

"This year, we are celebrating not one but two extraordinary individuals. Over the past two years, they have demonstrated remarkable courage to make a difference for our planet. For the fight against climate change, for the restoration of nature, and for the prosperity of less privileged people. One left a promising academic career in economics to pursue a bold dream. The other took a leap of faith, backing a risky environmental investment with no regulatory incentive—just a sense of duty."

The audience hushed.

"Ladies and Gentlemen, you have all seen the video of the Million Trees Project in Demba, and I am sure you are as moved as I am. Please join me in welcoming, here on stage: Ms. Ella Andersson, cofounder and CEO of startup Five Elements, and Dr. Thomas Cresta, founder and CEO of Cresta Software!"

Rainbow-colored confetti exploded from the rafters, raining down on Ella, Cresta, and the owner of the familiar voice: Lena Goldmann, CNBN's star moderator and host of the evening.

The massive screen in the background showed an oversized picture of Wanga, Andy, and several plantation workers standing in the backyard of Matipa Lodge, holding seedlings and shovels in their hands. Ella stepped to the microphone. Her voice trembled, then steadied.

"I would like to start by thanking Wanga Namira and her team at Matipa for their vision, patience, and..." turning to the cameras, "my God, how you stepped up to do the work. You simultaneously blazed the trail and cleared the path. I would also like to thank our partners at Walmera, and of course, you, Thomas, for your foresight and trust."

She scanned the room, shielding her eyes from the lights.

"Professor Turman, I know you're out there," Ella said, squinting. "This all started with you. You opened our eyes to the market failures and showed us a way to fix them. You also believed in us from the start."

She took a breath.

"And I need to thank my partners: Robin, Andy, and our families. I don't know why I'm standing here alone, because it started with you two and that horrible, hideous video. Winning the Canland Award fills us with immense pride and serves as a powerful inspiration to work even harder. Our commitment is to plant and protect more trees and promote solar power across Demba and beyond. Many thanks to all of you, many thanks, Canland, many thanks, Demba!"

Applause swelled. Ella waved to the audience and slipped backstage through a hidden door. A technician handed her a towel. The overhead lights shifted to a cool blue as Cresta took the microphone.

"At Cresta Software, we go beyond what is required and expected—both in our products and our responsibilities as citizens of Canland. Climate change is one of the most dramatic challenges of our century. Over the past years, we managed to significantly reduce the

CO_2 emissions linked to our software and our servers. We decided to support the Million Trees project in Demba to compensate for our remaining emissions. We do all that not because we are obliged to by law. We do this voluntarily because we believe it is the right thing to do. Doing well by doing good. This is our motto at Cresta Software."

A standing ovation interrupted Cresta's inspirational address. A few minutes later, he disappeared behind the hidden door.

After the broadcast, a lavish flying dinner unfurled for the award winners, influencers, and Canland's glamorous elite.

Robin clinked his champagne glass against Andy's. "Wow. Ella is a rock star."

It was a far cry from the infamous Cresta Gala disaster two years back, but something bothered Andy.

"Look around," he said. "People are staring at us, but nobody is talking to us. Are they scared? Or ashamed? Or even jealous?"

Robin squinted. "True that. Strange. And did you see Luke and Remy? They just passed by, and when I said hello, they looked the other way."

Ella joined them more than an hour later, smiling but visibly exhausted, the Canland Award in her right hand. One tip of the glass statue was broken off. A faint smudge of mascara clung beneath her eyes, and her eyeliner had softened.

She waved off the champagne Robin offered. "Water, please, I'm dying of thirst," she laughed. "At least ten journalists were waiting down in the media zone. Beatrix Lemore was all over the place. She wanted to understand our next steps, and she had hundreds of questions for Cresta. The poor man had beads of sweat on his face! But whatever." She downed the water. "Now I'm ready for a glass of champagne, and then let's call Wanga." She held up her phone. "Look at these messages! She managed to get a live stream at the Matipa Lodge! I've got messages from Morgan, Sophy, Nestor, and Tila! What a night!"

The room slowly emptied.

Ella had politely declined a chauffeur service sponsored by CNBN. She didn't feel like joining the after-party at the Laguna Club. Instead, they texted a few friends and agreed to meet for a nightcap at Brigitte's.

As they walked toward the bus station, passing the bicycle racks, Andy slowed.

"Isn't that Simon and Luke over there?" he asked.

Ella followed his gaze. Two silhouettes stood near the edge of the light. One of them held a racing bike.

"Yes," she said, frowning. "That's them."

She hesitated, then added, "I invited Simon over and over to join the award night. This is his baby, too. He never replied. Then last night— just one message: 'Pull out of the award before it is too late.' That was it."

She stopped walking. "So what is he doing here now?"

Before Andy could answer, the moon slipped behind a cloud. The figures moved, then vanished behind the little guardhouse at the entrance of the Convention Center.

Brigitte had called in sick that night—a rarity she blamed on "dusty lungs." Without her behind the bar, the Bungalow always seemed oddly hollow, as if someone had turned the volume down on the whole evening. Ella made a mental note to check on her the next day.

It was nearly 3 a.m. when Ella finally collapsed into bed, the night's confetti, champagne, and applause still swirling through her half-formed dreams.

Only hours later, a shrill ringtone tore through the dark.

"Ella—Ella, are you there?" a familiar voice panted.

"Huh?" She squinted at the clock. "Matt? What on earth is going on? It's six in the morning, Matt!"

"Ella, it's bad. Really bad. Lara just called. The new *Niburg Sunday Tribune* just went live.

The fog lifted all at once. Ella pushed herself upright. "What are you talking about?"

"The headline—" he swallowed, *"Canland Award for Greenwashing?"*

Her stomach dropped.

"What?" she said flatly.

"I'll read it. Just—listen." He fumbled. "Scandal overshadows Canland Awards. Last night, the founder of a giant software company, Dr. Thomas Cresta, won the prestigious distinction in the category 'Leader for a Better Planet'. But is he really acting for the climate? Major scientists call their carbon offsetting program into doubt."

Ella was fully awake now. "Scientists," she repeated. "Which scientists?"

"Beatrix Lemore wrote it. And she quotes—" he hesitated. "Luke Blackfield."

Silence.

"What?" Screamed Ella. "Luke's not a scientist. He's a theater major who shifted to pre-law."

"Well, it says here he's the lead scientist at Climate Warriors, and it quotes him. Listen: 'Cresta's servers consume massive amounts of electricity,' Blackfield says. 'Even if they've become more efficient over the years, Cresta has grown so much that their emissions are higher than before. Their tree-planting in Demba is pure greenwashing. What's more, the money mainly goes to Walmera, a giant forest logging company."

"Greenwashing?" Ella exploded. "After everything Cresta has invested—voluntarily? After all the work we've already done with the communities?"

"It gets worse. 'There is so much more Cresta must do. Their investment in Demba may have some benefits, but does it really move the needle? Cresta's priority must be on stopping all the carbon pollution right now. Cresta is greenwashing. Cresta's Canland Award must be revoked!'

"Damn, Ella, this is a catastrophe. No idea how Thomas will react to this blow when he wakes up. He was expecting some good news coverage."

"And what else is in the article, Matt? I saw that Lemore also interviewed Goldberg last night—"

Matt scrolled. "Yes. Here—Goldberg says she's 'surprised' with Blackfield's findings and that the committee will 'look into the matter.'"

"Findings?" screamed Ella, firing up her own computer. "Those aren't findings. They're just the ill-informed utterances of an imbecile."

"Ella, what do we do now?"

She paused as the Niburg Sunday Tribune opened on her computer, too. After a moment of silently scrolling down to the comments, she said calmly, "Matt, if there is one thing you can do now, then please print and show the article to Thomas, but try to make sure at least he doesn't go online to see the comments section. It's awful. I wonder who in Canland is getting up at six thirty on a Sunday morning to write disgusting comments like that? How frustrated are those guys, seriously?"

Matt darted to the comments and started reading them out loud. "'Not surprised about this greenwashing! Cresta's software is a scam!' Jesus. 'Ridiculous! Mr. Cresta pretends to be a climate hero, but in reality, he is just a greedy money man!' What the fuck? 'Climate change is nonsense—just an invention by the rich elite to sell overpriced software. Cresta should go to jail!' Fucking hell.

"Ella, can you wake up your gang and come over to the office? Lara just texted. She is on her way. We need to fire up our public relations company. We need holding statements. I am quite sure more journalists will jump on the topic once this Sunday Tribune story spreads."

It took ten missed calls from Ella to finally wake Robin up. But as he rubbed the sleep from his eyes and grasped what was happening, reality hit him like a bolt of lightning—the Voluntary Paradox.

Some companies go out of their way to do the right thing on climate— not because they have to, but because they believe it matters, Robin thought to himself. *And somehow, that's when the backlash hits. People start asking, 'Why didn't they do more? Isn't this just green- washing?'*

Meanwhile, the companies doing nothing at all? No one says a word. It's like donating $100 to charity, only to be confronted with the ques- tion, "Why didn't you give $200?"

This Voluntary Paradox had just hit Cresta with full force. It was the perfect cue for Beatrix Lemore to unleash her scandal story.

The Ideologies Paradox

Omar Lelong had founded his public relations company, Brunswick Lelong Partners, straight out of university. Cresta had been a client for decades, which made Omar the first call Thomas Cresta placed after the headline broke.

Omar sank into the dark-red sofa in the fifteenth-floor lounge in Cresta's high-rise office, loosening his jacket. The room felt muted—too quiet for a place that usually hummed with power.

"Here's the problem," Omar said. "The old tabloid instincts—drama over depth, heat over light—have gone mainstream."

Across from him, Thomas Cresta sat slumped, nearly unrecognizable from the triumphant figure of the night before. Lara and Matt flanked him, tension stretched taut like an invisible wire. It was just before noon, but the morning had already been long.

"Modern journalism thrives on controversy," he continued. "Some—maybe most—reporters have a mission to inform, but the spoils go to those who get the clicks, and the competition for attention is relentless."

He leaned forward. "Remember the first article in the *Niburg Daily Tribune* nearly two years back? When Andy showed it to me, I was skeptical. Beatrix Lemore hyped your startup like you'd already saved the planet. Just last month, she ran a euphoric interview with you, Ella. And I'm almost certain she was already in contact with Luke Blackfield."

"You think she planned it all from the start?" asked Ella.

"No, not the very start. She was just an intern when she scored a breakthrough with that story about your startup. Over time, she realized carbon credits were a goldmine—for drama, controversy, and headlines. She must have known about the greenwashing allegation of the Climate Warriors, and she just waited for the perfect moment to let the bomb go off. And the perfect moment to gain maximum traction for her story was, of course, the morning right after the Canland Award night."

A heavy silence followed.

Ella broke it. "Dr. Cresta and I were on stage together. We both won. Why put the spotlight only on him? She could have come after Five Elements. Let's be honest—there's no shortage of paradoxes in carbon markets. I'm sure she could've found something.

"And," she added, voice tightening, "she's never liked me."

Omar rubbed his temples. "That's what worries me. This wasn't about fairness—it was about strategy. Everyone knows your name, Thomas. You stir headlines. Five Elements was just another startup —until the award. By hitting you first, Lemore set the stage. The theme is out there now: greenwashing. The audience is primed. And once the debate gets traction, she'll move to Act II."

He leaned forward. "And here's the thing: You are between a rock and a hard place. You're too 'green' for the markets but too 'markets' for the green. Both sides are ready to take you down—for opposite reasons."

Cresta, pale and drained, cleared his throat. "This is all... unfortunate," he muttered. "But Omar, I have a more immediate problem. We closed our fiscal year in June, and our Annual General Assembly is around the corner—Wednesday, at the Niburg Convention Center. Around two thousand shareholders are expected."

He glanced at Lara and Matt, then back at Omar.

"Our climate commitment is front and center. We're set to announce a science-based target, which includes funding three new wind farms to power our server centers and several other investments to reduce our carbon footprint. Investment in carbon credits is another central part of our sustainability strategy. Our team has planned to mention the Canland Award as an encouraging signal showing that we are on the right path. But with this greenwashing allegation, we are now on the back foot. What should we do now?"

Omar scratched his head again. "First and foremost, precision. No half-measures. Instead of just introducing your climate strategy, you need to own it. Head-on. Make it a rallying point."

The Niburg Convention Center gleamed under the late-summer sun, the sky so blue it felt almost obscene to waste the day indoors. But Ella, Robin, and Andy were here again, for the third time, trudging into the same cavernous hall, but once more under different circumstances.

Thomas Cresta had asked them to join. The *Niburg Sunday Tribune* article had unleashed a firestorm, and media outlets had followed suit. The Canland Standard published a long interview with Remy Selnass of the Climate Warriors.

"Climate change is completely out of control!" she declared. "Ocean temperatures have reached record highs. Droughts are devastating entire countries. The small steps Cresta is taking are simply no longer good enough! Worst of all is their investment in carbon credits. With these credits, Cresta pretends to be on track to stop carbon pollution. This is not the case! Cresta must stop the greenwashing and radically cut its emissions. We must end carbon offsetting and initiate a giant leap forward right now!"

On the other side of the debate, Professor Turman had published a piece in the *Niburger Morning Chronicle* defending market-based solutions.

Cresta's communications team was stretched thin, scrambling to control the damage. Matt had spent four nights in a row polishing and fine-tuning his presentation of the Cresta Climate Strategy. He hoped to excite the shareholders with optimism, innovation, and a "can-do" spirit—precisely in line with Cresta's core values as he perceived them.

Droves of men in black and navy suits flocked into the convention hall in a steady, coordinated stream. Here and there, the sea of dark was broken by the shimmer of a lady's evening dress.

"I bought a few shares in Cresta," Ella said, joining the shareholders' registration line. Robin looked at her in surprise. "This way, I can vote."

Inside, rows of chairs stretched across the vast hall, the air buzzing with low, murmuring conversations. Was this really the same place where, just four days ago, they had basked in the glow of victory?

"If Five Elements ever gets this big, we're banning suits and ties at our General Assembly," Robin laughed.

The first hour dragged on, mind-numbing in its monotony. Ella dozed off on Robin's shoulder, her curls spilling over his face. He barely moved, half-lost in the scent of her shampoo. Then—he noticed it. The shift. The room had changed.

The financials were uninspiring, and Cresta had failed to impress. Then the chairman introduced Matt.

Omar had recommended a last-minute change from "strategy" to "vision" to sound more vague but also more engaging. When Matt had ended, you could have heard a pin drop. The large screen in the background indicated that two ladies in the third row and a gentleman in the first row had raised a hand.

"My name is Remy Selnass," said the first speaker.

Ella tensed. *Of course. She had bought Cresta shares, too.*

"Ladies and Gentlemen. The world is on fire! If we don't reduce emissions dramatically, global temperatures could reach three to six degrees above pre-industrial levels by the year 2100. This will mean unprecedented floods, droughts, heat waves, and masses of climate refugees arriving at the shores of Canland. Let me tell you, loud and clear: Large and hugely profitable companies like Cresta must lead the path and now commit to bold climate action. The current Cresta Climate Strategy is a joke. It is toothless and lacks the ambition we need now so urgently. I ask you to resoundingly decline this strategy, send it back to the authors, and urge the management to come up with a much more ambitious strategy that is worthy of a proud company like Cresta Software!"

Matt and Cresta sat on their chairs, thunderstruck. Ella, Robin, and Andy were now wide awake, staring at Remy in disbelief. A murmur rippled through the hall. The next speaker entered the stage.

"Christine Ghibber of Seaview Asset Management," a woman in a striking, bright-red robe introduced herself, her enormous, golden earrings swaying with every slight movement. "Mr. Chairman, esteemed Dr. Cresta, and Mr. Carter, many thanks for your presentations. And many thanks, Ms. Selnass, for your intervention. Let me please come straight to the point. At Seaview Asset Management, we are deeply concerned about Cresta Software's commercial performance last year.

"Let's be clear. Cresta grew revenues by 20%. Profit margin at 37%. But your competitors? They did better. We calculate that Cresta should be operating well above 45%. Instead, you squander capital on climate engagement. Climate change is a global issue. It requires global agreements. Why should Cresta move alone while its rivals do nothing? Your strategy puts this company at a competitive disadvantage.

"Instead of wasting precious capital on an inefficient climate engagement, it would be much more beneficial, also for the climate, if

Cresta instead raised its voice in support of stringent global climate regulations. Once again, and here we fully agree with Ms. Selnass, climate change is a global problem that can only be addressed if everybody contributes under the leadership of governments. Ladies and gentlemen," she turned around, every eye now fixed on her, "on behalf of the Board of Directors of Seaview Asset Management, I am following the proposal of Ms. Selnass. I herewith propose a share-holders' resolution to withdraw any further budget for the wasteful and inefficient Cresta Climate Strategy with immediate effect."

A stocky man in a black suit stepped forward.

"Stuart Roberts, Canland National Pension Fund," he said.

His presence commanded attention, and the room quieted in antici-pation as he adjusted his stance, ready to deliver his message. "Canland National has been entrusted by hundreds of companies as the custodian of their employees' hard-earned pensions, safeguarding their future wealth and well-being. As Ms. Ghibber has eloquently pointed out, in the current harsh macroeconomic environment, we consider it reckless of the Cresta management to embark on a unilat-eral so-called climate strategy, an effort that will cost our pensioners millions. We second Ms. Ghibber's proposal to cancel any further budget for the proposed Cresta Climate Strategy. Instead, Cresta should cooperate with industry peers and the government to advance globally valid and economy-wide climate efforts. This will be more beneficial for both the climate and Cresta. Thank you!"

Robin nudged Ella. "You're a shareholder, too! Take the mic."

She entered her name in the queue, and ten minutes later, she stood where she had four days before.

"Ladies and Gentlemen. I am aware that some of you believe Cresta is going too far in their climate commitment. And others believe that Cresta is doing too little. When it comes to climate action, views are very widely spread. But what does this fierce debate tell us? In my view, the fact that nobody is happy is a clear sign that Cresta has found a workable path in the middle. My name is Ella Andersson. I am 25 years old. In the name of all people who believe we must start acting now, as imperfect as the solution is, I beg you to support the Cresta Climate Strategy."

All efforts were in vain. The shareholders' resolution to cancel the budget for the Cresta Climate Strategy was approved with a majority of 51.6% of the votes present.

Ella stared blankly at the results on the screen. No cheers, no protests —just silence, thick and metallic.

Ella threw her Cresta General Assembly access badge into a trash bin on their way out.

"What a shitshow," she murmured.

"It's a paradox..."

"Robin! For fuck's sake! Shut up with your stupid paradoxes. I am not in the mood for that shit now!"

"No, Ella, just hear me out—this might be the craziest paradox we've seen yet. The Climate Warriors are rejecting Cresta's climate strategy because it doesn't go far enough. But, paradoxically, the investors are rejecting it too—because they think it goes too far.

That's the Ideologies Paradox. Opposing ideologies, both ends of the spectrum, united in blocking pragmatic steps to address climate change."

But Ella was already halfway to the bike racks.

The Perfection Paradox

Ella flipped on the television in her little studio. Robin played nervously with his bicycle key. Andy pulled out a cigarette. "Stop that!" shouted Ella. "Not in this room, please!"

The Friday Night Hot Seat was one of Canland's most-watched talk shows, a high-stakes arena where reputations could be made or broken in real time. The set was sparse and dramatic—three chairs, two in darkness, the one in the middle illuminated. On that chair sat a woman who moderated the Friday Night Hot Seat for the first time. Beatrix Lemore.

BEATRIX LEMORE

It is nine fifteen. Good evening, Canland! And welcome to the *Friday Night Hot Seat on CNBN,* your prime broadcasting network.

My name is Beatrix Lemore, principal editor at the *Niburg Daily Tribune,* and tonight, I have the great honor of moderating the *Hot Seat* for you with two very special guests, whom I will introduce to you in a minute.

Our topic tonight has already kept Niburg—I'd say all of Canland— in turmoil for the past week. Yes, I am talking about the greenwashing scandal that has overshadowed last week's Canland Award Night.

How could the founder of a renowned software company, Cresta, win this prestigious award for a toothless climate strategy paired with the inefficient and unproven instrument of carbon credits?

You will remember that Dr. Cresta won the controversial Canland award along with a previously unknown young lady, Ms. Ella Andersson. She is the founder of Five Elements, an opaque company that promises to develop carbon credits in the poor country of Demba.

Who is Ella Andersson, we ask in this show. The title of tonight's Hot Seat is: "After the Award Scandal: What's going on in Demba?"

And with this, let me introduce my guests sitting on the hot seats tonight. To my left, we have Ms. Rebecca Silver, director of FHA, the Fair Hope Alliance, a grassroots organization in Demba that supports local villages. Ms. Silver is an expert on Demba. She lived with the locals in Yolo village for over two months and knows firsthand what is really going on down there. Good evening, Ms. Silver!

REBECCA SILVER

Thanks for having me, Ms. Lemore. Glad to be here.

BEATRIX LEMORE

Now, to my right, we have Mr. Simon Andersson. Simon is not only Ella Andersson's brother but also a co-founder of Five Elements. Simon knows the company inside out, and I am sure he will have interesting details to share tonight, correct, Mr. Andersson? Welcome to the show! My first question goes to you, Ms. Silver. You are in regular touch with the people of Yolo. What did you hear? How did they feel when they learned that in Canland, the company Five Elements won an award? A company that pretended to help them by protecting their trees?

REBECCA SILVER

Devastated, Ms. Lemore. Devastated. I am just off the phone with Chief Emmanuel. He is the head of the Elders' Council of Yolo. To understand their suffering, you must understand their background. For centuries, the Nolé people of Yolo and Mutela have practised subsistence farming in their forests. The practice involves gently cutting and burning some trees to make space for plantations. Fifty years ago, the forest company Walmera cleared forests for palm oil and rubber plantations. And now, the same Walmera shows up again and tells them that the entire forest is now a conservation area. Just to create these carbon credits! Rangers and policemen with guns are now coming after the villagers when they want to burn a few trees, Ms. Lemore. It is awful!

BEATRIX LEMORE

Oh my god. Yes, this sounds horrible. And what do you hear about the projects that Five Elements is building up on the ground?

REBECCA SILVER

It's true. They have built a large secondary school in Yolo that includes sports facilities and a kitchen. But only in Yolo, not in Mutela! How unfair is that? How do we explain this to the mothers of Mutela? Are their kids less important? They have educated some 100 rangers. These people are now missing as workers in the fields! We hear worrying news from the Duiba area, too. They have expanded chimpanzee rescue stations. But chimps threaten the local gardens, and now their population is growing! Then, they plant trees in the Lester area. The water consumption will be enormous. The new trees will threaten the livelihoods of the villagers! And finally, they rolled out a solar power program. No more diesel engines! Can you imagine what that means for the many local diesel distributors? They go out of business. Unemployed! Entire families will be starving!

BEATRIX LEMORE

Unbelievable. What a scandal. Now turning to you, Mr. Andersson. You founded Five Elements together with your sister and two of her friends. But a few months ago, you quit the company in protest. Can you tell us why?

SIMON ANDERSSON

Yes, Ms. Lemore. About two years ago, my sister approached me for help on the investment case, and I was immediately very sceptical. The poor people of Demba need all our help. But not carbon credits! That's what I thought from the beginning. But then I reluctantly agreed to help her. She is my sister after all, isn't she? A few months later, she asked me to fly down to Demba to negotiate with the boss of Walmera. And check all the data on the ground for the investment case. At that moment, it all became clear to me. There are two fundamental problems with this carbon credits project.

REBECCA SILVER

Now we are all curious, Mr. Andersson. Let me guess. The first problem concerns Walmera!

SIMON ANDERSSON

Exactly, Ms. Silver! So here is the story. You must know that the basis of the carbon credits Five Elements wants to generate is forest concessions. Walmera owns vast amounts of such concessions. The government of Demba awards these concessions and allows Walmera to cut trees and plant palm instead. Five Elements and its local partner, Matipa, agreed to take over some of Walmera's concessions for their restoration and conservation projects. So here is what I found out. Walmera most likely obtained its concession illegally. I went online and found a blog post written by a political scientist a few years back. Yes, Walmera won a public tender to obtain the concessions. However, according to that paper, several private companies owned by certain senior officials of the previous government received overpriced contracts from Walmera in return for preferential treatment of their bid! I was wondering: How can my sister and her friends work with such a company? I urged them to stop and to find a different project, but they refused to listen!

REBECCA SILVER

I am not surprised, Mr. Andersson! This is precisely how Walmera behaves. And it gets even worse. I have evidence of collusion between Walmera and this strange cooperation partner, Matapi, or what was it called again, Matipa, something like that. Look here, look at this photo. It is from Yolo, at the inauguration ceremony of their carbon credit project, in front of the new school building. Here is a woman called Wanga Namira, who runs Matapi, and this here, this is a guy named Morgan. He works for Walmera. See how they are laughing together. They are best friends. I am sure there is a corruption case involved here as well!

BEATRIX LEMORE

But that person in the background, isn't that Chief Emmanuel himself? He appears to be quite happy.

REBECCA SILVER

All part of the scandal! They convinced Chief Emmanuel that he would benefit from the carbon credits. In the meantime, Emmanuel realized his error. Ah, it is all so depressing!

BEATRIX LEMORE

Absolutely, absolutely. But Ms. Silver, one more question about Walmera. I mean, quite frankly, we are all eating their products. You just had one of the cookies here on this table. They contain palm oil from Walmera.

REBECCA SILVER

Well... yes... I mean, again, it's another part of the scandal! With the cookies, we have no choice, do we? There is palm oil in all of them. With carbon credits, at least we do have a choice. We can actively decide to boycott them!

BEATRIX LEMORE

I am fully with you, Ms. Silver. Turning back to you, Mr. Andersson, you mentioned a second problem you encountered. Can you tell us more about it?

SIMON ANDERSSON

Yes, and this one is even worse. You know, Five Elements must strictly follow a calculation methodology to get carbon credits. The Five Elements team uses the Green Climate Standard. Over the past months, I have worked day and night to remodel all the calculations. I not only looked at Five Elements' Coltra East Emissions Reduction and Forest Conservation Project, but I investigated all other forest conservation projects certified under the Green Climate Standard. I then cross-checked my findings using new high-resolution satellite imagery. The result is shocking. Nearly all the projects receive too many carbon credits. I shared my results with several researchers, who all came to the same conclusion.

BEATRIX LEMORE

This is shocking. But isn't that a problem of the Standard? You cannot blame this on Five Elements, can you?

SIMON ANDERSSON

Well, no, you can't blame it on them. They did follow the Green Climate Standard methodology. But now that we know, they should immediately stop all projects and wait for a new methodology. I told them, but they didn't want to listen.

REBECCA SILVER

These carbon credits are a complete scam! Walmera, Matapi, or whatever they are called, the Green Climate Standard, Five Elements... They should just all shut down and go away. Just leave the Nolé people in peace!

BEATRIX LEMORE

Totally. At the same time, your organization, FHA, is present in Nolé villages, too, isn't it? Anyway, back to you, Mr. Andersson. Tell us more about Ella. Who is she? How did you experience her as a child?

SIMON ANDERSSON

Well, Ella has a good heart. But she has always been unbelievably ambitious. She had excellent marks at school, she had several boyfriends, and she won the school's tennis championship. She was the lead singer in a band. She moved out of our house shortly after our mother passed away. Her passion was always to drive and scale things. She never had the patience to take her time and work toward a perfect outcome. Now you see the results. Projects full of problems and scandals! And you know what? Before I managed to link her up with the right people in the government, she was about to sign a carbon credits deal with Rower, one of the most polluting companies in Canland. She believed that this would speed up the projects in Demba!

BEATRIX LEMORE

Seriously? Carbon credits for Rower? An oil company? That is greenwashing! Can you prove that?

The Carbon Paradox

SIMON ANDERSSON

Of course. Look at this photo. Ella and her two partners on the top floor of the Rower Tower. Here is the boardroom, next to the CEO's office!

Ella switched off the TV in her little studio. She had seen enough. A tear ran down her cheek. She shook her head. "What the fuck do you think you're doing, Simon?" she screamed out loud.

Robin sat slumped on the floor, his face buried in his hands.

Andy pulled out another cigarette. Nobody said a word. In the dark studio, his cigarette's faint, orange glow pierced the shadows. The soft crackling of the burning tobacco was the only sound breaking the room's stillness. The smoke curled upward, vanishing into the darkness as they sat there, lost in thought.

And yet another paradox, Robin thought late that night.

Everybody knows the world isn't perfect. Big companies cozy up with governments—that's no secret. And no one really expects you to build schools or launch conservation projects everywhere at once. Whether it's solar panels, forest planting, or protecting wildlife, there are always going to be hiccups. Imperfections.

Same with science. Models are just models—they get tweaked as new data rolls in. That's how progress works.

But somehow, when it comes to carbon credits, people expect perfection. No margin for error. If something goes wrong, it's not seen as part of the learning curve—it's seen as a scam. Like the whole thing was rigged from the start. Aiming high and striving for perfection may be well-intentioned—but paradoxically, it often leads to the opposite result.

I'd call this one the Perfection Paradox.

The Transparency Paradox

Robin paced the length of Andy's living room, a place once filled with ambition and possibility.

"Where the hell did Simon get those photos?"

Ella exhaled. "My fault. I synced my phone with our company server —figured it was a smart move in case we got stuck in the middle of the jungle with no internet. That's how Simon ended up with access to my private photos. I never imagined someone would abuse them. Especially not someone who knows us like Simon."

Robin stopped pacing. "What drives people like Rebecca and Simon to attack our projects so brutally? No one's claiming the projects are perfect. But does that mean they deserve to be dragged onto the *Friday Night Hot Seat* and eviscerated on national television?"

Ella looked up. "Rebecca? I think she fears competition. She sees herself as the voice of the Nolé people in Canland. Five Elements threatens her status—and her funding. She needs donations to continue with her work. But more than us, she fears Matipa. Wanga's legitimacy terrifies her. That's why she downplays Matipa. Pretends she doesn't even remember their name."

She hesitated before continuing. "But Simon is a different case. He means it. He hates injustice. He hates a world full of paradoxes and imperfections. Simon is intelligent. He is a sharp thinker. But there is a lot of bitterness inside of him. He is convinced that humanity must wake up and change our broken system. Only then will a better life be possible for all living organisms. In his view, any incremental effort that falls short of a perfect solution is a waste of time and a dangerous distraction—a temporary band-aid—and must therefore be opposed."

"I hear that," said Andy. "I think the same way sometimes."

"Sometimes?" Ella shot back, her tone edged with a skepticism that bordered on outright disdain.

"I'm an idealist, too," Andy said. "And I'm a perfectionist, but I know that a perfect world doesn't exist. Simon's a dreamer—he thinks we have to fix everything all at once, but he attacks the only projects that are actually making progress because they're incremental. Remy's talk of a 'giant leap' must have pushed him over the edge."

"Exactly," Ella sighed. "By demanding perfection, he achieves the opposite of what he wants. He makes himself an ally of the fossil fuel industry—whether he realizes it or not. A functioning carbon market would be really expensive for them. And the irony? The more he fails, the angrier he gets."

Just then, the front door swung open. Omar Lelong, sweaty and flushed from his evening run, leaned against the doorframe. "Sorry, guys," he panted. "Training for the Canland Marathon. Give me five minutes to shower, and then we can talk."

Omar emerged fresh, dressed in a sharp tracksuit, the image of a man always in control. He sat down, clapping his hands together.

"Alright," he said. "Here's the move: radical transparency."

No one spoke.

"I know," he added, reading the room. "Feels insane right now. But we've handled worse. If you play this right, this can actually flip."

"How?" Andy asked flatly.

Omar leaned forward. "You publish everything—data, maps, financials—you steal the media's favorite trick: the big reveal. If nothing's nebulous, there's nothing to uncover. And soon, people will ask why journalists are obsessed with a startup from Niburg while the world is on fire."

Andy frowned. "But Dad, we already do that."

Omar raised an eyebrow.

"Seriously," Andy said. "For six months, Maurice and I have been uploading everything—reports, spreadsheets, maps, satellite images, photos, and videos. It's all public on the Green Climate Standard registry."

"Exactly," Omar said. "And how many people are actually reading those documents, let alone understanding them?"

Andy hesitated.

"Right," Omar went on, "it's public, but it's buried. And even if someone finds it, they won't know what they're looking at. Science without translation might as well be secrecy."

"So, what are you suggesting?" Ella asked.

Omar shrugged. "What we need is something bold. Radical transparency. How about real-time information from your projects?"

Andy blinked. Then his posture changed.

"That could work," he said slowly. "All SunScore solar panels already log performance. Each village sends data to the cloud continuously. Cresta's software aggregates it. And for the forest projects—Lester Hills, Coltra East—we're already combining satellite and drone data with ground sensors to monitor progress."

He looked around the room. "Right now, we only publish data once a year because that's what the methodology requires, but the digital tools are so much better than when it was written. There's nothing stopping us from opening a real-time dashboard that anyone can access."

"Exactly," Omar said. "But—and this matters—you show the challenges, the mess. The delays. The trade-offs. The *paradoxes*, as Robin keeps calling them. Make it clear that you don't claim to be promising paradise on earth. You need to make it easy for people to evaluate you against viable alternatives and not imagined states of perfection."

Ella straightened in her chair.

"And if they still come for us?" she asked.

Omar smiled thinly. "Then at least they'll have to argue with facts—in public."

The next few weeks were a blur. Phones buzzed. Inboxes overflowed. Everyone wanted answers. Omar's advice: reply with one line—"Thanks for your question. We are committed to full transparency. You can soon access real-time data of our projects in Demba."

They were confident they could successfully counter Rebecca's allegations against the projects by providing real-time data. But Simon's allegations—shady dealings with Walmera and faulty methodologies—were thornier.

Wanga sighed. "I can't say Walmera is innocent. These things happen. Rarely do they make it to court."

Simon's second allegation—that the Green Climate Standard was built on flawed calculation methodologies—hit like a bomb. At first, officials scrambled to respond, issuing rebuttals and technical clarifications. But the counterattack crumbled under a landslide of follow-up accusations and expert critiques. Public trust in the Standard wavered—dangerously.

And the Five Element projects? They stood on that trust like towers on cracking ice.

"I just don't get it," Andy said, his voice tight with frustration. "I always thought the Green Climate Standard went through layers after layers of review and consultation—dozens of experts vetting every line before the methodologies go live. So how is it that the whole thing's collapsing now?"

But now wasn't the time for questions. The priority was to convince clients of the project's quality—by embracing full transparency, just as Omar had advised.

The team went straight to work. Matt pulled in Cresta developers. Sophy's team in Coltra East worked nights. Webcams went up. Data pipelines ran nonstop.

One morning, just as Robin and Andy were sipping their first coffees in the Cresta Tower office, a message from Maurice popped up in the group chat.

Guys, seen this? Our favorite friend is back... :)

Robin clicked on the article. Beatrix Lemore. The *Niburg Daily Tribune*.

The Carbon Credits Scandal: Novel Blockchain-Based Startup Provides Quality and Transparency

Lemore had featured the Cool Earth Chain. "We're not a traditional startup as you know them, with all their inefficiencies and flaws. We're fully digital, fully transparent. Fully on-chain," Lemore quoted HashRider, its founder. It went on. "Climate change is an existential threat. People are dying, you know! We're here to disrupt this entire broken carbon credit system. Full of flaws, full of fraud. No more gaming the system with the Cool Earth Chain. Every certificate is fully registered on our blockchain. Double-counting is impossible. Cheating is impossible. Full transparency. Full equality and inclusion. Full fairness."

Robin spilled his coffee. He scrolled further down. He read out aloud.

"With our blockchain, registries become obsolete. Immutable. Decentralized. Instant credibility."

"Full interoperability." "NFT-backed restoration." "Zero-knowledge proofs."

"Don't miss our initial Cool Earth Coin sale starting next week," HashRider beamed in the embedded video clip, his T-shirt featuring the words "Trust the Protocol" in bold letters.

Beatrix Lemore's quote followed just beneath in bold italics:

After all the greenwashing scandals, the Cool Earth Chain has set out to deliver the system we so desperately need—to fix climate change and to democratize climate action.

Robin shook his head, still scrolling. "Wow. They say the whole system's fixed. Do they even know how the Green Climate Standard works?"

Andy leaned over. "Yeah. They built a tokenized planet-saving protocol but haven't touched any of the stuff that really needs fixing."

Andy blinked. "Wait. Did he honestly say 'democratize climate action'?"

Robin scrolled back up to double-check. "Yup. And *Trust the Protocol*... What he means is a codebase he wrote last month."

Andy put on a serious face. "No, no, Robin—you've got it all wrong. What he really means is the Kyoto Protocol. He just... uploaded it to the blockchain!"

They stared at the screen for a long second. Then their eyes met.

It started as a smirk.

Then a quiet wheeze.

And finally, both of them broke—bursting into helpless laughter. Andy slid halfway off his chair, gasping for breath. Robin clutched his stomach, doubled over on the carpet.

"Cool Earth Chain!" Andy choked out. "A meme coin on a blockchain no one uses, for a problem they don't understand!"

Robin could barely speak. "It's... It's decentralized hope! With staking rewards!"

They laughed until their faces hurt, until they had to open a window to breathe. Somewhere beneath the absurdity, they both knew the punchline: someone, somewhere, was going to invest.

And someone else was going to write a white paper saying it was progress.

Three months after the infamous Canland Award Night, Five Elements issued a press release drafted by Omar:

"As a buyer of our carbon credits, you deserve maximum transparency. Visit our website to gain instant and real-time insight into the progress of all our projects. At Five Elements, full integrity is our North Star!"

Relief followed. Smaller papers ran the statement verbatim. The *Canland Business Review* invited Ella to write an op-ed, while the *Business Daily* wrote an elegant piece on the need to "demystify this most mysterious and befuddling of instruments." Only the *Niburg Daily Tribune* stayed silent. Perhaps Beatrix Lemore had moved on? Maybe she had lost interest, now that Five Elements had committed to radical transparency?

And their efforts finally seemed to be paying off. Before Christmas, new carbon credit buyers started to trickle in, searching for an opportunity to support the projects in Demba.

Then, snow blanketed Sova Valley. Robin's cabin was free.

The skiing was better than two years ago. The powder deeper. The silence sweeter. And the Sova Valley New Year's Party at Matt's hotel promised to be a glorious beginning of a new era.

But on New Year's Eve, as they kicked off their boots and reached for the showers, Ella noticed five missed calls from Demba.

She called back.

Wanga's voice trembled. "Ella, you need to come. Fast. Since you went live with the data, we're swamped. At first, it was researchers. Now journalists. From *the Tribune*. One is in Limata, another in Yolo, and they're blundering around, pestering people, asking all kinds of questions that don't make any sense. Now three others have shown up. What the hell is going on, Ella? What do these guys want?"

Ella began to answer, but Wanga pushed on. "I must be honest with you. I am growing sick and tired of these carbon credits! For decades, we simply received our donations from Rower. Every year, Rower covered our expenses here. We could not grow further, but we did our work, Rower paid, and we went about our lives..."

Another pause.

"And, Ella, we have a problem with Walmera. It's delicate. Come. Now."

They soon found out what it was all about. Beatrix Lemore's *Carbon Credits Revealed* series hit on the first Saturday of the year. A trilogy.

Carbon Credits Revealed, Part 1: The People of Limata. Left alone after the floods. Betrayed by the promise of carbon credits.

(...) In an exclusive investigation, editor Beatrix Lemore uncovers major disparities in how trees funded by carbon credits were distributed across the Lester Hills region.

Using the Five Elements Web Platform, Lemore tracked more than 100,000 trees that Five Elements and its local partner, Matipa, planted last year, then she sent local experts to the region for exhaustive field reporting.

Her findings: just 30.7% of the seedlings were planted in Limata, a region devastated by flooding. In contrast, 26.8% were planted near Duiba, and 42.5% around Zima and Letonga.

"The results are shocking," Lemore writes in her report. "Despite promises of support, Limata remains underserved. How come not even half of the seedlings are planted where they are most needed?"

Among the people she spoke to was Nulu, a mother of five, who pointed to the only surviving hut in the area. Her testimony is heartbreaking.

"Everything else got washed away," Nulu said. "They promised to come and plant trees, to hold back the floods. They promised to give us money from carbon credits. But most trees go to other regions, where the powerful people live. We are left behind. Once again!" (...)

Carbon Credits Revealed, Part 2: Is Solar Power the Cause of Malaria Outbreaks?

(...) A new report from the Faculty of Tropical Diseases at the University of Kewala documents a significant malaria outbreak in the villages surrounding Duiba and the greater Lester Hills region.

The study, obtained exclusively by editor Beatrix Lemore, shows that the outbreak unfolded over the past 12 months. This coincides with the rollout of the SunScore solar power program, which is part of the carbon credit scheme initiated by Canlandish for-profit company Five Elements and the Demban non-profit, Matipa.

Asked by your editor, the authors of the study did not deny a possible connection: "We mapped all existing solar power plants through the Five Elements Web Platform, and we believe such a connection is possible. The new solar panels have replaced a large number of diesel engines. We know that toxic exhaust fumes are an effective means of driving mosquitoes away!" (...)

Carbon Credits Revealed, Part 3: Are carbon credits putting Nolé culture in danger?

(...) Five Elements operates a carbon credits project in the forests of Coltra East. As part of the initiative, more than 100 forest rangers have been trained—including over 50 women—in efforts to curb illegal logging and monitor biodiversity across the region.

But in the Nolé culture, where religious tradition and gender roles remain deeply entwined, the presence of female rangers has sparked controversy.

Principal Editor Beatrix Lemore spoke with Father Nui of the Eternal Lights Mission Church in Yolo, who voiced strong opposition to the project's gender inclusion efforts.

The priest expressed his deepest dismay at what he considers a sincerely unethical project:

"We were able to access the live footage from the conservation area using the Five Elements Web Platform," the priest said. "We were shocked to witness no less than two romantic encounters between a male and a female forest ranger! This project deeply hurts our cultural and religious feelings!" (...)

The team gathered in Andy's living room. Despite his usual snazzy tracksuit, Omar looked worried that afternoon—disappointed, almost broken.

"Scandals, scandals, scandals," smirked Andy sarcastically. "Train only male rangers—scandal. Train female rangers—scandal. Don't train anyone –scandal. Solar power—scandal. No solar power –scandal. Plant trees—scandal. Don't plant trees?—Still a scandal. And our Five Elements web platform gave her all the data to fabricate her scandal stories."

Omar nodded slowly. "Our global media apparatus isn't equipped to tell complicated stories. Maybe it never was. Most reporters I know complain about that themselves. On top, now they're competing with social media—algorithms invite readers to assume the moral high ground, playing into a deep-seated human desire for what they perceive as justice, but is really just another shot of dopamine. Too many reporters are mimicking social media rather than competing with it. This may work in the short term, but in the long term, it makes traditional media even more replaceable."

"Ah, those types have always been around," said Andy. "Have you ever seen *Citizen Kane? Ace in the Hole? The Front Page?*"

"And with all their paradoxes, carbon credits are easy prey," Robin added. "It's a real hunting ground for sensational stories."

Ella watched. And listened. And then exploded.

"What a fucking shitshow! We gave them everything—every dataset, every update, even real-time access to our projects. We went above and beyond to be transparent. And that's exactly why they came for us. Our openness made us an easy target. That is now a fucking paradox, Robin! The more transparent we are, the more ammunition we hand Beatrix for her goddamn sensational stories!"

Robin gave a weary smile. "Let's call it the Transparency Paradox," he said softly.

"Really sorry, guys, think I misread the dynamics here," Omar tried to calm things down. "Looking back, it probably would've been smarter to do the exact opposite—just keep quiet. Say nothing, share no data, no information. Stay completely under the radar."

"That wouldn't have worked either," Ella said, burying her face in her hands. "Simon was hell-bent on destroying the projects and the company. He would've kept feeding the press with stories, no matter what we did."

The Quality Paradox

"Happy New Year!"

The words rang out just as Ella, Robin, and Andy stepped into their office at Cresta Tower. They froze. Dr. Cresta was waiting for them. His smile was tight—more porcelain than warmth. Something was off.

"I'm sure this doesn't come as a surprise," he began, skipping pleasantries. His voice was calm, but heavy with finality. "You saw the General Assembly. Our shareholders voted down the entire climate budget. You've read the headlines accusing Cresta of greenwashing. The Green Climate Standard is under fire—its credibility questioned, its data challenged. And as ridiculous as her breathless, scandal-chasing stories are, Beatrix Lemore's carbon trilogy has only added fuel to the fire."

He exhaled sharply, eyes narrowing.

"As a result, Cresta is terminating its contract with Five Elements. We can't fund the expansion of conservation zones. We can't subsidize more solar panels. The program ends here."

A beat of silence followed.

Then he softened—just slightly. "But I still believe in what you've built. I believe in the projects. I believe in the credits. That's why I'll continue funding at least some of the ongoing work out of my pocket."

He reached for a folder on the table. "There's more. You'll need to vacate this space, but I've arranged something. I spoke to Professor Turman. He's offered you an office at the University of Niburg's Startup Innovation Hub."

He looked at each of them, eyes lingering.

"Remember the sky, the animals, the mountains, the forest, and the endless ocean? They're still out there. They just need us to find them again. A famous president once essentially said, 'It is not the critic who counts, but the man in the arena—the one who fights, fails, gets up again, and dares to do great things. His place is not with those cold and timid souls who know neither victory nor defeat.' You will come back, and more people will take inspiration from you—I am convinced of that!"

***

Two days later, Ella and Andy boarded a night plane back to Demba. Robin saw them off in the departure hall.

As he kissed Ella goodbye, a sharp ache pierced Robin's chest. He couldn't help but think of those high school days, sitting with her in the back row, playing chess during dull lessons.

"One day we'll open a dive center on a remote island off the Demban coast," Ella had joked back when she started her economics classes and Robin chose engineering. "I'll run the shop, and you'll handle the boat and the gear!"

Now she was actually heading to Demba—not for a dive center, but in a bold attempt to rescue their shared dream: to make a difference for the forest, for the people, and for the climate.

But Robin kept his feelings to himself.

"Giving up isn't an option," he said, forcing conviction into his voice. "Not after everything we've endured. Not after how far we've come."

Matipa Lodge. Ella closed her eyes. She let the thick, humid air envelop her, absorbing the vibrant sounds of the jungle—the chirping of insects and the distant calls of exotic birds. Only now, sitting on the balcony of Lester Villa, did Ella realize how much she had missed Demba. Andy sat next to her, smoking, lost in thought. She realized how much the past few months had drained her energy levels. Traveling back to Demba with Andy was also therapy for her, she thought, an escape from Canland, a break from the steady stream of questions, comments, and well-meant advice.

Wanga had alerted them the day before that Morgan would arrive at Matipa Lodge just before lunch.

A large Jeep pulled up on the little square in front of the office building shortly after eleven. It was a private car without the Walmera company logo. Morgan emerged from the rear door.

Is it just me, or does he look much older compared to when I first met him nearly three years ago? Ella thought. To their surprise, another man emerged from the passenger seat. It was Hubert Spencer himself, the chief executive of Walmera.

It was a joyful reunion as they gathered around the small board table in the meeting room. Spencer had always admired Ella and made no effort to conceal it. "Remember that night at the Wildlife Reserve?" he said, laughing. "When we planned to save the whole world with carbon credits, and Andy ruined it by pointing out their limits?"

Then, just as quickly, the laughter faded. Spencer's face turned grave.

"Listen, we have a problem," he said. "You know that Walmera also owns the concessions North and East of our current project in Coltra East, beyond Mutela."

Andy nodded. "Of course. We were planning to expand there soon."

Spencer scratched his head. "Well, this is exactly the problem. To come straight to the point, our competitor, Kewala Palm International, has submitted an offer to our Board of Directors to purchase all those concessions from us. Honestly speaking, their offer is very attractive. Particularly in light of the low prices of palm oil, soybeans, and rubber these days. No idea how Kewala Palm wants to make money this way. I fear that they simply bet on achieving a higher scale. They own two refineries already, so the more palm oil they produce, the lower their costs. Moreover, our board has heard a lot of criticism about carbon credits. They are aware that the Green Climate Standard is under pressure. They are getting cold feet and prefer to get out of carbon credits."

Ella and Andy sat frozen in their chairs as Spencer continued: "For our Board, selling the concessions would solve an additional problem. Remember, the largest buyer of our products is Canland Foods. They are under increasing pressure from the public to stop deforestation in their supply chain. Last year, they told us very directly that if we started deforestation in Lomba, they would blacklist us and no longer buy our palm oil. You see where I am getting to. If we just sold these concessions to a competitor, we would get rid of all these problems!"

"But this is outrageous!" shouted Andy. "You sell the concessions, Kewala Palm takes over and cuts the trees?" Spencer shrugged apologetically. "Kewala Palm sells its products elsewhere, not to Canland. They don't face the same pressure from their clients as we do."

"So in the future, Canland Foods can publicly claim that there is no deforestation in their supply chain, but in reality, this is just because Walmera sold its remaining forest concessions to a competitor, who just goes ahead and cuts the trees? This is absurd!" Andy insisted.

Now, Ella went all-in. "Mr. Spencer, you simply cannot do that! Remember your own words when we met for the first time at the Wildlife Reserve? You said: 'Walmera has a firm commitment to the environment. Achieving net-zero carbon emissions is our target!' Why don't you stick to your words? Why don't you stick to your promise?"

Spencer exhaled. "I'm the CEO, but I'm still an employee. It's the shareholders and the Board who decide."

A long silence. Then Spencer leaned forward.

"There might be another way. What if Cresta buys the concessions? In return, they'd own all the carbon credits—forever. The price of credits will rise. This could be a smart play for them."

Ella and Andy exchanged glances.

"Mr. Spencer," Ella said. "I don't think Cresta will go for it. They just pulled out of our contracts."

At the back of Matipa Lodge, the chimpanzee rescue station had grown.

"There, in the back, next to the jackfruit tree," Wanga said, pointing. "See the one with the funny white spot on the front head, that's Bobby, the chimp we rescued when you were here for the first time."

The chimps groomed each other, rolling in the dust, their movements easy, instinctive.

"I wish our climate community behaved a bit more like these chimps," said Andy thoughtfully. "In case all goes wrong, at least we can say that carbon credits funded this large chimpanzee rescuing station."

Ella looked up. "Andy, honestly, I don't know what to do now. Cresta is out. The Green Climate Standard is still floundering. And now Walmera wants to get rid of their concessions. Perhaps Simon was right after all. We should never have worked with this company. Perhaps we should have never come to Demba."

Wanga threw a few figs into the cage. Several young chimps raced to fetch them, stumbling and rolling on top of each other. "Demba is not an easy place to work. Remember I told you that the very first time we met? But giving up now is not an option. We have come so far. Let's walk together until we succeed!"

"And Canland is not a particularly easy place to work, either," scoffed Andy. "At least not if you try to run a business with a purpose."

Wanga continued unperturbed. "We need to find new buyers. And fast. Listen, here is an idea. Before Matipa engaged in carbon credits, we used different external standards to earn quality labels for our projects. There is the Rainbow Standard. It provides an in-depth assessment and verification of all the community benefits you claim to achieve. It is costly, takes at least six months to complete, and you must repeat it yearly. But donors often rely on it. Then, there is the Fair Biosphere Standard. It certifies any forest restoration and forest conservation project regarding its contribution to biodiversity. You pay a fee per hectare of certified forest."

Andy blinked. You could almost see his analytical brain rotating. "Yeah, I have heard of them. Actually, two new outfits just launched —Carbon Plus and Delta Impact. They both focus on assessing the quality of carbon credits. Popped up in response to all the recent backlash."

Ella raised an eyebrow. "Do they visit project sites? Reverify stuff?"

"No, that's the thing—they don't. What they do is rerun the numbers. Recheck the calculations. Then they dig into the assumptions behind the Green Climate Standard."

"Seriously? But it took years to perform all the measurements and verifications—expert panels, public feedback, all that."

Andy shrugged. "What can I say? Trust in the Green Climate Standard has gone. Maybe, if we show that additional quality checkers have vetted us, we can pull some clients back. It's kind of like poker—we're down to our last hand. Might as well go all in."

Ella frowned. "I don't know. Maybe. I guess we have no choice. Well, let's try it. Let's apply for all four of them. If this is what it takes to convince new clients and to prevent Walmera from selling their concession, then why not?"

It's another paradox, thought Robin late that night, after Ella and Andy had informed him about the events unfolding in Demba—*the Quality Paradox*.

Everyone wants integrity, right? Quality, credibility—who's going to argue with that? If carbon markets are going to work, they have to be solid. So in come the audits, the verifiers, the third-party reviews. Certify this, verify that.

But here's the thing—rigor has its price.

Each new layer of scrutiny adds cost—consultants, monitors, analysts, reports. And it all slows things down. What should be urgent climate action turns into a paperwork obstacle course. And ironically, the standards meant to keep critics quiet? They just invite more criticism. Too little oversight? It's greenwashing. Too much? It's wasteful. Damned if you do, damned if you don't.

As he drifted off to sleep, he found himself on a rust-red desert that stretched endlessly in every direction. Above, a dust-choked firmament pressed down, its dim sun a cold, distant ember. Instinctively, he felt that he was on another planet: Mars. Suddenly, a fissure split the crust in front of him, and from it rose a colossal obsidian hydra. Its necks unfurled like question marks against the thin, greyish-violet sky. Between glossy green-black scales burned rows of ember-orange eyes, and every mouth whispered a riddle at once:

"Can a footprint ever be zero?" "Does a baseline exist without an observer?" "If a tree falls in a forest and no one is around to hear it, does it make a sound?"

Robin drew the long silver blade from his belt. With a roar, he severed the nearest head—but two new throats sprang forth, thrashing more fiercely than the first. He hacked again and again; with each strike, the hydra multiplied until the air rang with a cacophony of contradictions.

Spent, Robin let the sword fall. In that moment, from the sky glided a long-tailed bird, shedding prismatic sparks like a comet. Clutched in its beak glowed a cobalt shape: a triangle that twisted back upon itself without any surface being curved. The bird released it, and

Robin caught the impossible object, a Penrose triangle, its mirrored facets holding the infinite alien sky inside.

He stepped forward and offered the symbol to the hydra instead of striking. The heads recoiled, then leaned in, entranced. Necks coiled around the triangle, looping into a living knot. A single sonorous "Ohm..." rose; the hydra melted into the sand, and the fissure sealed as though healed in time-lapse.

Robin blinked: the red plain had become an earthly meadow, warm with dawn light; he was on Earth, the mother planet. Everything was suddenly, implausibly, at peace.

He woke before sunrise, heart steady yet mind spinning. What was the dream trying to tell him, if there was even any meaning to it?

The Novelty Paradox

Ella and Andy decided to stay in Demba a little longer. Ella hired a local photographer and a film crew to visit the project sites. Trying to counter Beatrix's scandal stories was pointless. But it was worth capturing some footage, just in case a journalist ever wanted to hear the other side.

Meanwhile, Andy was preparing documentation for verification under four additional quality standards. Fortunately, their Five Elements web platform generated real-time performance data, which meant much of the required information was already at their fingertips. Still, the process proved frustrating—each standard asked for similar data, but in slightly different formats and through different submission portals.

Luckily, Cresta had prepaid a significant amount for their carbon credits, so the decision to terminate the contract had no immediate impact on the existing projects. However, they urgently needed new funding commitments to support the project extensions. Without this backing, the remaining forest concessions in Coltra East would likely be sold to Kewala Palm, marking the end of an ancient forest that has stood for thousands of years.

The projects had been registered at the Green Climate Standard in

August of the previous year. Now, six months later, it was time to verify the production of carbon credits for the first time.

The seedlings at Lester Hills were still too small. They had yet to accumulate enough CO_2 to make a verification worthwhile. However, the other projects had avoided substantial emissions during the six months. They were ready for their first verification and issuance of carbon credits.

According to their Cresta monitoring platform data, the SunScore solar project had avoided 5,742 tons of CO_2 emissions, while Coltra East forest conservation had generated 43,109 tons of verified emissions reductions.

One morning in early May, while Ella and Andy were in Yolo, trudging through another site visit with a verifier from the Rainbow Standard—some well-meaning functionary eager to count the number of students attending the new secondary school—Robin called, his voice hovering somewhere between hope and anxiety.

"Ella, I think you need to come back to Niburg. Next month, the annual Canland Climate Summit starts. We're invited to present Five Elements and our projects on the main panel. Think Cresta somehow arranged that. He's still a sponsor. Who knows, this may be our chance. Lots of potential clients will be there!"

Ella frowned. "That sounds great, but where will the conference take place?"

"In the Niburg Convention Center again," Robin replied hesitantly.

"No way!" shouted Ella. "That goddamn place has brought us bad luck three times already. I'll come back to support you, but you are going to speak, Robin!"

A few weeks later, Ella flew back to Canland. She pressed her forehead to the window. Below, the forested mountains looked like piles of rotting broccoli. *Jesus, they look sickly*, she thought to herself. *How long must this drought have been ongoing?*

241

It was a bright summer morning when she met Robin outside the small guardhouse by the entrance of the convention center. He looked good in his new suit—sharply cut, just the right shade of professional confidence—but she could tell he felt absurd in it, like a man in borrowed clothes. Robin belonged in jeans, a fleece jacket, maybe a windbreaker if he was feeling formal.

At 8:30, she hugged him and watched as he disappeared through the speakers' entrance.

A new message lit up her phone screen. Matt.

Her stomach tightened.

> Sorry, Ella. Please tell Robin. Cresta has to pull out of the panel. Too risky, they say. After all the backlash against our climate strategy. Need to keep a low profile. Really sorry.

Robin now faced the panel alone.

Good luck, Robin.

Minister Paul Becker opened the conference with a speech. Measured. Scientifically correct.

Then Lena Goldman entered the stage.

"Dear Minister, Excellencies, dear friends, good morning, and welcome to our first panel here at the Canland Climate Summit. As Minister Becker pointed out, climate change is no longer a future threat. It has arrived, here and now, and it affects the lives of our citizens, farmers, fishermen, and all of us.

"We urgently need climate solutions that scale fast. I am pleased to introduce our session titled 'Nature or Technology: Which one to solve climate change?' Today, we have two Canlandish industry heavyweights with us.

"Please welcome Mr. Ross Murphy, CEO of the energy company Rower. And..."

The moderator put a hand on her ear.

"And... ehm... very unfortunately, I am just being informed that... ehm... Dr. Cresta is not able to be with us today due to an unforeseen, very urgent business trip.

"But we do have two startup founders with us. Please welcome Ms. Amy Dupont, founder of Deep Capture, a breakthrough technology that stores CO_2 deep beneath the ocean.

"We also have Mr. Robin Trebon, founder of Five Elements. They focus on forest restoration and conservation in Demba.

"So Robin, to start with you. Less than a year ago, your girlfriend, ehm... excuse me, your high school friend and co-founder, Ms. Ella Andersson, won the Canland Award as Leader for a Better Planet."

Ella, sitting in the third row, blushed and looked down.

"But ever since, a stream of negative news has rocked carbon credits from forest conservation. Robin, do you still believe you are on the right track?"

Robin defended himself bravely. He closed his short introductory statement with a call to action:

"Our projects in Demba are installing one million solar roofs. Planting a million trees. And they are protecting hundreds of millions of trees. When you buy carbon credits from our projects, you are not only helping to preserve and restore the forest in Demba. You are not only bringing benefits to the local villages. You are also buying into one of the most cost-efficient climate solutions.

"I am happy to announce that within a few weeks, we will get our first verified carbon credits. Fully certified against the Green Climate Standard, with additional quality labels from the Rainbow Standard and the Fair Biosphere Standard.

"On top of that, we got a positive rating from both Carbon Plus and Delta Impact!"

He earned a round of polite applause.

Then Amy Dupont leaned forward.

"I am a big nature lover!" she began, flashing an easy, charismatic smile. "You know, I spend most of my weekends hiking and biking in the forests and mountains. Don't you agree that nature is a source of happiness, unlike this dark and gloomy conference hall?"

People in the room chuckled and applauded.

"Haha, yes, yes, thanks. So, while nature is great and should be protected, unfortunately, it is very unreliable as a climate solution."

Her face suddenly became grave.

She's a great actor, thought Ella.

She turned to Robin. "I deeply respect what you're doing, Robin. I really do. But we have to be honest—nature is fragile. Forests burn. Land is logged. Projects like yours are vulnerable."

She let the words settle before delivering the pivot, the smooth turn into the heart of her pitch.

"This is where Deep Capture comes in. We have a patented technology that permanently stores CO_2 in rock layers, over 400 meters beneath the seabed. The potential is massive.

"The ocean is vast—so much bigger than land, right? That means no conflicts over resources, no competition between trees and crops.

"And most importantly, unlike the challenges you're facing with the Green Climate Standard, we have no trouble with calculation methodologies.

"At Deep Capture, we count every ton of CO_2 we store." She smiled. "Simple. Easy."

This time, the applause was more than polite.

Goldman beamed. "Truly fascinating, Ms. Dupont." She turned to Ross Murphy. "Mr. Murphy, as the CEO of Canland's largest energy company, you have unparalleled expertise in reducing CO_2 emissions —or, well, producing them."

Scattered laughter. Murphy smirked, his gold watch flashing under the sleeve of his tailored suit.

"Indeed," he said smoothly. "Which is why I'm thrilled to announce a joint venture between Rower and Deep Capture. Over the next few years, we plan to install carbon capture units on all our new ultra-deepwater oil platforms off the Demba coast."

Ella's stomach dropped. Ultra-deepwater oil platforms.

"As Ms. Dupont said, the potential is enormous. We are confident that by 2050, we will be able to capture all the CO_2 linked to our oil extraction in Demba and store it right back underneath the seabed. We will lock it away, safely and permanently!"

He let the words hang in the air.

Why isn't Goldman intervening? Ella wondered. *Doesn't she realize what a sham this is? He talks about CO_2 from extraction—but what about emissions from combustion?*

"At Rower, we believe in thinking big. In my office, I have a plaque: 'Go big or go home.'"

The audience erupted. Applause. Cheers.

Goldman's smile radiated joy and hope.

"And how far advanced is your technology, Ms. Dupont?"

"We are making huge progress, Ms. Goldman," Amy replied. "Our pilot project is fully operational at the Department of Engineering, University of Niburg. Last year, we managed to capture almost a hundred kilograms of CO_2! Rower has kindly provided us with a fully equipped research lab on their premises. Over the next two years or so, we should manage to increase the absorption capacity by a factor of ten!"

Goldman, Murphy, and Dupont engaged in a vivid discussion on the scaling potential of Deep Capture technology.

"We aim to become a publicly traded company in a few years from now, so everybody in Canland can become part of our mission," Dupont promised.

Excited applause erupted through the hall once again.

Robin was sidelined on the panel.

Shortly before time was up, he insisted on getting the mic once more.

"Ladies and gentlemen, technologies like Deep Capture are exciting. But to effectively fight climate change, we now need all the tools in the toolbox, and all at the same time. Let's not make this a fight between nature and technology. Let's do both, let's do it all!"

———

Ella watched as people gravitated toward Murphy and Dupont, toward the gleaming Rower–Deep Capture booth, where an espresso machine whirred, churning out free lattes. Delegates walked away with glossy brochures and sleek giveaway keychains shaped like tiny oil drops.

Ella and Robin spent the afternoon at their own booth—decorated with photos of forests, solar panels, and clean water projects. A steady trickle of visitors wandered by.

Not to visit the Five Elements. But because the line for the women's bathroom started right there.

"It's insane, Robin," Ella said when she returned from the Rower booth with two paper cups of espresso. "You'd think people would be excited about our solar projects. Or the work we're doing to grow and protect forests. It's all proven. Scalable. Ready to go. And it helps the people in Demba. But no—they're obsessed with some shiny new tech that hasn't even made it out of the lab. They actually believe that's what's going to save the world."

"That's just how human brains work," Robin replied. "Tree planting, solar power—it's familiar. People have heard all the flaws, the controversies. But Deep Capture? It's so new, no one's picked it apart yet. The fantasy of a perfect fix is still intact."

He smirked. "Let's call it the Novelty Paradox."

As Ella and Robin were about to leave, a figure stepped into view.

"Ella? Robin?" said Janice Hanratty, holding up her media badge reflexively. "I saw your names on the speaker list—figured I should say hello."

"Janice!" said Ella. "What a surprise. Must have been three years since we met back at Port Kewala airport—"

"But I visited your projects in Demba last year with Wanga and Andy."

"Did you ever run a story?" asked Robin.

"No," said Hanratty. "I pitched three different backgrounds to three different editors, and they shot them all down."

Robin frowned. "Why?"

"No hook. Not punchy enough. But mostly, I suspect, because they wanted something more black or white," she said. "A hero. A villain. Either a piece that proves carbon credits are great and all the critics are totally wrong. Or one that proves the exact opposite. Balanced backgrounders have a hard time these days. They don't attract attention. They don't spark emotions."

She paused, searching for the right words.

"I kept digging—interviewed forestry and climate finance experts, started reading more. And honestly? Carbon credits are complex."

Ella raised an eyebrow. "We are aware of that. How many paradoxes did you find already, Robin? We all stopped counting."

Hanratty nodded. "Exactly. It's a rabbit hole. Every answer leads to three new questions."

"It's bizarre," said Robin. "When we launched three years ago, everyone wanted to hear the simple story. The dream of saving the world with carbon credits. Rescuing a baby chimp. Working with the communities. We tried to talk about uncertainties and complexities, but nobody bothered..."

"Yes, because you were the bright, shiny new thing then," said Hanratty. "That's why they call it *news*, not *olds*."

"Funny," said Robin, smiling at Ella. "That's yet another angle of the Novelty Paradox."

Hanratty tilted her head. "The what?"

"Ah, nothing, don't worry," Robin replied. "We realized that carbon credits might never save the planet, but they're an endless source of fascinating paradoxes. So we started to give them names."

For a few seconds, Hanratty's eyes drifted, as if locking onto something far beyond the room. Then she gave a slightly pained smile. "Interesting. Anyway, I'll give you a call after the Climate Summit. Let's grab coffee. I won't give up trying with that story."

When Ella returned from the bathroom, she found Robin sitting on a cardboard box filled with Five Elements flyers. The box was still almost untouched.

"Robin, hello, what's up? Are you day-dreaming?" said Ella, gently nudging his shoulder.

"Sorry, Ella. It's just... these paradoxes. They're getting to me. Twisting around in my head. Slowly eating at me."

Ella tried to smile, though her eyes searched his. "Come on. Let's go to Brigitte's Bungalow. My last drink there was in December—right before we left for Demba."

Robin gave a long sigh. "Yeah. Let's do that. I haven't been back either. It didn't feel right without the two of you."

They unlocked their bikes and began the quiet ride. The path traced the railway tracks, the hum of the city increasing with each turn of the wheels. As they crossed into the park, the night train heading north crawled out of the station behind them like a dark-blue serpent, windows glowing dimly like tired eyes.

Science Square lay ahead, ghostly in the faint streetlight. The university campus loomed in silence, heavy and still. They pedaled over the cobblestones, their tires crackling faintly, until the narrow alley that led down to the harbor came into view.

But something was wrong.

The alley was dark. Deserted. No thrum of punk rock. No laughter spilling from open doors. Ella slowed first. Robin followed, both of them dismounting quietly, as if instinctively sensing the shift in the air.

Plastic straps cordoned off the front of the bar. No lights inside— except for one.

A glass bowl sat near the door, shielding a flickering candle from the night breeze. Next to it, a photograph. Brigitte's face, smiling in stillness, danced in the candlelight. A piece of cardboard leaned beside it. The words, hand-scrawled but deliberate, struck like a drumbeat to the heart:

"You stood for the many, not the few. Rest in peace, comrade."

For a moment, neither of them spoke.

Then Ella stepped closer, and Robin reached for her without a word. They stood together, arms wrapped tight, as grief swelled and spilled into the still night. Tears ran down their cheeks freely, quietly—no longer held back by duty, or words, or time.

The Price Paradox

The heavy-duty tree harvester moves forward with relentless force, inch after inch, its crawlers cutting through the underwood like a knife through paper. The roar of the engine drowns out any sounds of life. Birds fly out of the branches, screaming in terror.

The forest floor behind the machine, soft and rich just a few seconds ago, is churned into mud. Broken branches, upturned earth, and destroyed small trees, reminiscent of ghostly skeletons, are all that the harvester leaves behind. Dust and debris fill the air.

The machine briefly pauses to switch directions. With a loud blast, it cuts a swathe through another untouched piece of forest.

The harvester comes to a halt in front of a massive kapok tree. The ancient tree, its vast canopy towering 50 meters above the ground, its thick, wonderfully folded roots a home for countless inhabitants, stands like a fortress in the forest.

The felling head of the machine is struggling to encircle its massive trunk. Its hydraulic arm presses a powerful chainsaw against the dense bark, buzzing and vibrating as it begins to cut into the wood.

The engine lets out a gruesome roar, reverberating through the forest, the chainsaw biting into the bark with a harsh, grinding sound. As the blade bites deeper, splinters fly, and the tree shudders under the force.

But the kapok, a giant of the forest, resists; its fibers are strong, and its wood is dense, built to withstand storms and natural forces over centuries.

The machine pushes harder, its metal jaws trying to grip and control the enormous weight above.

When it finally breaches the heartwood, the kapok lets out a long, groaning scream—an almost mournful sound—as it begins to lean, its majestic crown swaying ominously. The surrounding vegetation trembles. Animals and birds scatter in panic.

With a final push, the harvester forces the tree to surrender, and the towering giant collapses in a thunderous crash that echoes for miles.

The ground shakes. The engine of the heavy machine stops. Then everything goes quiet.

A terrible, ghostly silence engulfs the forest. An eerie stillness replaces the cheerful chorus of birds, insects, and rustling leaves. It's as though the forest is holding its breath, mourning the fallen giant.

With another roar, the tree harvester's engine fires up again.

"No! Stop!" shouts Robin now. He stumbles through the mud towards the giant machine. He reaches the massive crawlers, jumps up, and hammers against the machine's cockpit window, his fists pounding with desperation and fury.

"Stop the engine! Stop it!" he shouts.

He can now see inside the cockpit. Hubert Spencer and Ross Murphy turn around, catch sight of his face, and burst out laughing.

Murphy pulls a large handle. The crawler on which Robin stands begins to move. Robin starts to tremble and loses his balance. He crashes into the mud.

"No! Please stop!" he screams in horror. The hydraulic arm with the chainsaw comes closer. "Stooop!"

"Robin! Robin! What's up, Robin? Can you hear me?"

"Stop, no!"

"Robin, calm down. Listen to me. Robin!"

"Ella! Come! Help me! Quick, Ella!"

"Robin, calm down!" She took his hand.

"Ella. Where are we?" Robin opened his eyes. His T-shirt was soaked with sweat.

"You are on my floor, Robin. You're having a nightmare. Come on. I'll brew us some ginger tea."

Robin sighed and attempted to calm down. He rose from the camping mat and sat down at the kitchen table.

"We're failing," he said as Ella poured ginger tea into a cup in front of him. She briefly ran her hand through his tousled hair. He shuddered. "We will lose the trees of Coltra East."

Ella reached into her cupboard for a second ceramic mug. She found a colorful one with the name of a city printed on it, a remembrance of her last holidays abroad with her mom, more than ten years ago.

"I know. I fail to understand it. All it would take was around ten dollars per carbon credit. If we found somebody to front-load that money, we could buy Walmera's forestry concession. And we would still have enough money to build the health clinic at Mutela. Probably also a secondary school building."

Robin nodded and blew into his tea, which still was too hot to drink —the earthy smell of ginger spread through the kitchen.

"And you know what?" Ella continued, "When I was queuing for our espressos at the Deep Capture booth, I asked one of their staff how much they needed to promise the removal of a ton of CO_2 in the future. She said it was about one thousand dollars."

Robin almost spat out his tea.

"It's crazy, Robin. It's a hundred times more than what we need to save the trees of Coltra East! And so far they have captured less than a single ton of CO_2, that's what Amy admitted herself on stage."

Robin took a sip. His hands were still shaking.

"I know, Ella. Nobody cares if it's gigatons, megatons, tons, or even only kilograms. Yesterday, sometime later, a sustainability manager from a transport company stopped by our booth. I told him if he buys a big batch, we might be able to sell them at nine fifty, maybe lower.

"You know what he said?" Robin snorted. "He said, 'Your credits are so cheap, they can't possibly be of high quality.'

"And then he says, '*I'm* more convinced by Deep Capture. No one can accuse me of greenwashing if I pay one grand per credit.'

"I then asked back, 'So can you really afford to offset all your emissions with such expensive carbon credits?'"

He shook his head, mimicking the reply.

"'Of course not,' the guy says, laughing. 'But nobody offsets anymore. It's greenwashing. But we'll commit to buy a few carbon credits from Deep Capture in the future. The key thing for us is to show commitment and leadership by supporting an emerging technology!"

Robin's voice turned bitter.

"Then he adds, 'We don't actually need the credits until 2050. That's when our net-zero target kicks in.'"

He looked straight at Ella, eyebrows raised. "They haven't even captured a full ton yet—and he doesn't care. In fact, he almost seems to love it. Paradoxically, the later the credits arrive and the more expensive they get, the better. That way, no one can accuse them of greenwashing. They're too slow and too costly to be suspicious."

Ella nodded. "From an economic perspective, it makes no sense. Carbon credits were created to cut emissions at the lowest possible cost. The cheaper they are, the more climate impact you get per dollar."

"Exactly," Robin said. "That's what Amina Keita said—'cutting the cost in half means doubling the impact per dollar spent.' But paradoxically, it's the opposite in people's minds. The more expensive the credit, the higher the quality."

Ella gave a wry smile. "Maybe we should call it the Price Paradox."

He leaned back, exhausted.

"The world is upside down."

"Robin, let's try to get some more sleep," Ella said gently, after a long pause. "We'll call Andy in the morning. Figure out what's next."

Robin stretched out on the camping mat on the floor. When he closed his eyes, he could see a giant kapok tree, its leaves moving slightly in the wind. It was as if the tree wanted to tell him something.

Like the old oak tree on Niburg Hill, back on that cold afternoon in January when the idea to create catchy names for their carbon credit projects first came up.

That's a long time ago, Robin thought. He stared at the ceiling.

Then—softly, from the dark:

"Robin," Ella whispered. "I'm cold. Can you come up here?"

Robin's heart skipped a beat. A shiver raced across his skin. He moved very slowly, carefully sat on the edge of her bed, pulled up the blanket, and gently lay down beside her.

Ella reached up and wrapped her arm around him. She felt the tension in his body begin to ease; his heartbeat slowed.

No one said a word. At that moment, all his worries about the future, the forests, and the people of Demba appeared to fade behind a beautiful wall of flowers full of humming and singing birds, which surrounded him in this precious moment.

"Ella, did you notice that Lena Goldman stupidly mentioned on the panel that I founded the company along with my girlfriend?" Robin said after a long while.

Ella softly pinched him in the back and murmured, "You know, even those who speak only nonsense can occasionally stumble upon the truth without even realizing it."

She closed her eyes.

The Size Paradox

Summer refused to leave Niburg.

September came, but the heat only grew more brutal, the sun glaring down like punishment. City fountains dried up. Trees dropped their leaves in defeat. Ella and Robin started dropping into the city's crammed swimming pools—kept open by mayoral decree as the heatwave stretched on, unrelenting.

Andy remained holed up in Demba, determined to finalize the first verification of their carbon credits—a fragile win in a collapsing market. After the media storm, climate finance had all but imploded.

"Hang in there," Professor Turman had told the Five Elements team on the third anniversary of their company's founding. "In market economies, everything comes and goes in cycles."

But cycles return to where they began—up and down, like a pendulum. This was different: an upward spiral, each turn hotter, drier, and more dangerous than the last, with no path back to the cool seasons they once knew.

"Remember three years ago?" Robin asked, stretched out on a sun-bleached towel. "When we rode out that heatwave in your library?"

Ella smiled and kissed him lightly. "We were clueless. Naive... but inspired."

Robin gave a dry laugh. "Now we're smart. Informed. And dull. The only thing that hasn't changed is the temperature—rising, year after year."

Climate change had arrived in Niburg—not as a warning, but as fact.

The university's meteorological institute once calculated the odds of a three-month drought in the region at just 0.01%. That figure now seemed like a cruel joke. This year's drought eclipsed even the devastation of three summers prior.

"Those forests in Canland never recovered," Ella murmured. "They're a tinderbox waiting for a spark."

The spark came soon enough—an overheated generator at a full moon party nearly 50 kilometers to the north.

The blaze spread like a living thing, ravenous and relentless. Five months without rain had turned the land to kindling; firefighters never stood a chance. Within days, flames reached the outskirts of Niburg. Entire neighborhoods in the Niburg Hills were evacuated under choking skies.

The fire raged for weeks, unstoppable—until the rains finally came, just before Christmas. The "Niburg Fires," as the media came to call them, were the deadliest and most devastating natural disaster the city had seen in living memory.

That winter brought another first: for as long as anyone could remember, the ski slopes on Sova glacier never opened. Too many crevasses. Too little snow.

It was a cool, brilliant afternoon in early spring—the kind of day that used to draw them up to Niburg Hill without thinking. The path was familiar, etched into their memories from years of walks, talks, and late-summer sunsets. But this was not the place they remembered.

Plastic tape flapped in the wind, cordoning off the trail's edge. "Danger! Leaving the path is strictly prohibited!" the signs warned in stark red letters. Ella, Andy, and Robin walked in silence, passing beneath the blackened stumps where towering oaks once stood. These ancient trees had survived centuries of storms and human intrusion—but they had not withstood the inferno that tore through the forest after five relentless months without rain. Now, only charred remnants remained, the air still tinged with the faint scent of ash.

"What story would they tell us today, if they were still alive?" Robin wondered aloud. "Would they even talk to us? Or shake their branches in disbelief about human stupidity to destroy itself? Or would they share an idea of how to solve the paradoxes that stand in the way of funding climate action? Or would they just smile, wondering why we humans attempt to control forces far beyond our power?"

When they reached the platform, the sun was sinking low on the horizon, casting a golden glow over the city, the ocean, and the blackened remains of what had once been Niburg's proud forest. The skyline shimmered in the warm light, its glass towers catching the sun's final rays, each reflection a flicker of fire. The entire scene was awash in amber, beautiful and haunting all at once.

Ella stepped closer to Robin, and he gently draped his arm around her shoulders. Rower Tower stood out like a rock in the surf, proud and immovable. "Life in the city goes on as if nothing had happened," she murmured.

Andy had returned from Demba. His work, for now, was complete. All projects had passed their first verification of carbon credits, and even the new trees on Lester Hills had absorbed their first tons of CO_2. Every now and then, a client would still buy a few carbon credits. But the excitement—the hope that this might be the next big lever to help save the climate—had long since faded. Or rather, it had gone up in smoke—along with the trees on Niburg Hill.

The city of Niburg had been keen to reopen the restaurant on the hill as soon as possible, demonstrating a sentiment of normality to its citizens after the catastrophe. In the playground nearby, three children embodied that hope. Here, among the charred hills, they chased each other in circles, their laughter ringing through the air. But nothing was normal anymore. "Ella, remember us standing here on this platform, when you first had the idea of the million roofs and the millions of trees?" Andy asked.

Ella smiled. "That was three years ago. Back then, we thought carbon credits were an obvious and simple instrument—pay for your remaining carbon emissions and fund the roofs and the trees. Help fight climate change. Not sometime in the future, but right now. Now we know better. Carbon credits are full of imperfections, controversies, and paradoxes."

Robin cleared his throat. "But why? Look at all the destruction up here. Carbon credits don't solve climate change alone. But they could fund real projects. Instead, all our efforts in Demba are now at risk. Why do carbon credits spark such an enormous controversy, while in reality the market is absolutely tiny?"

Andy got excited. "That's what I've been thinking about a lot these past weeks. I even did some research online."

He pulled out his phone.

"Like you said, the global market for carbon credits from projects like ours stands at about a billion dollars annually, right?"

Robin nodded.

"Compare that to the global market for soft drinks—it's nearly 1,000 times larger," Andy said. "And everybody knows sugary soft drinks are bad for your health. Yet, unlike carbon credits, soft drinks remain largely free from controversy and are sold to kids every second."

"I've been doing the same exercise," said Robin. "Here's an even crazier example—the fashion industry. It's nearly two trillion dollars. Fashion is 2,000 times larger than the carbon credits market. Everyone knows it's one of the most polluting industries on the planet. It produces masses of waste and consumes mountains of chemicals and water. But do we hear much public controversy? Not really."

Ella pointed at the Rower Tower, its large windows reflecting the sun's rays. "Well, let's talk about fossil fuels. That industry generates around eight trillion in global revenues—8,000 times bigger than our market. It damages the planet by emitting all that CO_2, and yet, when Remy and Luke protest against Rower at a gala dinner, what happens? The police usher them off the stage, and the world returns to normal. No drama. No controversy."

"Yeah," said Robin. "This tiny carbon credits market, designed as a force for good, triggers so much controversy, while massively larger markets that create obvious damage don't.".

He gazed at the horizon, where two giant container ships were leaving the harbor, and scratched his head.

"I think carbon markets are attacked not *despite* their small size, but *because* of it," he finally said. "It's a paradox: the Size Paradox."

"He's back!" said Andy.

"Think about it," said Robin. "Compared to its small market size, carbon credits attract an absurd amount of criticism. And paradoxically, the small market size itself is the main reason for this illogicality."

"I don't follow you," Andy said.

"Large, mature markets are regulated," Robin explained. "Governments have set clear standards to address their paradoxes long ago. These industries also have experienced lobbyists and public relations teams trained to manage public perception.

"Carbon credits cannot scale without strict regulation. But, paradoxically, there's little urgency to regulate them properly. As long as the market remains small, governments simply won't bother."

Andy grunted.

"All this is true. All these paradoxes exist. And many more. We've discussed them back and forth. But now, the question is: how do we move on? Or can we?"

They stood in silence for a moment, gazing over the city and the black stumps.

He's right, thought Robin. *What's next? Or are we humans simply too ignorant to save ourselves, even if we know the science and see the evidence?*

Is that the biggest paradox of all? The more we know about the danger of climate change, the more we bury our heads in the sand?

He glanced down towards the forest's edge. "This would be a good moment for the two deer to shoot out of the trees and inspire us with new ideas," he said with a wry smile.

No deer appeared. They were all gone. Yet something else moved—subtle at first, then unmistakable. A solitary figure emerged from the tree line far below them, winding his way up the steep final stretch of the hill. He wore a dark trench coat, his face partly hidden beneath the brim of a brown felt hat.

Robin tilted his head slightly. "You guys see that?"

Ella and Andy looked up from the railing.

"Yeah," said Ella slowly. "That guy... doesn't he look familiar?"

Andy squinted. "Wait—is that Paul Becker?"

Robin straightened up, brushing off the railing as Becker finally approached the platform. Ella stepped forward, offering a polite smile.

"Good afternoon, Dr. Becker. It's great to meet you here!"

Becker paused, breathing heavily from the climb. His glasses had fogged up, and he wiped them off with his shirt before returning Ella's smile.

"Ella Andersson," he said, a little startled. "Now that *is* a pleasant

261

surprise!" He glanced at the others. "And your friends, excuse me, what are your names again?"

"Robin Trebon and Andreas Lelong, Minister," Ella replied. "Andy just got back from Demba. We've completed our first verification of carbon credits."

"I see, I see," Becker said, dabbing a few drops of sweat from his brow. "And how's it going in Demba? How are your projects getting along?"

Andy shifted uncomfortably. "Well, Minister, what can I say? You delivered the keynote at the Canland Climate Summit last year, and you saw the panel that followed it. Robin tried his best on stage, but it's tough."

"I missed that, but I read Hanratty's piece in *The Standard*. I was quite impressed with the way your school withstood those floods. It perfectly illustrates what I've been saying all along—international climate finance doesn't just reduce carbon; it saves lives."

He paused, glancing at Robin, who gave a quiet nod. "Yeah," Robin said, "She actually visited our projects about two years ago. But last fall, another horrible flood happened, this time in Yolo. I guess that was the hook she needed to get the story published finally."

He turned to the Minister. "But when it comes to carbon credits, Minister... the tide's turning against us. People want simple solutions —like Deep Capture. A silver bullet to magically remove all carbon and store it deep underground. To put it mildly, the complexities of forest conservation have rendered us somewhat unfashionable. And now, after this fire, critics feel vindicated. *'Trees burn. Trees aren't stable.'* That's the line. The hotter the planet gets, the more fragile forests become—and the less reliable they seem as a climate solution. That's the new narrative, while the reality is we now have to manage forests like never before."

Becker's eyes darkened. "Which is exactly why we need to turn back now. Get out of this paradox."

Ella broke the silence. "There's hardly any political support left," she said quietly. "To be honest, we're lost. The whole idea feels like it's collapsing under its own contradictions."

Becker slowly shook his head, a sad smile crossing his face. "I know, Ms. Andersson. I've followed the news closely. You and your friends, you've tried everything. We've failed. We've failed as a society and as scientists, but above all, we've failed as politicians. Our system rewards those who pollute our planet and deplete the resources of future generations. It does not reward those who preserve nature."

His voice grew heavier. "Every year, I go to climate conferences. Every year, the same conversations: loss and damage, carbon markets, climate justice. We form alliances, launch task forces, issue declarations. But progress? Minimal. You remember when you visited my office? When we talked about Article 6 of the Paris Agreement?"

Ella nodded, a shiver running down her spine. The mention of that day brought Simon to her mind, unbidden. She hadn't thought about him in a while. What was he doing these days?

"After years of negotiations, we were able to approve basic rules," Becker went on. "But the system isn't working. It's too complex. Too controversial. We need something different. Something simpler. More workable. And we must find a way to bring in the private sector. Taxpayers alone can't cover the costs, especially now, with political priorities shifting heavily toward security and military."

He paused, glancing around the hilltop as though searching for inspiration. "That's why I walked up here today. To reflect. To think about what I might have overlooked. And now I meet you here. What a coincidence!"

Ella smiled at his sincerity, but Becker's face turned serious again.

"Listen," Becker said. "I don't want to take up your whole afternoon. But would you join me for tea at the restaurant? Just half an hour. I have some questions."

When they emerged, four hours later, it was pitch black but for the fossil-fueled skyline below.

"I'm still trying to wrap my head around all of this, Minister Becker," Andy said. "It's hard to believe we're actually having this conversation."

"We most certainly are, Mr. Lelong," Becker replied confidently. "This plan can work, and we're not alone. I know Amina Keita well. She's the Demban Environment Minister and one of the strongest advocates of international climate finance."

Becker's driver had been waiting patiently outside the restaurant. The electric limousine hummed softly as the doors slid open.

"I was just wondering how we'd get back to the city," Ella laughed, as she and Robin climbed in beside Andy.

Part Five

The Rebirth of the Dream

The Call

MINISTER AMINA KEITA

Paul, can you hear me?

MINISTER PAUL BECKER

Loud and clear, Amina. How are you?

KEITA

Paul? You are still on mute!

BECKER

Ugh... Now?

KEITA

Ah, here you are! Twenty years of this stuff, and we still make the same mistakes.

BECKER

All these new apps... same old... My goodness, Amina. Twenty years... reminds me of our negotiating days. Remember Copenhagen? Furious delegates shivering for hours in long waiting lines? Then that horrible, crowded meeting room, when we tried to establish a video call with the Demban president in the middle of the night?

KEITA

Jesus Christ. CoP 15. What a nightmare that was. And then your prime minister fell asleep on the panel, remember? I will never forget that scene.

BECKER

It was unbelievable. What did we do wrong, Amina? That conference had fifty thousand participants. Everybody was so keen and excited. We believed in a big breakthrough to extend the Kyoto Protocol. We expected a massive boost for international finance. And then it all collapsed.

KEITA

It was insane. We couldn't even start discussions, because the translators were stuck in the queues at the entrance...

BECKER

Yeah, the beginning of the Crowd Paradox...

KEITA

The what?

BECKER

The Crowd Paradox. A paradoxical situation. The more people get excited about climate action, the less progress we seem to achieve. One of the many paradoxes we need to overcome, Amina. But how are you? All good?

KEITA

Hanging in there. But we're falling behind, Paul. You saw the floods two months ago—this time it was Yolo. How's Canland coping after those forest fires?

BECKER

It's been rough. The official line is: "Canland, look ahead with resolve. Let's move forward—together!" But honestly, it's all PR.

KEITA

Sure, people need reassurance. But we can't keep pretending. Canland's targets still fall far short.

Demba is ready to pull its weight—our emissions are one ton per person. Yours are ten times that.

You've been pumping emissions for a century. When your forests burn, the insurers pay. When our rivers flood, our farmers lose everything. The imbalance is glaring.

BECKER

I fully agree, Amina. This imbalance is exactly what's slowing things down in the negotiations.

But things in Canland aren't simple, either. You saw the last elections. The True Canlanders Movement swept by outright denying climate change—calling it a hoax, a fabrication. And they've turned our carbon tax into a political punching bag—saying it punishes working people, steals their heating, their holidays.

KEITA

Of course, their leader happens to own your country's largest oil import business. But that's a story for another day.

BECKER

Unfortunately, yes. We're miles from meeting our Paris goals. Right now, we're just trying to keep the carbon tax alive—and that alone's a fight.

Speaking of fights—have you heard of Matipa? They're working with a Canlandish firm called Five Elements.

KEITA

Of course, I do. Wanga Namira is a force here in Demba. Their work in Coltra East—especially the new school in Yolo—was a lifeline. One of the few buildings that didn't get washed away.

They've won a lot of support in government, but they're under pressure. No one wants to buy their carbon credits. If we could finance those projects through the Paris Agreement Crediting Mechanism, it would change everything.

Remember, we discussed that many times, Paul. You kept insisting that Canland's priority is on emission reductions at home.

BECKER

That's still true—we *should* reduce emissions at home. But I've come to realize it's not enough.

A few weeks ago, I met with the kids who started Five Elements. That conversation shifted something in me. Frankly, even with all the confusion around carbon credits, we don't have the luxury of waiting for a perfect solution.

That's actually, that's why I arranged this meeting. Five Elements says the forest project in Coltra East is at risk. If they don't find a buyer soon, the landowner will sell—and the forest will be cleared.

That's the same area that flooded, isn't it?

KEITA

Exactly. That's the project I meant.

Matipa approached us about buying back the concession, but our hands are tied. International lenders would punish us for taking on more debt.

Now, if Canland could help through Article 6—through real cooperation—that would unlock fiscal space. We could cover 25% ourselves. Do you think that's a realistic path forward?

BECKER

It could be. I've tested the idea with the cabinet—they're on board, in principle. But the numbers are brutal. After years of defense spending, we can't foot the whole bill. Not politically. The True Canlanders would pounce. I see only one viable path forward: we must bring in the private sector. Companies, foundations, even individuals—everyone would need to contribute.

And that won't be easy. Carbon credits are facing a severe reputational crisis, especially after the latest wave of criticism from the media and civil society. But...

KEITA

Oh, come on, Paul, give me a break! Did you read those stories your Canlandish journalists wrote about our country and our projects?

BECKER

I did, and you're right—they stripped out the context.

Frankly speaking—and please keep this between us—a journalist admitted to me recently that he knows the quality issues, but the editorial line is clear: Reports about Demba must focus on conflicts, corruption, or crises. Other narratives are hardly possible to include.

KEITA

Tell them to come down to Demba, see the work, talk to the people actually managing the land.

BECKER

The Canland Standard ran a much better piece, a much fuller picture. But you're right. The expertise is where you are—

KEITA

—and the money's where you are. This isn't charity, Paul. We're providing an ecosystem service—managing our lands for the benefit of the global climate.

BECKER

Indigenous communities know how to do that better than anyone.

KEITA

And we're going to make sure the world knows it too!

Too often, we're treated like colorful backdrops—people to take selfies with—rather than land managers operating under difficult circumstances with minimal resources.

BECKER

I couldn't agree more, Amina.

Still, a large part of the answer lies with us—me, you, all of us in government: we signed the Paris Agreement over a decade ago. Article 6 rules have been in place for five years. But the process? Still a maze of shifting rules, conflicting standards, endless approvals.

KEITA

Because we've avoided the hard conversations—about trade-offs, tensions, and what really happens on the ground.

This is a communications failure as much as a policy or implementation failure.

BECKER

And here in Canland, we've failed to give the private sector real guidance.

We regulate labor. Safety. Data—but when it comes to sustainability, we suddenly go quiet.

So what counts as a real climate action? What's a scam? What crosses the line into greenwashing? Who decides? Without clarity, no wonder people lose trust.

KEITA

Then let's turn this around, Paul! The urgency is obvious. We've all heard the arguments—yes, carbon credits are messy, but what's the alternative? The Paris Agreement gives us a starting point. Now it's on us to make it work.

On the Demban side, I'm ready. I'll bring the ministries together and push for clear rules—something solid, built on Paris. If forest countries and indigenous people don't lead, who will?

BECKER

That would be a big step. And on the Canlandish side, I'll make an effort to bring the key actors on board. Not by pretending carbon finance is a silver bullet—but as one crucial tool we can't afford to ignore.

Better regulation won't solve all the paradoxes, but at least we can provide guidance on how to move forward in a complex situation.

If this works, I'm confident I can secure approval for Canland to step up—to be a first mover. We could purchase enough credits to let your government buy back the forest concession in Coltra East. Before it is too late.

KEITA

We're aligned on this, Paul. That said... there's still something I can't shake. Maybe we can convince other ministers and technical experts. But what about the public? The youth? The farmers? The ones losing faith?

They're watching this whole thing unfold and think, *climate action is just another scam to help the rich and punish the poor.*

How do we win them back—not with promises, but proof? Proof that this transition can actually be fair, inclusive, and full of opportunity?

BECKER

I know. It's not easy. As governments, we can certainly help resolve some of the paradoxes through smarter regulation. But we can also lead by example—act as first movers to spark momentum. But in democracies like ours, the public decides in the end.

Our role is to build the platform—the framework. To create the conditions. Not to dictate the outcome, but to cultivate the space for it. Think of it like a garden: we prepare the soil, provide the tools, and ensure access to water and sunlight. But people still choose what to plant, and how to make it grow.

Speaking of the garden... Amina, both our countries celebrate National Day on August 15, right?

KEITA

Yes, we do indeed, Paul—though for us, it's "Independence Day," and the timing is by design. Our resistance leaders launched the revolution while your colonial governors were celebrating National Day. Now we host our own celebrations all across the country, with music and dances.

BECKER

Here in Niburg, our National Day celebrations have always centered on Niburg Hill. It used to be a lush garden—filled with flowers, trees, and life. Now, it's all dust and ash.

But maybe that's our reason to come back. Not to mourn—but to rebuild.

This year, what if we joined our celebrations? Canland's National Day and Demba's Independence Day—two celebrations of freedom, side by side.

We'd invite our people—not to follow a script, but to make something tangible with their own hands. Clear the ash. Plant new life. Show what renewal looks like, right here, right now. Not just trees— but something deeper: a sign that this transition isn't about ideology or mandates. It's about *us*—our histories, our land, our future. If we can rally around that, maybe we're not so divided after all.

KEITA

I love the idea. Paul, perhaps that could also be the day when we announce our cooperation for climate action under Article 6?

BECKER

Let's get to work, Amina. Talk soon!

KEITA

May the sky, the animals, the mountains, the forest, and the ocean be with us!

The Letter

One rainy morning in October, Ella had just poured herself a coffee from Professor Turman's old machine when a registered letter arrived at the Five Elements office.

Government of Canland
The Ministry of Environment
Minister Dr. Paul Becker
68, Brown Valley Avenue
10001, Niburg

Ms. Ella Andersson
CEO, Five Elements Ltd.
Startup Innovation Hub
University of Niburg, East Building
3, Science Square
10025, Niburg

Subject: Invitation to Collaborate under Article 6 of the Paris Agreement

Dear Ms. Andersson,

On behalf of the Ministry of Environment, I would like to extend my sincere appreciation for the engaging and insightful discussion with you and your co-founders at Five Elements. The depth of your expertise and commitment to innovation left a strong impression.

I am pleased to inform you that, following extensive deliberations, the governments of Demba and Canland have officially signed a Memorandum of Understanding establishing a framework for cooperation under Article 6 of the Paris Agreement.

Within this framework, we are now inviting proposals from developers of high-impact climate projects in Demba, with a view toward official certification and potential co-funding. We understand that the initiatives led by Matipa, in collaboration with Five Elements, have been positively recommended to us as promising candidates.

Please be aware that any successful project will be required to demonstrate a meaningful financial contribution from the private or non-governmental sector, as the funding share from the governments of Canland and Demba will be capped at a maximum of 50%.

If this opportunity aligns with your interests, we warmly invite you to respond to our official request for proposals. You will find the details on our website.

We look forward to the possibility of working together in pursuit of meaningful climate action.

On a separate note, you may have heard through the media that Canland and Demba intend to host a joint National Day celebration under the banner of climate action. We would be delighted to see Five Elements participate as a contributor to this important event.

Sincerely,
Dr. Paul Becker
Minister of the Environment

"Guys! You need to see this—now!" Ella shouted across the open-plan office, waving the envelope above her head.

Several heads popped up from behind laptops.

Robin grabbed and skimmed the letter. Once. Twice. A third time.

"This is... unreal," he breathed. "Becker was serious. He actually did it. He must've reached out to Keita and floated the idea of buying back Walmera's forestry concession."

Andy frowned. "But is that even possible now? Wanga said Walmera and Kewala Palm have already signed a pre-agreement. KP's running due diligence as we speak."

Ella glanced at the letter again. "Still. The governments got a memorandum of understanding in just a few months. That means they believe this could work."

"What about the private sector side?" Robin asked, already pacing. "Should we call the team at Rower?"

Andy shook his head grimly. "Don't bother. They'll laugh us out of the room. I read this morning that they're tripling their Deep Ocean pilot. Bragging they'll soon absorb one thousand kilograms of carbon."

Ella stopped in her tracks, took a breath, and straightened. "Then I hate to say it—but our only shot is Cresta."

Robin winced. "Seriously?"

She held up the letter like a flag. "Remember that god-awful Cresta General Assembly two years ago? When the guy from the Canland National Pension Fund stood up and said that Cresta would only act if the government stepped up first? Well, this is that moment."

———

Ella disappeared into their narrow phone cubicle.

"Ella? What's up? Been a while! Did you catch some of that fresh powder from that freak blizzard after Easter? With the Sova glacier closed, we had to fly up North. But man, that was fun. First tracks all along, I waited the whole winter for this!"

"Good to hear your voice, Matt! Yeah, long time no see. No, I missed that. Shame. Hope we can do a few sessions next winter. Provided there will still be some snow. Listen, Matt. I have big news. The governments of Canland and Demba have agreed to cooperate on carbon credits. They might come in and fund some of the projects. But the condition is that the private sector is tagging along. What do you think? Could Cresta play here?"

"Whoa. That's a surprise. I thought they'd given up on credits ages ago. Hm... I guess I could bring it up with Thomas."

He lowered his voice. "Between us? Since we shut down the carbon-neutral program two years ago, we've saved millions. It's absurd, I know, but nobody complains and nobody cares."

"Matt, come on. Remember that General Assembly? People shot down your climate plan with that tired line about needing government leadership. Well, here it is. That excuse doesn't work anymore."

"Yeah. You're right. All that talk about greenwashing and optics and... Look, truth is, we're not doing anything at all now. And yeah, it sucks. But hey, the world sucks, right? What can we do? Better enjoy the powder as long as we can!"

"Matt, seriously. This is the chance to turn that around. What would it take for Cresta to come back in?"

"Honestly? We can't afford another front-page scandal. You remember what the *Daily Tribune* did to us. Thomas barely kept his job. The moment we pulled back? Silence. No activists, no journalists, nothing. It's like the outrage machine only kicks in when someone tries to *do* something."

"The Voluntary Paradox, and the Claims Paradox. I know, Matt. We've been there. But let me ask you this. What if we could get the Climate Warriors behind this effort? What if we could win their support? Would you then give it a shot?"

"That could change the game, I guess. We would have to find a new storyline. A new narrative. Something different, breaking the old silos and the old controversies."

"I'll call you back, Matt. Maybe—just maybe—these fires have changed something. Climate change is here. We simply don't have any more time to bicker around, stuck in the same old debates."

"Let me know, Ella. And good luck!"

———

"How'd it go?" Robin asked as Ella emerged from the cubicle.

She looked worried. "Guys, we need to talk to Remy."

"To Remy?" Robin's eyebrows shot up. "Why? If the Climate Warriors get wind of that letter, they'll instantly spin it into another greenwashing scandal."

Ella didn't flinch. "Let's be realistic. The government's commitment is a major opportunity—but they expect the private sector to step up. Cresta could be a player. But they've already been burned by the whole carbon credit mess. Spent a fortune and ended up with nothing but bad press. Why would they risk that again? If we want them back at the table, we need to get some sort of truce with the Warriors. They don't need to cheerlead carbon credits—but at the very least, they'd have to somehow accept them as one of the tools to fix climate change."

Andy played around with a ballpoint pen, lost in thought.

"Should I email her?" he proposed after a while.

———

They spent the rest of the day in a tense silence, downloading the project data from their Cresta monitoring cloud, clicking through their PowerPoint presentations, updating their documentation. When Robin had just finished a first draft of an answer letter to the Ministry of Environment, Andy's face lit up in excitement.

"Remy replied!" All heads turned towards him.

Hi Andy,

It's been a while, great to hear from you. Yes, you're right. We're losing the battle. To greed, to ignorance, to apathy. I've seen the footage from Yolo. It's devastating. We are sleepwalking to climate collapse.

And, here at home, if the burning of Niburg Hill can't jolt us into action, I genuinely wonder what will.

Regarding carbon credits: I understand the argument. In a political climate where few are willing to fund meaningful climate action, carbon credits may appear to be one of the few tools remaining.

I also concede that some of our messaging led to a feeding frenzy by some reporters. Believe me, that was not our intention.

Unfortunately, the fundamental problems of carbon credits are unsolved. Offsetting emissions is riddled with uncertainty and can still serve as a tool for greenwashing. Carbon credits can still provide an excuse to not reduce emissions here in Canland. If you really want to breathe new life into carbon credits, then you'd have to change the narrative fundamentally. Until that happens, I really don't see how we could change our stance.

Anyway, keep up the good work, and talk soon!

Best, Remy

The Professor

"So... now what?" Robin finally broke the long silence.

"Without Climate Warriors' support, we can't win Cresta. And without Cresta, we'll never land the government deal. No government deal means no chance to revoke the concession to cut the forest at Coltra East. No forest, no credits. And no Five Elements. This isn't a paradox. It's a puzzle. We're missing a piece."

"The Five Elements, yes..." Andy murmured, rolling a cigarette between his fingers now instead of his pen. "Changing the narrative..."

"What are you babbling about?" Ella asked.

"It's just... funny," he said. "Remy talking about a 'new narrative.' Most people think that just means better messaging—PR stuff."

He paused. "But I remember my dad saying once, it's more than that. Narrative is how we think. How we make sense of everything."

Ella raised an eyebrow. "So you think Remy's sending you some cryptic message?"

"Well, I think she has a point."

He leaned back, eyes distant for a second.

"Wanga and I had that conversation, too. It was back during those rough weeks last year—while you two were still battling it out at the climate summit. I was holed up in Demba, drowning in questions from four different rating agencies."

He exhaled slowly, resisting the urge to light up.

"One night, Wanga and I sat down and came to the same conclusion —carbon credits, the way they exist today, aren't working. If they're ever going to work—*really* work—we need more than tweaks. We need a new way of thinking. A new way to understand carbon credits."

He turned to Robin.

"Your paradoxes? They need to be named. Faced. Resolved, if they can be."

He looked up at them, more focused now.

"Wanga believed the Belé wisdom held a key. A deeper framework. A way of seeing carbon not just as a commodity—but as something rooted. Interconnected. Alive, even."

He hesitated.

"We actually started drafting something. Sketching out what we called a new approach—based on the Five Elements of the Belé."

"And then?" Robin asked.

"Then came the noise. The setbacks. I shelved it. Forgot about it."

Ella blinked. "Wait—*that's* what you were working on at Matipa Lodge?"

Andy nodded.

"Do you still have the notes?" she asked, voice rising a little. "Can I see them?"

Ella glanced around the cramped office, taking in the same cluttered bookshelves and sun-faded maps. She and Robin had sat in these very chairs four years ago, pitching a wild idea about carbon credits in Demba. Now they were back—older, and with heavier questions.

"What happened to your colorful Pigouvian tax graph?" she asked, nodding toward the bare patch of wall behind Turman's desk. "Ah —needed the wall space for more shelves," the Professor said. Then he paused.

"But honestly, it's more than that."

He leaned back, his voice more thoughtful now.

"For most of my career, I believed the Pigouvian tax was the answer to almost everything. The idea is simple: if pollution causes harm, then polluters should have to pay for that harm. That way, markets reflect the true cost of environmental damage.

"In theory, it works beautifully. You charge companies for their emissions, use the money to support those reducing their impact, and let the market correct itself. That was the dream—that the 'invisible hand' of economics could guide us back into balance. Not just on climate, but across social and environmental issues."

He glanced at the empty spot on the wall again.

"It's called 'internalizing externalities.' It means making sure the people who cause harm are the ones who pay for it. Not society, not the poor, not future generations.

"So yes, I loved that graph."

He smiled more warmly now.

"And I remember when you two first came in here with your Demba proposal. I probably didn't hide how excited I was. You were going to test the theory—take it out into the real world. I was proud then. I still am. You made real progress. Emissions were cut. Local people benefited. And the polluters paid for their emissions. Somewhere, I imagine Pigou is smiling."

Robin blushed and shifted in his chair. "I am sorry about the term paper, Professor," he said. "We did complete a draft version, but I'm afraid the content is completely outdated. After all we've learnt."

Turman's expression turned serious again. "I'd actually like you to finish it. Because the problems you ran into go beyond carbon credits. They go deeper.

"And that brings me back to why I took the graph down. Because after following your work, I've come to realize Pigou's ideas are right in principle. But the real world isn't a clean model. People bring politics, beliefs, fears, history. You can't solve that with equations."

He shook his head, half in frustration, half in recognition.

"What struck me most wasn't the activists—it was my own colleagues. Brilliant economists, quick to dismiss carbon credits as flawed. But no one asked the most critical question: What were carbon credits supposed to do? Were we aiming for perfection? Or were we building a tool—messy but useful—that could get us closer to real climate progress? If we throw them out, fine. But then what's our plan? How else do we turn theory into action?"

Robin nodded. "Climate projects—and their paradoxes—can only be understood if you've seen them with your own eyes and worked with them."

Turman nodded slowly. "And not only that. Some colleagues seriously claim that buying carbon credits would remove the incentive for companies to reduce their own emissions. But a quick cut with Ockham's razor—the simplest test of common sense—shows how nonsensical that is: anyone who doesn't want to do anything anyway is certainly not going to buy certificates. They simply do nothing and save the money. After all, these are voluntary payments."

"Exactly!" exclaimed Robin. "On the contrary, companies that voluntarily purchase carbon credits are setting their own carbon price. They are creating an incentive to avoid their own emissions—because every ton costs money. And the more expensive the projects become, the more it costs."

Turman smiled. "You really should have studied economics, Mr. Trebon. Some of my colleagues don't seem to understand the damage they are doing with their one-sided criticism—especially since there is no reasonable alternative anywhere near for financing such projects in Demba."

Ella added quietly, "Criticizing projects is also alarmingly easy. There is so much data on the internet that researchers can comfortably produce endless articles, studies, and meta-studies from their laptops without ever having set foot in Demba. Robin calls this the transparency paradox."

Turman nodded again. "I also fear that much of the debate is ideologically driven—not factual. Even professional journals are not immune to this. But be that as it may: The hard truth I've come to accept is this: just because something makes economic sense doesn't mean it resonates with people's minds—or their hearts. To make the system work, we'll need far more than sound economic theory. We'll need to understand—and work with—human nature itself."

Ella sat up straighter and looked Turman directly in the eye. "Professor," she began, "there's something we'd like to show you—and we'd appreciate your advice.

"You're right: the carbon credit system, at least as we've known it, has failed to scale. Instead of building momentum, it's become trapped in endless, often bitter controversy. We agree that—even if it's intellectually and technically sound—a purely economic approach just isn't enough.

"A few months ago, our partner, Wanga Namira in Demba, and Andy started rethinking things from a different angle. They turned to the Five Elements of the Belé culture—the sky, the animals, the mountains, the forest, and the ocean. Each of these elements represents a core virtue, a worldview, and shared principles that bring the Belé people together. At their heart, these values embody unity in diversity.

"Wanga and Andy reinterpreted those principles to create something new—a narrative foundation rooted in culture, not just markets. It's a new way of thinking, one that could breathe life into the idea of carbon credits and help them grow into something meaningful. In case you see merit in this idea, we wanted to ask you if you'd be willing to reach out to Remy Selnass. If this idea is to go anywhere, we'd need the buy-in of the Climate Warriors."

Andy reached into his bag and pulled out a slim, transparent folder. Inside were five neatly stacked sheets of paper. He handed it to Professor Turman, who removed his glasses and began to read.

After five minutes of silence, Truman put his glasses back on. He nodded slowly. Then smiled. "That would mean the rebirth of the dream... I suppose I'll have to clear some shelf space again—for that old Pigouvian tax graph to go back on the wall."

The Elements

The cafeteria on the fourth floor of the East Building overlooked Science Square. At the far end, scaffolding and plastic sheets clung to the remains of Brigitte's Bungalow—once home to the Earth Cinema. The days of chaos, passion, and purpose felt impossibly distant now.

Ella, Andy, and Robin sat by the glass, watching students drift across the square like shadows from another life.

Then Remy appeared. No signature boots, no sharp attitude—just jeans and a breezy green shirt. She spotted them, paused, and offered a hesitant wave.

"Sorry, I'm late," she said, approaching. "Luke's right behind me. What are you having?"

Ella stood, smiling. "I'll grab for both of us. Vegan chai, right? Some things never change."

Remy's smile softened. "Thanks."

Minutes later, they returned with steaming cups—chai for everyone but Luke, who nursed a cappuccino.

"The world's gone mad," Remy said. "Forest fires here last year, floods in Demba, and another heatwave already announced for summer," she continued. "And what does the government say? 'Nature is stronger than humans. We must stay strong and stand together, hand in hand. Thoughts and prayers.' Honestly? What a heap of bullshit. We've completely failed as a society."

"Looks like it, yeah," Ella replied, sipping her drink. "Did you hear about the climate festival the government wants to host on National Day? Do you think anything meaningful will come out of it?"

"I don't really trust governments. All they care about is the next election cycle," Remy said with a shrug. "Still, I was surprised they even announced something like that—especially with all the pressure from the True Canlanders. We're not sure yet if Climate Warriors will take part."

She glanced around the table. "But tell me—how are you all doing? With all the attacks on carbon credits lately... I really felt for you."

"We're more worried about the projects in Demba," Andy replied. "One of them is in Yolo—right where the flood just tore through. The price of carbon credits has completely collapsed. We just can't fund them anymore under current conditions."

Luke leaned back in his chair, frowning. "Listen, it's not personal. It never was. But carbon credits simply don't work. Too many flaws. Too much controversy. We need to think of something bigger— something more robust, something with real impact. There's been so much talk... and so little to show for it."

"Exactly," Robin said, dry as ever. "We call it the Size Paradox. Massive outrage over a small sector trying to do good—while mining, fast fashion, and fossil fuels keep tearing through the planet, and no one blinks."

Ella leaned forward, voice firm. "And that's exactly why we wanted to talk to you. Yes, carbon credits—in this current configuration— don't work well. The whole system is full of paradoxes. We know that."

Remy cut in. "I've heard the 'paradox' argument before. It sounds like a clever way to avoid taking responsibility for all the failures."

"Remy, you're right—mistakes happen. But not just with carbon projects. They happen in mining, farming, construction—everywhere. And worse, even if a project is perfect, many paradoxes still remain. Some are unsolvable."

Luke looked genuinely perplexed. "Okay, so what's your point? That nothing works?"

Ella exhaled slowly, then looked each of them in the eye. "No. What I'm saying is this: even with all its flaws, if we don't have a mechanism that rewards real climate impact, then how exactly are we going to fund projects in places like Demba? We've been looking for alternatives for decades, and we still haven't found one that can scale."

Robin sighed and cut in: "Maybe this is the paradox that holds all the others—the *Carbon Paradox*. That a tool with such power to do good is tangled in so many contradictions. And yet, despite all the flaws, it may still be our best hope."

He paused, then continued. "So here's the real question: can we agree on a new framework? A concept? Maybe even a shared vision —for how this climate finance tool could work despite the paradoxes?" His voice dropped. "Because if the answer is no, let's not kid ourselves. These projects won't get funded. Not fast enough. Not at the scale we need. Forests will keep vanishing. Tree restoration efforts will stall. Solar power will stay a luxury for the rich—while the poor get left behind."

A hush settled over the table. Outside, students drifted across Science Square, their laughter rising faintly through the glass. They moved in easy rhythms—toward bike racks, toward the tram stop, toward ordinary lives.

Robin watched them absently, a hollow weight pressing against his chest. *If we'd just stuck with our engineering classes,* he thought. *We'd be working for some mid-sized Canlandish firm by now. Chess on weekends. House parties. Why the hell did I click on that godforsaken video of the drowning girl that night?*

Remy broke the silence, her voice quieter than before, almost vulnerable.

"So listen, Professor Turman told me that you might have an idea about a new framework—or a vision—to rethink the concept of carbon credits. What do you have in mind?"

All eyes turned to Ella. She didn't speak. Instead, she looked at Andy.

He hadn't moved. It was hard to read him—his face drawn, his shoulders tight with exhaustion. But there was something in his eyes. A flicker. A spark.

As if he knew this was it—his moment.

After all the fights. After the endless meetings, the sleepless nights, the destructive controversies—this was perhaps their final chance to lay the cornerstone of something new.

A shared vision—clear, ambitious, honest. One that could face the paradoxes, not run from them. One that could unite the people still willing to try. Andy leaned forward.

He cleared his throat and shifted in his chair.

"My parents are from Demba, but I had the privilege of a safe childhood and an excellent education here in Canland," Andy began, his voice trembling slightly. "Nearly five years ago, a devastating flood wiped out a village near my mother's birthplace. That was the moment I knew I couldn't just talk about climate anymore. I had to do something. Something real. Something transformative.

"And I kept asking myself: if capitalism can fuel a trillion-crown global machine to extract oil—why can't that same system ignite a trillion-crown movement to remove carbon? To restore balance instead of destroying it? That question—that mission—lit the fire in us."

He paused, gathering breath.

"We started full of energy, full of belief. But it didn't take long to realize just how unbelievably complicated climate finance really is. Every step forward was met with a wall—legal paradoxes, political contradictions, cultural divides. What began as a clear goal started to drown in controversy and conflicting worldviews."

"Then, two years ago, we were told that instead of protecting the last forests in Coltra East, Walmera was considering selling its concession to Kewala Palm—for conversion into palm oil plantations. It felt like the floor had been ripped out from under us."

His voice softened.

"One evening during that difficult time, Wanga, the founder of our local partner Matipa, sat me down. She said, 'Andy, I think you're making a mistake. You're trying to turn carbon credits into a commodity—like palm oil, rubber, or timber. And sure, if you could pull that off, it might scale like those other markets. But that's not how carbon credits work.

"Palm oil becomes cookies. Rubber becomes tires. Timber becomes homes. They're raw materials. They have form. Function. Demand.

"But carbon credits? They only exist because we agree they matter. Their value is constructed. Created. Chosen. Maybe carbon credits are less like commodities... and more like music. Or art. Or literature. They only scale when enough people perceive meaning."

Andy paused. The silence was complete.

He glanced around the table. Everyone was watching him—fully present.

Ella gave him a slight, almost imperceptible nod.

"Wanga pointed to the emblem of the Belé culture hanging on the wall of the Matipa Lodge," Andy continued, his voice steady now. "It was carved into a round wooden disc—simple, yet powerful. 'Do you see the five elements of the Belé?' she asked me. 'The sky, the animals, the mountains, the forest, and the ocean. Together, they represent unity in diversity. A common vision, despite our differences. This philosophy has guided our people for thousands of years.'

She paused, then added, 'Maybe this—this—holds a clue for the future of carbon credits.'"

Andy glanced down at the table, a small smile crossing his face.

"So we pulled out a notepad and started scribbling ideas. It was one of those rare moments—light and intense at once. We didn't solve everything, but something took shape. Then life pulled us away. I only found them again a few days ago."

He reached into his bag and pulled out the same slim, transparent folder that he had produced in Turman's office. He removed the first sheet of paper and held it up.

"The Sky," he read aloud. "It stands for Purpose and Vision.

Carbon credits must always serve the purpose of increasing climate ambition—not reducing it. They should drive emissions down in the most effective, most meaningful ways. They must never be used to replace responsibility or delay action. They must always add to a climate target—never substitute for one."

Andy looked up. Everyone was quiet.

"I believe we can address some of the major paradoxes—if we can all agree to live up to this vision," he said carefully. "Take the Offset Paradox. Or the Voluntary Paradox. These aren't unsolvable... not if the framework is grounded in integrity and shared purpose."

He reached for the second sheet and held it up.

"*The Animals—they represent the complementarity and diversity of climate solutions,*" he read. "*Carbon credits are just one tool among many. Like a single species in the jungle, they play a role—but only in harmony with the others. You can't solve climate change with carbon credits alone. But without them, you lose a powerful opportunity to get closer to the goal. Likewise, we should welcome a wide range of approaches to reduce and remove carbon.*"

Remy exchanged a glance with Luke, her eyes narrowing slightly. He gave a subtle nod.

Ella leaned in. "We all see the world differently," she said. "But maybe that's not the problem. Maybe the problem is we've forgotten how to hold disagreement without losing solidarity."

She paused, scanning the faces at the table.

"What if we agreed—just this much: that whenever someone acts sincerely for the climate, we support them. Even if we don't agree with every method. We can't resolve paradoxes rooted in fundamentally different worldviews—the Ethics Paradox, the Ideology Paradox. But we can name them. Respect them. And we can even flip the Crowd Paradox back around."

She looked toward Remy. "The climate movement used to be a force for unity. Now it feels like we're constantly fighting each other."

Luke gave a half-smile, the first in a while. "Yeah," he said quietly. "Remember Fridays for the Future? Those were the magic days."

Remy blinked. "True that. Those peaceful climate demonstrations were huge." Then she leaned back, crossing her arms. "But can I be honest with you? You guys ruin that force for unity yourselves! At Climate Warriors, we were always scratching our heads. You carbon credit folks already have a hard enough time defending yourselves. So why are you constantly tearing each other apart? I mean, come on— your infighting makes it really easy to campaign against you. Just a friendly hint."

Her tone was playful, but the edge was real.

Robin nodded. "Ah, yes. The Avoidance Paradox. The Novelty Paradox. And the worst of them—the Intentions Paradox. Some of the most painful, and honestly, the most pointless. We've burned so much energy fighting battles we never needed to fight."

Remy's face turned serious again. "I agree on the need for diverse approaches. But if carbon credits are really supposed to play a bigger role, you need better regulations."

Andy smiled and pulled out the third sheet.

"The Mountains," he said. *"It stands for robustness, transparency, and regulation. Like mountains against wind and time, carbon credits should be grounded in strong, reliable systems—regulated where possible by governments and guided by international principles, ideally those of the UN Paris Agreement. Instead of being scattered and fragile, carbon credits must become solid. Like rocks."*

Luke leaned forward, nodding slowly. "Government supervision would be a lot more credible. More transparent. More democratic. Not like the tangle of private standards and shadowy quality ratings you've got now. "

Ella glanced at him. "On that we all agree," she said. "Problem is, the UN's carbon market collapsed after the global financial crisis—almost twenty years ago now. It lost momentum, and the private sector stepped in to fill the gap. The problem? No consistent rules. No shared baseline. With proper government regulation, we could finally tackle some of the trickiest technical paradoxes—like the Additionality and Baseline Paradoxes. You can't eliminate them completely, but you can create fair rules that apply to everyone."

"And we could finally address the Quality Paradox," Andy added. "Right now, too much money disappears into overlapping standards and endless certifications—funds that should be going to actual projects. Clear, unified regulation would cut waste and get more money where it matters."

"Well," Robin said dryly, "assuming the government doesn't make it so bureaucratic that we're stuck in endless paperwork."

Ella nodded. "And it's not just governments. Science has to step up —objectively. Researchers and institutions must examine carbon credits without prejudice, without falling into ideological traps. The goal isn't to prove or disprove their value abstractly, but to identify what delivers the greatest impact. We need evidence-driven analysis that cuts through noise and focuses on results—on the actual carbon saved, biodiversity protected, or livelihoods improved. Otherwise, we risk letting assumptions cloud progress."

"Exactly," Andy said. "The point is to make the system better—not perfect in theory, but more effective in practice. But even if one day carbon regulations are great, we still miss perhaps the most important ingredient we need for scaling the impact."

He drew out the second-to-last sheet with care.

"The Forest—it stands for wonder, beauty, and excitement. But it wasn't always so. For much of human history, forests were shrouded in

danger and mystery, even as they sustained us. Today, we also see them as sources of inspiration, renewal, and creativity. That's precisely the kind of narrative shift we need for the climate.

Climate action has long been framed in terms of sacrifice—costs, austerity, and giving things up. That mindset has to change. When we think of meeting the climate challenge, we must think about jobs, innovation, opportunity, and prosperity. We need to unleash the excitement of solving climate change—not the fear of it."

Andy's words stirred something in them—a spark of the hope and can-do spirit they'd almost forgotten. For a moment, silence settled over the table as each of them drifted into their own thoughts.

Andy had one final sheet left in his transparent folder. He paused, took a deep breath, and began reading:

"The Ocean—it stands for endless learning. For deep mysteries, the last real frontier on Planet Earth. The unfinished. The contradictory. It reminds us that carbon credits will never be perfect. Some paradoxes will always remain. But like the ocean, they offer vast opportunities—if we're willing to learn, adapt, and evolve."

He looked up, eyes steady. "Here, we encounter the truly unsolvable paradoxes. The Control Paradox. The Communities Paradox. We've faced them again and again."

"The Leakage Paradox is my personal favorite," Robin said with a grim chuckle. "The nasty thing about that one is how the unintended consequences tend to show up years after your well-intended project is launched."

Andy nodded. "Anyway—that's the framework Wanga and I came up with. The Five Elements of the Belé.

So here's what we wanted to ask, Remy and Luke: would the Climate Warriors consider supporting carbon credits if we commit—all of us—to this framework? Could we stand together? Not as rivals, but as allies. Fighting not each other, but the real enemy—the ones who still deny climate change and keep pumping money into fossil fuels."

A long silence followed. Remy and Luke exchanged a glance. Then Remy sat up straight, her expression clear and serious.

"Look," she said, locking eyes with Andy. "I'll be honest. I'm still not a fan of carbon credits. Governments should be stepping up and doing their job. Period."

She paused. "But I'll also be realistic—we're out of time. Completely. And I know some of your projects do make sense."

She turned to Ella. "Remember Rebecca Silver?"

Ella froze. A chill ran through her—goosebumps pricked her arms. "Of course."

"She's representing the Climate Warriors in Demba now. On a recent call, she told me something that stuck with me. Your new school building? It survived the flood. And the forest you planted around Limata? It likely spared the village from much worse. That matters."

Remy took a breath.

"You know, back when the UN still regulated carbon credits, the Climate Warriors initially supported the system. It turned out not to meet the expectations. Maybe it's time we consider it again. And your framework—the Five Elements of the Belé—it's powerful. Honest. Grounded in something bigger than politics."

She leaned in slightly. "But can we agree on one thing?"

Andy, Ella, and Robin looked at her, tension tightening in the space between them.

"Can we change the name?" Remy asked. "Carbon credits—it's outdated. The word 'credit' still sounds like permission to pollute. We need something new. Something that speaks to funding the future, not offsetting the past. Call it a Climate Coin or something —anything that signals a shift in thinking."

Andy looked at Ella. Ella looked at Robin. And for the first time in a long while, the silence at the table wasn't heavy.

It was hopeful.

The Festival

On this fifteenth of August, life returned to the burnt, barren Niburg Hill. For one day, the blackened slope bloomed—bursting with sound, color, and scent as the Canland Climate Festival unfolded.

Flags snapped in the breeze, balloons bobbed above the crowd, and the air vibrated with laughter, music, and the low, steady murmur of thousands of voices woven into one.

Families spread blankets across the slope. Children shrieked on the newly built playground. A brass band yielded to a rock trio on the makeshift stage beside the still-closed observation tower and the increasingly cheerful din from the large beer tent. From behind the restaurant drifted the aromas of food trucks offering specialties from Demba and Canland. Beyond them, small exhibitions and jewelry stalls lined the path, street performers beckoned with juggling pins and painted faces, and Demban braiders worked deftly, fingers flashing as they parted, twisted, and wove intricate plaits.

Even the Climate Warriors had set up a booth, where children competed in sack races to outrun an imaginary flood. Only after they started jumping did they discover the game was rigged: some sacks were filled with stones, others with wood shavings, and others with scraps of paper. "You're a farmer from Demba—and she's a farmer from Canland," Remy would explain. "Sometimes the storm hits harder in one place than the other."

From the neighboring Five Elements booth, Ella watched it all unfold. She and Robin had chosen the exact spot where, four years earlier, they'd seen the deer burst from the forest—and where they had unexpectedly run into Minister Becker.

"I'm not sure this really motivates the little ones to take action for the climate," she laughed, handing out squares of dark Lester Hills chocolate.

A few tents away, visitors slipped on virtual-reality headsets at the Deep Capture stand, descending into digital oceans to glimpse where Amy Dupont and her team planned one day to bury the captured CO_2.

The real highlight of the festival, however, lay about a hundred meters further downhill, at the edge of the charred forest. Two landscaping companies had spent months clearing away ash and debris and painstakingly restoring the soil. A large wooden sign announced in proud green lettering:

"We are making Niburg Hill bloom again!"

Dozens of people queued up to receive a fragile sapling and gently place it into the freshly turned earth.

The True Canlanders had also set up a booth. Their banners fluttered near the parking lot:

"Give Niburg back its National Holiday!"

"Driving and flying—only for the rich?"

"No to climate terrorism."

But amid the bright festival colors, children's laughter, and the eerie remains of the burned forest, their protests felt strangely hollow—like a shrill echo from a bygone era.

A Canland folk band finished its third encore to thunderous applause when Lena Goldberg stepped onto the wooden stage.

"Ladies and gentlemen, dear children," she called out, "we have a surprise for you!"

An e-bike shot up a ramp and landed cleanly beside her. The rider wore full downhill gear—a sight that made every biker in the audience feel a pang of nostalgia for the days when Mount Niburg had been crisscrossed by countless trails. He came to a stop beside Goldberg, removed his helmet and gear—and laughter erupted.

Paul Becker, the Minister for the Environment, shook out his hair and raised both hands in mock triumph.

Behind him, the massive screen flickered to life, its glow washing over the upturned faces, the festival momentarily suspended in anticipation:

"Canland Climate Festival. Yes, we act!"

"Good afternoon, dear compatriots—esteemed women, men, and children of our beloved Canland," Becker began. "On this National Day, I stand before you with pride, humility, and a deep sense of responsibility. Today, we are united—not just by our shared love for this country, but by a growing recognition of the challenge that defines our time: the fight against climate change."

For a moment, everyone on Niburg Hill fell silent. Then, the picture on the screen changed. It was a little shaky at first, but then a colorfully decorated square with beautifully dressed people appeared.

"As you can see, we are not alone on Niburg Hill today," he continued. "Please welcome my esteemed colleague, Minister Amina Keita, Minister of Environment for the Republic of Demba. She joins us live from Port Kewala, where a parallel celebration is taking place—today also marks Demba's Independence Day."

He paused for applause. "Our warmest congratulations to the people of Demba! We've chosen to unite our national celebrations this year as a symbol of something greater: our shared commitment to tackling the climate crisis and to building a future rooted in sustainability and solidarity. It's a powerful reminder that the challenges we face don't stop at borders—and neither does our determination to meet them, together. We're truly excited to link our two festivals in spirit and in purpose and to celebrate the growing unity between our nations in this defining fight of our time!"

On the screen, Keita appeared before a sea of flags and dancers. For a moment, the live stream nested inside itself—Keita framed within Keita within Keita—until the camera steadied and the image resolved.

Port Kewala's main square blazed with drums and color. The Parliament building rose on one side, and Walmera Tower on the other. Smoke from countless street stalls drifted upward in fragrant spirals. Dancers in Belé costumes spun in widening circles as the crowd pressed closer to the stage.

Off to the side, Matipa had set up the "Climate Tent," where Wanga and her team curated a powerful exhibition: photographs from Limata and Yolo, taken before and after the floods. "Save Our Trees. Save Our Culture!" was emblazoned in large letters above the entrance.

Keita lifted her hand.

"Today I have the great honor of making an important announcement," she said. "As you know, Demba's economy depends heavily on the export of raw materials: palm oil, timber, soy. Many forest concessions were granted to agribusinesses for this purpose. But we face a dilemma: if we lose our forests, the spiral of climate change accelerates ever faster."

She lifted her head. "Our government has therefore taken a historic decision. We will buy back and revoke all remaining logging concessions. These lands will return to nature. We will expand our national parks—and preserve our green heritage for future generations."

Applause surged across the public squares in both countries.

"But that is not all," she continued. "We will reforest the Lester Hills and accelerate the transition to clean energy. Solar power and clean fuels will soon reach every village and every family. This is not a promise—it is a commitment. Yet we cannot carry it alone. That is why we have agreed on a partnership with the Canland government under Article 6 of the Paris Agreement. Our program rests on three pillars: the Dembanian government, the Canland government, and private partners from both countries. It is open to all—companies, organizations, even individuals. Climate protection belongs to all of us. We act together—or we fail together."

Thousands of kilometers apart, applause broke out at the same time —for a brief moment, Port Kewala and Mount Niburg sounded like a single place. Then the live stream switched back to Canland. Paul Becker reappeared on stage, removed his goggles, and polished them with a handkerchief.

"Not with his shirt?" Robin whispered with amusement, nudging Ella.

Becker stepped forward, his voice resolute, the setting sun casting long golden shadows across the hillside.

"Today, we celebrate all those already taking action—organizations, companies, and individuals—committed to reducing CO_2 emissions. Canland has set ambitious goals in the global fight against climate change. And I stand here with pride because the progress we have made—together—is real, and it is meaningful.

"But one thing is also clear: we can win this fight only through bold, determined international cooperation.

"For years, global negotiations dragged on. We talked, drafted, argued, hoped—and yet an effective global mechanism for climate finance remained a patchwork. More than thirty years ago, CO_2 certificates were invented to fill precisely this gap. The idea was to involve every country, every company, every individual directly. But that dream was worn down by controversy and contradiction— enough to fill an entire book."

He paused briefly—and Robin thought he detected an almost imperceptible wink in the direction of the Five Elements booth.

"After the Niburg fire and the devastating floods in our sister nation, Demba, one thing became painfully clear to us: we cannot afford to simply set aside an instrument as important as climate finance. CO_2 certificates may be flawed, imperfect, at times frustrating. But we must admit to ourselves: over the past decades, we have not found anything better. That is why we sat down with countless partners from Canland and Demba to search for a solution.

Some of you may be familiar with Article 6 of the Paris Agreement. It provides the legal framework for international cooperation. Our first step was therefore to translate that framework into clear, workable rules—for governments, markets, and companies. But we soon realized that alone is not enough."

He paused. "I am a physicist. I am trained to look at numbers, not at stories. But today I must admit something I would never have said before: for this mechanism to work, we need more than facts. We need a shared vision. CO_2 certificates must no longer be a necessary evil. They must become a symbol—for technological progress, effective climate action, and genuine international cooperation."

Becker turned toward the screen, where images from Port Kewala reappeared.

"So we asked ourselves: where should this vision be born, if not in Demba—a country where people have lived in harmony with nature for millennia? And so I now return the floor to Minister Amina Keita, who will present the new concept to us. Just one more thing, ladies and gentlemen ..."

He smiled. "We decided that we need a new, simple name—one that expresses cooperation across all borders. So today I say goodbye, CO_2 certificates. And welcome, Climate Units!"

The broadcast switched back to Port Kewala. Keita stepped forward.

"Sisters and brothers—today you've heard the call. The Climate Unit, as you will soon see, is more than a new instrument; it's the living heartbeat of the Paris Agreement's Crediting Mechanism. Each unit represents one ton of CO_2 reduced or removed from our atmosphere—one more step toward our shared ambition. Yes, Minister Becker reminded us, Climate Units are a complex tool, riddled with paradoxes that in the past have sparked devastating controversies. But today is different. Today, an international coalition of Demban and Canlandish organizations and scholars—led by the Climate Warriors—has forged a new framework. A framework rooted in the Five Elements of the Belé people, one of Demba's indigenous nations. Let me share them with you:

"The Sky means vision. Each Climate Unit will elevate our climate ambition. A Climate Unit shall never be used instead of, but always on top of, emission reductions.

"The Animals mean complementarity for all climate solutions and all project types. We need everything, everywhere, and all at once.

"The Mountains mean robustness. Clear rules and regulations for the production and use of internationally approved Climate Units.

"The Forests mean wonder. Climate action shall inspire us, challenge us to innovate, to create, and to cooperate across all borders.

"And the Ocean means eternal learning. The acceptance that we live in an imperfect world, where we must continue to try harder. Always."

As Keita finished, enthusiastic applause surged through both festivals, and several cannons shot thousands of flowers, which rained down on the crowds.

Local bands entered the stage, and the dance floor on Niburg Hill quickly filled up. Several bars started serving sundowner cocktails.

Visitors continued to flock to the Five Elements booth, eager to learn about Climate Units and to play around with the online tool that calculates their emissions from the past year. The products directly sourced from a Yolo farming cooperative, honey, spices, and natural skin lotion, were sold out long ago.

"It's insane," whispered Ella. "We've sold more Climate Units since we doubled the price. We can fund the next stage of Lester Hills plantations with the proceeds from the first round of sales!"

"The Price Paradox, you know...," laughed Robin, as a woman approached from the crowd, with a *Niburg Sunday Tribune* badge hanging around her neck and an audio recorder in one hand. "And please shut up. Beatrix Lemore is right over there!"

Beatrix waved at them, smiled, then disappeared in the crowd.

"With this Five Elements framework, Climate Units are simply not an attractive target anymore," Ella said. "She is now digging deep into recycling. Just last week, she had a big article on greenwashing in the plastics industry."

"Talking about Beatrix, I wonder what actually happened to the Cool Earth Chain. Did they ever launch?" asked Robin. He pulled out his phone and found HashRider's feed.

> CareCoin. Initial coin offering in 4 days.
> Democratizing healthcare. Don't miss out!

The sun had set over the ocean, leaving the sky above Niburg Hill washed in a mystical blend of oranges, pinks, and purples. It was one of those endless twilights mid-August, where time appeared to stand still.

Most families had left, but the bars and the dance floor were still buzzing with energy and laughter.

Before dismantling their Five Elements booth, Ella and Robin called Andy and Wanga in Demba, who showed them around the parallel festival in Port Kewala that was still in full swing, too.

"How much I miss Demba," Ella thought, when suddenly a last visitor tapped her shoulder.

"Doctor Cresta!" she exclaimed joyfully.

"Ella, come on, after all these adventures, please call me Thomas!" Cresta laughed.

He reached into his bulky-looking briefcase, but instead of pulling out a laptop, his hand emerged with something round. It was a bottle of Château Margaux, then a corkscrew, and five cups.

"Thomas! We cannot seriously drink Château Margaux from plastic cups, can we?" asked Robin.

"Of course we can. As with Climate Units, the content counts, not the packaging. And by the way, these cups here are biodegradable!"

Ella and Robin exchanged glances. Lemore was out of sight.

"Global discussions about carbon credits have been entangled in debates over context and surrounding circumstances for too long. The core issue often got lost in these debates—the content," Cresta added, undeterred.

Wanga and Andy in Port Kewala swiftly got themselves a beer, ready for a virtual cheer.

"On Climate Units. On the rebirth of our dream! And on you—the pioneers who dared to take the plunge!"

A beautiful crescent moon hung low over Niburg's western hills, and next to it a bright light—Venus—pierced brightly through the last remaining purple shades of the sunset, as if to give its celestial blessings.

The Five Elements team had dismantled their booth and stored the boards and poles in a Cresta company truck.

Robin had lit up a torch. "Let's walk down," he had proposed.

In the flickering light, they spotted a man leaning against the railing, someone they hadn't noticed before.

A racing bike was parked behind him.

"Ella," Simon said as he slowly moved closer, his face glowing in the dim torchlight.

"Ella, Robin, I have a client for you. I have returned to work for the Canland International Finance Corporation. I asked them to become a Global Climate Supporter and buy Climate Units from Five Elements to support your projects. They agreed. I hope that's okay with you?"

Ella didn't reply.

The faint light of the torch cast a warm, golden glow on the two siblings as they embraced for a long time.

Then, they walked down towards the city, passing the garden where the kids had planted the new seedlings. "It will take a while before you become old oak trees. But here you are! Good luck!" whispered Robin.

The Rebirth

Robin didn't recognize the number, and caller ID was blocked. But he answered anyway.

"Robin, how's life?"

It was a familiar voice: Remy.

"Andy is back in Niburg, right?" she continued. "Can you meet us at 8, in front of the Science Square entrance? Bring Ella and Andy. Luke and I have a surprise."

Robin was skeptical. Surprises from Remy hadn't ended well.

Still, just after 7:30, he pumped his bike and whizzed down towards Niburg University on that fresh evening in late September.

This is the same route I took five years ago, he thought, as the clip of the drowning girl spun again through his head. *Same route, same people, same destination—minus the Bungalow. What a roller coaster this has been...*

Ella and Andy had already locked their bikes on the rack next to the main entrance to East Building when Robin turned the corner.

Andy sniffed theatrically. "Well, the campus isn't on fire yet."

"Not funny," Ella said, laughing anyway and nodding towards Remy and Luke, who just emerged from a side alley.

"Here you are!" Remy shouted cheerfully. She was dressed as a bartender from the fifties. "Come on, follow us. We want to show you something!"

They crossed the square, toward the corner where Brigitte's Bungalow once stood. Robin felt a pang as they neared the construction slats. Luke halted, pulled two planks aside, and motioned them through a gap in the plastic sheeting.

And there it was: the familiar façade. Faded letters still read *Brigitte's Bungalow*. Tables were stacked against the wall. The door looked unchanged—worn but sturdy.

Luke pulled out a key, opened the door to the bar, and switched on the light. What awaited them behind the door let their jaws drop. All the walls had been freshly painted and beautifully decorated. The old bar table—still the same wooden structure, behind which Brigitte used to stand—was totally refurbished. "Climate Bar" was engraved in large letters above the long display of colorful bottles. A smaller banner was fixed to the opposite wall: "The place of co-creation. Where ideas have sex!"

"How on earth...," stuttered Ella. "You reopened Brigitte's Bungalow? But wasn't this place about to be smashed and replaced by a clothing boutique?"

"It was indeed," smiled Remy. "Brigitte had no heirs. So after a long back and forth, the city of Niburg decided to enter into a leasing agreement with a real estate developer. But then, when we cleared out our stuff from the bar, we found Brigitte's testament between folders on a bookshelf in the office. Initially, nobody believed us. But two independent laboratories confirmed that it was the genuine handwriting of Brigitte. It stated, black on white: "This plot of land and this bar are a place of resistance, a place of co-creating, of tolerance and of stubborn optimism. I herewith donate it to my two best employees and climate activists, Remy Selnass and Luke Blackfield, under the condition that they run the place in the spirit of diversity and inclusion, and foster a place where all views are welcome, and where you support each other to fight the world's biggest challenge: Climate change.

They all stood there in silence for a minute. A tear ran down Ella's cheek.

Then, Luke went to the back of the bar. "I brought the old fridge back, I simply couldn't let that one go..." He produced five Demba Lagers.

"On the Five Elements!" he toasted.

They laughed—real, full laughter.

And somewhere, Brigitte was watching them with pride. Somewhere, she was watching and cheering.

Reflections

By Renat Heuberger, 1.5.2025

One beautiful morning in the spring of 2024, I sat on the terrace of my temporary home in Bali, the island that had welcomed me so many times for inspiration, for adventure, for laughter, for healing.

Why is climate action so controversial? I asked myself.

Why is it that in 2021, in my home country, Switzerland, a proposal on a new climate legislation got voted down with a majority of 51.6% —by an unholy alliance of the political right and the radical green? "Too much!" shouted the ones. "Too little!" the others.

Why are carbon credits—the only climate finance instrument that ever managed to scale—the source of so much heated debate and controversy, which appears to spiral endlessly around the same arguments?

Why were the pioneers, who took risks and started funding climate projects decades ago, attacked so harshly by the media?

Why is the discussion on the correct response to climate change being led with so much furor?

The climate community is a paradox, I concluded. You would expect more members, more views, and more diversity to lead to more action and better outcomes. The opposite appears to be true. The more climate activists, the more infighting on the right approach—and the more controversies for the fossil fuel lobby and the media to exploit, hampering climate action.

But why, then, are there so many controversies within the climate community? Because the solutions to climate change, it appeared to me, are full of paradoxes as well.

Take energy efficiency. The more efficient you become, the more carbon you reduce. Really? Well, not always. The more efficient you get, the cheaper your product becomes, and the more of it you produce.

Take forest conservation. The more trees you protect, the better for the planet. Really? Well, the more funding you have for conservation, the more attractive it might become for a country to wave with the chainsaw: Give me money, or else I will cut this forest!

Ok, then let's forget about all that and fund only solutions that directly capture carbon from the atmosphere. Well, another paradox. Those happen to be the most expensive solutions with the least benefits to communities.

It occurred to me that the controversy around carbon credits is not happening in isolation, but is a prominent example of the broader controversies around climate finance, impact investment, and climate action in general. How was humanity able to address global problems such as the ozone hole or the COVID-19 pandemic with swift, decisive action, while climate action has stalled for decades? One important reason is a paradox at the heart of the issue: those with the greatest financial resources and political power to act on climate change are also the ones best positioned to adapt to increasingly extreme weather.

The paradoxes started to fascinate me. I compiled some of them and sent the list to my South Pole co-founders, Christian, Christoph, Ingo, Marco, Patrick, Thomas, and a few other climate aficionados. I didn't have to wait long for answers. "Nice list, but you forgot this paradox..."—"Here is another one..."—"In my view, the key paradox is here..." Soon, the list grew to over 50 paradoxes.

The initial idea was to write a scientific paper on the paradoxes of carbon credits. But severe doubts overcame me soon. Thousands of scientific papers exist on all aspects of climate change and climate action—would anyone read *this* one on carbon paradoxes? Wouldn't folks get frustrated and turn away after encountering five out of fifty paradoxes?

How about writing fiction instead? This would allow me to illustrate the paradoxes by combining various examples, situations, and projects. For too long, the climate debate has been dominated by experts, while journalists have found it all too easy to sensationalize carbon markets with decontextualized stories. We concluded that a meaningful public debate requires something different: enabling a much broader audience to understand how climate finance actually works.

Marco, Christian, and Christoph agreed to join forces. We narrowed down the list of paradoxes to 25, avoiding any duplications, ensuring that each paradox stood on its own feet.

When the manuscript was half-written, I dared to expose it to a daunting test. What would an international expert like Steve Zwick think about it, one of the most outspoken and knowledgeable journalists on carbon markets? Would he just send it back, saying this makes no sense?

Instead, Steve reacted in an unexpected way. "We have debated these paradoxes so many times. None of them is new. But never have we compiled all of them in one place. I wanna be part of this!"

"Everything should be made as simple as possible, but not simpler," Albert Einstein once famously said. That principle turned out to be one of the greatest challenges in shaping this book.

But how do you distill the vast, tangled world of global climate finance—decades of shifting carbon markets, thousands of project examples across hundreds of countries—into a narrative that's both accessible and accurate?

We hope that the adventure story following Ella, Robin, and Andy through 25 paradoxes offers a constructive path between the two extremes of the Perfection Paradox.

Yet the most challenging question concerned the ending of the book. We knew it would not be enough to simply guide readers through the paradoxes or to encourage debate and deeper understanding. We wanted to offer a vision of how these paradoxes might be overcome —and how climate finance could once again emerge as a truly impactful instrument.

What if we managed to come together around a shared vision, allowing different climate innovations to flourish side by side, and chose collective action over endlessly pushing one another down in debate? What if a genuine "can-do" spirit re-emerged within the climate community? What if mistakes were no longer treated as failures, but as opportunities for learning and progress?

And what if governments stepped up, providing clear guidance and regulation to address some of the paradoxes that cannot be resolved by markets alone?

The fifth part of our book—set in the not-too-distant future—became The Rebirth of the Dream.

Two years after sitting on that Bali terrace, climate action is at a crossroads. With the new American administration quickly and radically dismantling climate-related science, subsidies, and support programs, it is clearer than ever before: Our climate community wasted precious years debating, instead of supporting each other to scale climate action.

Can we still turn around?

To move beyond the controversies, the first and perhaps most crucial step is to try to listen to each other. Understand and acknowledge the different viewpoints. Find common ground. Find compromises.

May the sky, the animals, the mountains, the forest, and the endless ocean be with us.

Renat Heuberger

Acknowledgments

This book is dedicated to all the real-life Robins, Ellas, Andys, and Wangas—hundreds of passionate entrepreneurs and environmentalists who have fought against these paradoxes, often against overwhelming odds. Your passion, your spirit, and your stubborn optimism are needed more than ever.

We would like to thank all the friends and supporters who provided invaluable feedback and encouragement along the way, especially these contributors:

Adam Rogers, Agus Sari, Dr. Alexandra Soezer, Almir Narayamoga Suruí, Andrea Gori, Prof. Dr. Anna Broughel, Antoine Geerinckx, Dr. Axel Michaelova, Barbara Franzen, Barbara Ryter, Brigitta Heuberger, Carl Thong, Carolin Güthenke, Prof. Charles Bedford, Chiyedza Heri, Chris Leeds, Christian Dannecker, Dr. Christoph Grobbel, Dang Hanh, David Antonioli, David Greely, Prof. Dr. Estelle Herlyin, Eva Tamme, Prof. Dr. Fabrizio Ferraro, Florian Reber, Francisco Renteria, Prof. Franz Josef Rademacher, Giulia Gervasoni, Prof. Gregor Dorfleitner, Ingo Puhl, Jen Stebbing, Jeremy Freund, Jim Pittman, Jonah Busch, Josep Oriol, Joshua Bishop, Jost Hamschmidt, Juan Carlos Gonzalez, Katherine Pineault, Dr. Kruthika Eswaran, Lisa Neuberger Fernandez, Mahua Acharya, Max Zeckau, Michael Jenkins, Dr. Mike Poltorak, Nathan Truitt, Nick Aster, Patrick Bürgi, Peter Kilesi, René Velasquez, Reto Gerber, Ricardo Bayon, Rich Gilmore, Sebastian Manhart, Stephanie Larkin, Tanjung Sentosa, Thibault Sorret, Thomas Camerata, Tilmann Lang, Tim Reutemann, Vasco van Roosmalen, Vilhelmiina Vulli, and Wil Burns.

We remember with gratitude the late Mikkel Larsen, whose support and encouragement continue to inspire us.

And above all, our deepest thanks go to our families and our friends, for your unwavering support and all that you have done to carry us this far.

About the authors

Renat Heuberger

Renat Heuberger is a Swiss climate activist, serial entrepreneur, and impact investor. He has launched and led several pioneering sustainability organizations, including myclimate, South Pole, and Terra Impact Ventures.

Over the course of his career, Heuberger has helped mobilize billions of dollars into nearly 1,000 climate projects across more than 50 countries, contributing to the reduction of over one billion tons of CO_2. In recognition of his impact, he has been named a Social Entrepreneur by the World Economic Forum's Schwab Foundation.

He serves on numerous boards and is an elected member of Switzerland's InnoSuisse Innovation Council. In 2024, he cofounded the Carbon Paradox initiative to foster open, constructive dialogue on the challenges and complexities of climate finance.

Raised near the Swiss Alps and having spent five years working in Asia, Heuberger developed an early passion for social justice, entrepreneurship, and nature. He enjoys hiking, mountain biking, snowboarding, diving, or kite surfing. He lives in Zurich with his wife and their four daughters.

Steve Zwick

Steve Zwick is an environmental consultant, analyst, and journalist who has spent his adult life trying to forge peace between the opposing forces of economy and ecology—and chronicling that effort in plain language for non-experts.

He is a senior advisor to ESG consultancy Responsible Alpha, runs the boutique advisory Bionic Planet, and produces the Bionic Planet podcast. Previously, he served as Managing Editor of *Ecosystem Marketplace*, shaping it into a globally respected crucible of climate policy and environmental markets, and later as Senior Manager for Special Projects at Verra, the leading carbon credit standards body.

Zwick's journey began in the trading pits of Chicago, where he saw how information asymmetries stacked the deck for the privileged few. That realization pushed him from futures markets to grassroots environmental activism, and then to Germany, where he worked to make economic systems understandable to all—covering European business for *TIME* and *Fortune*, earning two shortlistings for Business Journalist of the Year. He also produced and hosted Deutsche Welle's *Money Talks*.

He grew up on the south side of Chicago and is married to a Kenyan attorney who teaches human rights law. They own two bicycles, no car, and a pile of transit cards.

Marco Hirsbrunner

Marco Hirsbrunner is a Swiss serial entrepreneur and impact investor. He co-founded Terra Impact Ventures, where he leads operations and drives the growth of sustainability-focused startups. He also serves as co-CEO of Svarmi, an Icelandic company specializing in geospatial and nature data.

Previously, he co-founded South Pole, where he played a key role in scaling the company into a global leader in climate finance by establishing and leading offices in East and Southeast Asia. In parallel, his focus on operational excellence and digital solutions helped South Pole scale its work and manage one of the world's largest and most complex carbon project portfolios.

Fluent in multiple languages, he holds an M.A. in Media and Communication Studies and Chinese Studies from the University of Zurich, where he developed a deep fascination for ancient Chinese philosophical concepts.

A lifelong enthusiast of logical puzzles and scientific paradoxes, he is especially captivated by unsolved mysteries like the *Fermi Paradox*—the central enigma of astrobiology, which asks why, in a universe so vast, we have yet to encounter another civilization. One sobering possibility—later dubbed the "Great Filter"—is that the same technologies capable of carrying a civilization to the stars may also hasten its destruction. Another, no less terrifying idea is that we are actually alone. In either case, we are called upon to truly live up to our responsibility toward all life on our home planet.